Love Finds You
in
Sisters
OREGON

Love Finds You in Sisters

OREGON

BY MELODY CARLSON

summerside
PRESS

Love Finds You in Sisters, Oregon
© 2009 by Melody Carlson

ISBN 978-1-935416-18-0

All scripture quotations are taken from the King James Version of the Bible.

Front cover photo of mountains by Steve Gardner, PixelWorks Studios, www.shootpw.com.

Front cover photo of Cascade Avenue in Sisters, Oregon, by Rick Schafer, Rick Schafer Photography, LLC. www.rickschafer.com.

Back cover photo of downtown Sisters, Oregon by Jonathan Barsook.

The town depicted in this book is a real place, but all characters are fictional. Any resemblances to actual people or events are purely coincidental.

Cover and Interior Design by Müllerhaus Publishing Group, www.mullerhaus.net

Published by Summerside Press, Inc., 11024 Quebec Circle, Bloomington, Minnesota 55438, www.summersidepress.com

Fall in love with Summerside.

Printed in the USA.

MORE THAN THIRTY YEARS AGO, MY HUSBAND AND I honeymooned near Sisters, Oregon. We stayed in a Camp Sherman cabin situated on the pristine and beautiful Metolius River. We always loved this section of Oregon, where the majestic Cascade Mountains go from rain forest to desert within a few miles. But because Sisters was a small and struggling tourist town, we could never quite figure out a way to make a living here—until about fifteen years ago when God opened a door, and without thinking too hard, we ran right through. We dragged our teenage boys with us and bought a fixer-upper cabin that's located in a ponderosa pine forest with deer, rabbits, raccoons, coyotes, and the occasional cougar for company. We're twenty minutes from both downhill skiing and a little lake great for fishing and boating in summer. Town is minutes away, and since we moved here, it's expanded into quite a fun place. Sisters looks like a western frontier town, and the shops and activities are numerous. So, whether it's our "Biggest Little Rodeo," our "Largest Outdoor Quilt Show," or any of the various music festivals (Folk Fest is our favorite), Sisters is a great place to live.

Melody Carlson

Chapter One

It was Hope Bartolli's experience that grief and guilt were as inseparable as peanut butter and jelly, Siamese twins, or maybe even Barnes & Noble—although in her line of work, she knew that corporations sometimes restructured. Still it seemed that one emotion never showed up without the other one—grief and guilt, hand in hand. And as the small commuter plane bounced through the turbulence above the snowcapped mountains, Hope felt as if grief and guilt, like playground bullies, had her cornered.

But why should a semi-mature thirty-two-year-old woman feel guilty about returning to her hometown? Especially when it was to grieve the death of dear Nona? Hope's grandmother had lived a long and mostly happy life. And throughout Hope's entire childhood, she and Nona had been close—even closer than Hope had been to her own mother. Not that she wanted to think about that right now, since it came with its own truckload of guilt and grief. But really, when it came to going home, why couldn't Hope just be happy?

The pilot announced the arrival time, "five-thirty-five," and weather conditions, "a breezy seventy-two degrees," as the small jet began its descent. Anyone who hadn't experienced landing in Central Oregon on a blustery day might've been startled by the way the lightweight plane bumped in the air, but Hope knew better. And besides, what was the difference between a plane crash and a train wreck? Either way, she felt headed for disaster.

But the pilot managed to land the plane and, all too soon, Hope was making her way down the rickety stairs and retrieving her carry-on from wherever it had been stowed in the small plane. She hadn't bothered to pack a checked bag this morning because, despite taking a week off from the firm, she had no intention of staying more than a day beyond Nona's funeral service tomorrow afternoon. Hello, good-bye, see you next lifetime.

With the wind whipping, she carried her oversized handbag with one hand and used the other to roll the carry-on over the bumpy tarmac. She wished for a third hand to tame her wildly flying hair and to smooth down the front of her rumpled jacket. She knew the navy Ralph Lauren suit was overkill for a town like Sisters, but it was what she wore to court when it mattered. And for whatever reason, her first impression seemed to matter today. She wished she'd thought to freshen her lipstick and to make sure she didn't have cracker crumbs stuck to the sides of her mouth. Even more than that, she wished she didn't care so much.

Hope braced herself for whoever was picking her up in the terminal. She didn't want to see either of them just yet. Why hadn't she politely declined the offer of a "free" ride and arranged for a rental car? Really, what had she been thinking? Obviously, she hadn't been thinking at all! At least she wouldn't stay with them. That's where she would draw the line, and she'd already booked a room at the Ponderosa to prove it.

Her punishment for not getting a rental car would be twenty torturous minutes as she was taxied to Sisters by either Cherry (her younger sister) or Hope's former high-school sweetheart, Drew Lawson (AKA Cherry's husband of nearly thirteen years). Just then,

Hope's carry-on bag, buffeted by the wind, flipped over and nearly tripped her. Feeling like a total klutz, she knew these Christian Dior heels weren't exactly practical footwear in Central Oregon. And she knew that she was obsessing over minor details that no one but her would even notice.

Just breathe, she told herself. *And grow up.* As she slowed down, she reminded herself that what had happened was ancient history. And she should be so over it by now. Good grief, she hardly ever thought of any of this anymore. And, if she did, she felt mostly relieved—like she'd missed a bullet. But that attitude was easier to maintain from a distance. And now that she was close and getting closer, she wasn't so sure.

If she were to be honest with herself, which she normally wasn't when it came to the marriage of her ex-boyfriend and baby sister… the wound still ached. Was it really the pain of betrayal…two loved ones who'd let her down? Or was it just her selfish pride that stung? Would she ever know for sure? And why focus on this now, when all she wanted to do was to act natural and get the next couple days behind her?

As she entered the terminal, she repressed every feeling related to Cherry and Drew. She neatly filed it in a drawer labeled "Old and Useless Junk." She held her head high, put on her confident face—the same expression she used to face a judge when defending a corporation that probably didn't deserve her sacrifice either. And she willed herself to smile. Not too big. Just enough to show that she was in charge. She. Was. In. Charge.

"Hope!" Drew waved in her direction, looking like he was actually glad to see her.

Hope's smile increased slightly. Not because she was happy to see her ex-boyfriend. And not even because she was amused, although she was, to see his paunchy midsection or pale, thinning hair. Her smile was for the young, dark-haired girl standing next to Drew. She knew it was Avery—her eleven-year-old niece.

"Hi, Aunt Hope," Avery said politely.

"Look at *you*." Hope bent slightly to hug Avery. "You've gotten so tall. And so grown-up." She touched the soft cheek. "And so pretty." She smiled at Drew. "I'll bet you have to beat the boys off with a big stick."

He chuckled. "I'm getting ready for the onslaught."

"Oh, Dad." Avery glowered at him in a typical preteen way.

Drew reached for Hope's carry-on, and she turned her attention back to Avery as they walked toward the exit. "Did you get your birthday card?" Even though Hope rarely saw her niece and nephews, she always sent cards and checks for birthdays and other holidays—another little something she had learned from Nona.

Avery smiled wide enough to reveal straight white teeth. "Yeah, thanks!" Then, just as quickly, the smile faded. "Oh, I'm sorry, Aunt Hope. I forgot to write a thank-you card. I meant to do that as soon as school ended…then Nona died." She sighed.

"Yes, don't worry about a thank-you now." Hope put an arm around Avery's shoulders as they went outside. "Dear old Nona." Hope gave Avery a squeeze. "I know she was very fond of you, Avery. She wrote about you often. It sounded like you and she had a lot of good times together."

"And Nona always said that I'm a lot like you." Avery's stride matched Hope's. "She even said I look like you, Aunt Hope."

"And I heard you're good in sports, too." Hope ran her hand down Avery's shiny dark hair.

"Our soccer team won the championship."

"Congratulations!"

"Here we are," Drew announced as he unlocked a sage green SUV, opened the passenger door, and waited for Hope to get in. Avery hopped in the back, still chattering about soccer and how she had played several positions.

"Cherry is having some family over for dinner," Drew said as he climbed into the driver's seat and started the engine. "It was supposed to be small, just immediate family, but it sounds like it's growing bigger by the minute."

"Well, Nona has a lot of descendents." Hope fidgeted with a button of her jacket, willing herself to just relax.

"And your dad and Cindy should be getting in around five or so," he continued filling in details. "And Faye and Monroe showed up just before we left."

Hope hadn't seen her older sister in several years. Not since Faye had brought Monroe to Portland for his eleventh birthday. "Jeff's not coming, too?" Hope asked absently.

"You didn't hear?"

"Hear?"

"They split up." Drew was putting down his window to pay the parking fee now. But Hope was still trying to absorb what he'd just said. Faye and Jeff had split up? After sixteen or more years of marriage? It didn't seem possible.

"Did I hear you right?" Hope asked as he pulled away from the booth. "Did you say Faye and Jeff split up?"

He nodded then sighed as he shook his head.

"Aunt Faye says she wants to move back to Sisters," Avery said from behind. "But Monroe says no way."

"Naturally, Monroe doesn't want to leave his home and his school," Drew filled in. "Most kids would feel like that."

"I know I would," Avery offered. "I love my school and my friends. I'd hate it if my parents broke up and I had to move away."

"Well, you don't need to worry about that, Sweet Pea." Drew made what almost seemed a forced laugh. "Both your mother and me love our town. And as far as I know we're not planning on breaking up."

"Are you going to stay with us, Aunt Hope?"

"No, I already reserved a room at the Ponderosa." Hope glanced at her brother-in-law. "And if you don't mind, Drew, you could just drop me there first, and I'll walk—"

"Please, please, stay with us," pleaded Avery. "I helped Mom fix up the guest room with flowers and everything. I even put a mint on the pillow."

Now Hope felt torn. She hated to disappoint Avery. And yet she needed to draw her boundaries. Her counselor had told her that more than once. "How about if I spend tonight at the hotel?" Hope suggested. "And we'll see about tomorrow later."

"Or you could stay at Nona's," offered Avery. "At least you'd be close."

Too close, Hope was thinking. Nona's house was right next door to the home where Hope and her sisters had grown up—the house that Drew and Cherry and their kids currently occupied. Convenient then, but awkward now.

"Cherry thought you might want to use Nona's car while you're in town," Drew told her. "It's not much to look at, but it runs decent."

Hope considered this. "That's not a bad idea. Why don't we swing by your place first and I'll say hey to everyone then use Nona's car to drive myself back to the hotel."

"Sure." Drew nodded. Then the car grew silent, and Hope tried to think of something to say.

"Monroe has a tattoo," Avery announced suddenly from the backseat.

"Really?" Hope felt her brows rise. That did not sound a bit like her conservative Christian sister. But neither did the splitting-up news. "What kind of a tattoo?"

"A skull."

"Oh…" Hope frowned. "I wonder what his mom thinks about that."

Drew chuckled. "Faye's not real happy with Monroe at the moment."

"And Monroe's not real happy with Aunt Faye," Avery added.

"Faye's looking into renting an apartment at the Fourth Sister."

Hope kind of laughed. "Faye living at the Fourth Sister…now that is funny."

"Why do they call it that anyway?" asked Avery. "Everyone knows there are only *three* sisters." She giggled in a cheery way, like a typical eleven-year-old. "And now all *three* Bartolli sisters are in Sisters—all at the same time! How cool is that?"

"Faith, Hope, and Charity," Drew said quietly.

"I love that Grandma named her three daughters after the mountains," Avery chattered. "I wish I could've known her. Your mom seemed like a really cool lady."

"Yes…she was…" Hope was looking out the window and trying not to gasp as the familiar mountains came into view. The three snowcapped mountains looked regal and stunning against the clear blue sky—so much so, it nearly took her breath away. How long had it been since she'd seen them from this angle? Oh, she'd seen them from the sky while flying to places like Denver or Chicago or Salt Lake. But like this…well, they really were beautiful.

"Mom got out an old photo album right after Nona died," Avery continued. "She was looking for a picture of Nona for the funeral. But there were pictures of your parents, too—back when they were young. They were a really good-looking couple, don't you think?" Before Hope could respond, Avery continued. "And there were pictures of your mom in her hiking clothes and on top of the mountains. Aunt Hope, did you know she climbed all three of the Sisters?"

Hope sighed. "Yes…and she died on her way to one of those mountains."

"Mom said Grandma was going to climb the Middle Sister that day."

Hope pressed her lips together and just nodded.

"That's the one you're named after, Aunt Hope. Does that make you sad?"

"Yes…sometimes it does." Hope felt her chest tighten.

Drew cleared his throat. "Avery," he said in a warning tone. "Give your aunt some P and Q, okay?"

"P and Q?" ventured Hope.

"Peace and quiet," Avery said softly.

"Oh, that's all right." Hope forced cheer into her voice. "I think it's nice that you're learning some family history, Avery." Although she did wonder just how much Avery actually knew about their family. How much had Cherry told her preadolescent daughter about the Bartollis?

And then, as Drew pulled into the driveway of Hope's childhood home—the same house that their father had practically given to Cherry and Drew while he was still grieving for his deceased wife—Hope wondered just how much she knew, herself, about her own family. How much did she want to know?

Chapter Two
....

"Hope!" exclaimed Faye as she wrapped her arms around her sister. "It's so good to see you." She held Hope back and examined her more carefully. "Wow, you look fabulous. Did you lose weight or something?"

Hope just shrugged as she set down her bag. "Not really." Then she looked more closely at Faye, suppressing the urge to say, "Have you gained weight?" But it was obvious; not only had Faye put on at least thirty pounds since they'd last been together, her hair appeared to be turning gray. And Faye wasn't quite forty! Hope would never say this to anyone, but in this moment she felt Faye could easily pass for fifty…or more.

"How are you?" she asked Faye as they went into the living room together.

"Oh, you know…so-so."

Hope was surprised to see that nothing looked the same in her old family home. New paint, new furnishings, and even the wall that used to separate the living room from the kitchen had been removed. It was an improvement, of course, and yet it was slightly irritating, too.

"I suppose you heard," Faye continued as they stood by the same fireplace. The same fireplace where all three girls had taken turns posing for prom pictures so long ago, only now it was covered in slate and the mantle was a peeled log. Hope tried not to think about the two years when she had stood in that very spot with Drew by her side. Or the following year, after Hope had graduated and gone on to college, when Cherry had taken her place and posed right there with Drew.

"Is it true?" Hope dragged herself back to the present. "You and Jeff?"

"He had an affair."

Hope tried not to look too shocked. "But you guys seemed so strong in your faith and you went to church and—"

"He had an affair with someone from church."

Hope made a face. "That's too bad."

"She worked in the women's ministry, too."

"Oh…" Hope shook her head then hugged her sister. "I'm sorry."

Faye sniffed. "Yeah, me, too."

"Hey, sisters!" called out Cherry. Avery was tugging her mom into the house through the opened French doors (another improvement over what had previously been aluminum sliders). Was nothing the same?

"Hi, Cherry." Hope tried to appear genuinely happy to see her younger sister. And she wasn't even surprised that Cherry didn't look much different than the last time Hope had seen her, although it had been years. Still blond and petite and bubbly. Trim and fit, sporting a golden tan, and those pretty white teeth that shone when she smiled, which she did often and with ease. Cherry was the perennial cheerleader type. She'd probably still look perky and cute in her nineties.

"We're all here together again." Cherry came over and gave Hope a big hug—or as big as her petite five-foot-two frame would allow. "Wow, you look great, Hope. Is life treating you well?"

Hope kind of shrugged. "All things considered."

"It *was* sad to lose Nona." Cherry's eyes grew somber as she turned to Avery. Hope was surprised to see mother and daughter were nearly the same height now. "Hey, Sweetie Pie, will you go and take a head count so we can figure out if we need to make another run to the store for buns or meat?"

Avery trotted back outside to where other family members, probably ones Hope hadn't seen since childhood, were gathered in the backyard. It even sounded as if a game of horseshoes was being played. So quaint and sweet…like old folks at home.

"At least Nona died in her bed," Cherry continued. No surprises that she'd take the positive angle. "Not a bad way to go if you think about it."

"That's how I want to go," Faye said soberly.

"I don't know." Hope knew it was juvenile, but she wanted to show off just a bit right then. "I'd rather go doing something exciting. Like mountain climbing or skydiving or maybe even BASE jumping."

"You and Mom." Faye just shook her head like her sister was a lost cause. "*Thrill seekers.*"

Hope just laughed. But the truth was, she hadn't done any thrill seeking for quite some time. Still, her family didn't need to know everything.

"Do you still do rock climbing?" Cherry asked with concerned eyes. "Just yesterday I saw on the news that a woman died from a fall over at Smith Rocks. She was in her early forties."

"I haven't done any climbing lately." Hope stood straighter. "But I might do some climbing while I'm here." Okay, she knew that was a complete lie, but she just couldn't help herself. As childish as it seemed, she needed something to own—or to call her own.

"Do be careful."

"Of course." She smiled at her sisters and wished for this day to be over.

"You're a mountain climber like Grandma Bartolli used to be?" asked a boy who had been sitting nearby, playing on a handheld video game. Hope studied him, realizing that he had to be her nephew since he looked just like his dad. It took Hope a second to remember his name, but then she recalled how Cherry had named him after her favorite actor.

"Harrison," Hope exclaimed. "Just look at you. You're half grown already."

He stood straighter and smiled to reveal a pair of large front teeth. "I'm nine and a half, Aunt Hope."

"And I hear you're good at sports," Hope said. "Like your dad."

"But I want to climb mountains, too," he said hopefully. "Like my grandma used to do...before she died."

"She was a good climber," Hope told him. "She taught me how to climb."

"Will you teach me to climb?" he asked eagerly.

"Why don't you run outside and see if Daddy needs help with the hamburgers?" Cherry suggested as she nudged him toward the door.

"But I want Aunt Hope to teach me to—"

"Not *right now*, Harrison." Cherry's voice was firm.

He went outside, dragging his heels all the way.

"Ever since he saw old photos of Mom, he's been obsessed with mountain climbing." Cherry shook her head. "I've told him he's too young."

"It's too dangerous for children," Faye added.

"Mom took me up when I was his age," Hope reminded them.

"Mom was nuts," Faye said in a matter-of-fact voice.

"Mom was nuts?" Hope stared at her older sister. "How can you say that?"

"Because it's true." Faye narrowed her eyes. "What kind of a mother leaves her children to go climb a mountain?"

"A mother who wants to have a life," Hope stated.

"A mother *has* a life," Faye protested, "and that life is to take care of her children, to put their needs above her own. But since you don't have children, I wouldn't expect you to know that."

Hope blinked.

Faye just shook her head. "I'm sorry. There I go again, saying things that I don't really mean…hurting people's feelings." Her eyes filled with tears. "I don't know what's wrong with me."

Hope put her arm around Faye. "What's wrong is that you're hurting, Faye. Anyone can see that." Now Hope felt tears coming, too.

Just then, their dad and stepmom entered the room. "Anyone home?" Dad bellowed as he pulled Cindy into the living room. "Oh, there they are now. The three sisters, in all their glory." He came over to hug his daughters. "Say, you girls shouldn't be crying for your Nona. She had a good life. Ninety-two years is a long time to live. She wouldn't want you to cry."

"They're not crying for Nona, Dad," Cherry said quietly. "Faye and Jeff are split up, and Faye's having a hard time with it."

"Oh, well, you kids can patch it up," Dad assured Faye in a dismissive way. "Love gets rocky sometimes, but that doesn't mean you give up. *Right?*"

Faye just shrugged.

Now Dad placed his hands on both sides of her cheeks and looked intently into her eyes like she was still a little girl. "What you need to do is fix yourself up a little, Faith. Lose some weight. Buy a new dress. Then go back to Jeff and show him what he's missing. He'll come around."

Faye pulled herself away from him and, with a choked sob, went running down the hallway.

"That was great, Dad." Hope rolled her eyes.

"What'd I say?" He held up his hands in a helpless gesture.

"Oh, Vitto," scolded Cindy. "There you go putting your foot in your mouth again."

"What?" he persisted. "What'd I say wrong?"

"I'll go talk to her," Hope offered. The truth was, she had no idea what she could say to encourage Faye, but she was eager to get away from the rest of her family.

She found Faye in the bedroom that had once belonged to Hope, but now it appeared to be a guest room—because there were the fresh flowers and a mint on the pillow. Of course, with its slate blue paint and craftsman-style furniture and formal-looking Oriental carpet centered on the refinished hardwood floor, it looked nothing like Hope's old room. And, although she wouldn't have expected them to leave it the same, she still missed the pale pink walls and those eyelet curtains that she had sewn herself with Nona's help. She sat down on the bed next to Faye. "Are you okay?"

Faye fished a ratty-looking tissue out of the pocket of her sweater and loudly blew her nose. "That's so like Dad to say, 'go fix yourself and win back your man.' Our father is so clueless."

"He's from another generation."

"Another planet is more like it."

Hope laughed. "He loves you, Faye. And, being a man, he thinks he needs to say something to fix things and make it all better."

"And instead he just makes it all worse."

"But you can't blame him for trying."

"No...," she sniffed. "I suppose not."

"Hey, where's Monroe?" Hope asked.

"Who knows?"

"Did he really get a tattoo?"

"I think it's his way of getting even with his parents for letting their marriage fall apart."

"Where is it?"

"What?"

"His tattoo."

"Oh." Faye kind of smiled. "His left cheek."

Hope's hand flew to her mouth. "On his face? He tattooed his face with a skull? Didn't the tattoo artist know that it's illegal to tattoo a juvenile? You could sue the pants off that—"

"No, Monroe didn't get a tattoo on his face, Hope."

"But you said his—"

Faye pointed to her behind. "His *other* cheek."

Hope laughed. "Didn't it hurt?"

"Who knows."

"Well, at least you don't have to look at it."

"Except when his baggy pants slip too low."

Hope made a face. "Is he into that gangster look? You'd think that would be so yesterday by now."

"Not as long as we have rappers around to keep it alive. And if he can find any new way he can rebel these days, Monroe will try it out. Honestly, he's making me crazy."

"Too bad. But it's probably just a phase." Hope remembered what a sweet little boy Monroe once had been. Red hair and ruddy cheeks like his dad, sparkly blue eyes like his mom…the kind of boy who would cry to see a dead bird on the sidewalk. How did someone go from that to skull tattoos?

"I hope so."

"Avery said you're thinking about moving back to town."

"I'm not thinking about it, I'm doing it."

"Seriously?"

"I've already put a deposit down on a condo unit."

"At the Fourth Sister?"

"No. I found a better place in Pine Meadow Ranch yesterday. It's really nice and, because it's been sitting there empty for six months, it's a good deal. And it's close to school and town."

"And you're really going to do this?"

Faye held her chin up. "I am."

Hope wondered how realistic this plan was. Could Faye really manage this? "Are you still going to teach? Are they hiring here?"

Faye shrugged. "Maybe…or not. I don't really care. Monroe and I could easily just live off of alimony and child support for a while… until I figure things out."

"Are you *already* divorced?"

Faye nodded. "It was final last month."

"Seriously? How long ago did this all start?"

"I found out about the affair last Christmas. I made Jeff leave, and I thought I'd keep the house. But I've been so miserable there. It's like my whole life was blown to pieces when he did that to me. I gave my notice two months ago. Today was actually the last day of school, but I took this week off for bereavement time. I wasn't doing a very good job in the classroom anyway. I doubt the kids even missed me."

"I'll bet they did."

"But I'd already decided I didn't want to live in that house anymore. And I reminded Jeff that I'd put a lot of my own money into it from Mom's insurance. I made him refinance to repay me my share, which I should be getting by the end of the month. Jeff can do what he wants with the house now—keep it, sell it, burn it to the ground like he did our marriage."

"What about Monroe?"

"He's furious at me."

"You can't really blame him, Faye. I mean you said your life was blown to pieces...what about Monroe's life?" She wanted to ask what about Monroe's right to have his father nearby...what about Jeff's right to shared custody. But she decided not to let the lawyer in her take over.

"I can't help that." Faye looked at Hope with watery eyes. "I feel like I'm hanging on by a thread here. And for some reason, it just felt right when I came to Sisters. I drove out here the same day that Cherry called to tell me about Nona. And as soon as I got to town, something in me just clicked. I saw those mountains and I knew I was home. I started looking at real estate immediately." She blew her nose again. "Monroe will have to get used to it."

"What did Jeff say about it?"

She gave Hope the blankest of blank looks.

"He doesn't know, does he?"

"For months I didn't know he was having an affair, Hope. Do you think he really deserves to know?"

"You're not moving here to spite him, are you?"

"Weren't you listening to me? I said that something just clicked inside of me. I got home, and I knew I was home."

"But what about custody…?"

"What about it?"

"Well, you've crossed the state line…and I assume you and Jeff share custody of Monroe."

"So?"

"So…Jeff could press for full custody now, and he'd have a pretty strong case." Hope didn't add that it wouldn't help matters that Monroe was fourteen and wanted to remain in Seattle. A good judge would take that into consideration.

"And your point is what, Counselor?"

"I don't know, Faye. I just would hate to see you lose your son as well as your marriage."

"Jeff wouldn't dare."

"Divorce does strange things to people, Faye."

"Tell me about it." Faye rolled the tissue into a tight ball then tossed it toward the waste basket by the dresser and missed.

"Jeff could use this against you in court."

"I thought you were a corporate lawyer. Have you suddenly taken up family practice?"

"No, but I'm not stupid."

"Are you saying I am?"

"I'm only saying that I don't think you've given this enough thought, Faith." Following her parents' examples, Hope only called her sisters by their real names when she was aggravated at them. Like now.

Faye suddenly stood. "All I've done is *think* about this. My heart's been ripped from my chest. I feel like my life is over. If I can't come home—to the only place I feel like I might really be at home—well, then I just don't care anymore." And Faye walked out of the room.

Feeling like a failure as a family counselor, Hope stooped to pick up Faye's tissue wad then lobbed it into the waste basket.

"So you decided to stay with us after all?" Drew smiled at her from the hallway.

Hope blinked and suddenly felt self-conscious over the fact that she was standing in her old room, the same room that she'd sneaked Drew into a few times back in high school. She refrained from putting a hand to her cheek, where she could feel her face warming with the flush of embarrassment over this thought. "I was just in here talking to Faye." She came into the hallway, closing the door behind her. "But I must've offended her because she walked out on me."

"That used to be your room, didn't it?" His voice sounded casual, but his eyes looked intense.

"Yes. It's changed some. Nice shade of blue. I'll bet Cherry picked it out." She was trying to keep her tone light and disconnected.

"She's the one with all the taste." He frowned. "I'm just the one who pays all the bills."

"Well, you guys have fixed this old house up really nice." Hope smiled blankly as she made her way past him.

"So, how about it, you want to stick around and be our house guest?"

"No, but I appreciate your hospitality."

"Too bad."

Her back was to him now, but something about the way he was acting and the way he said *too bad* made her uncomfortable...and yet she was curious. Had he really been insinuating what she thought he was insinuating? She paused and turned to see him looking at her with what seemed like longing.

"Pardon me?" she asked as if she hadn't heard him right.

He stepped toward her now. "You're sure looking good, Hope. The years have been kind."

She acted oblivious. "Thanks. But I suppose we're all starting to show our age some."

He ran his hand through his thinning hair. "Some of us more than others, I expect."

"And thanks for the offer of a room, but I'll be more comfortable at the Ponderosa."

"Well, I put your bag in the back of Nona's car for you. But if you change your mind, I'll be happy to go and—"

"Thanks, but no thanks." She laughed lightly then turned away. But as she walked down the hallway, returning to the now vacated living room, she remembered something she'd read in a magazine— if a guy cheats once, he's likely to do it again. But surely Drew wouldn't consider turning the tables by cheating on Cherry to be with Hope now. And even if he would stoop that low, Hope would never—not in a million years and even if he were the last man on the planet—give him the chance!

Still, it brought her a tiny sliver of guilty pleasure to think that Drew might've been thinking along those lines—that he might still find her attractive or even wonder why he'd let her go in the first place. And yet she knew it was wrong to feel that way. Especially at her sister's expense.

Cherry might not have thought twice about stealing Hope's boyfriend twelve years ago. And to be fair, Hope had broken it off with Drew at the time—mostly because she wanted the freedom to date a certain guy on campus. Even so, Hope would not repay her sister's evil deed in kind. Hope would remain on the high road.

Chapter Three

....

In an attempt to avoid Cherry, and mostly because she had nothing to say to her, Hope went out of her way to visit with all of her other relatives. Not that there were so many, but Nona had borne four children by her first husband, a non-Italian man named Charles Emerson. And then she'd had two more children with her second husband—the Italian husband—Antonio Bartolli. Vitto Bartolli was Nona's youngest child, and everyone assumed her favorite since he looked so much like his father.

As a result of these six children, who were now in their sixties and seventies, Nona was survived by seventeen grandchildren, thirty-eight great-grandchildren, and by Hope's best estimate, several dozen great-great-grandchildren. Not even half of Nona's descendants were expected to attend the funeral tomorrow, but many of them were already in town, and most had descended on Cherry's house for this impromptu barbecue. So it was a bit like a family reunion, and Hope found it somewhat interesting if not exhausting getting reacquainted with some of her now middle-aged cousins and their offspring.

However, after an hour or so, Hope grew weary of answering the same old questions. "Are you married yet?" Or "How did a pretty girl like you avoid the trip down the aisle?" Or "Any children in your future?" And so she made her apologies to Cherry, saying she had a headache, which was actually the truth. Then, Cherry gave her the keys to Nona's old Rambler, and Hope attempted to make a graceful exit, but instead nearly plowed down the attractive thirty-something man who was unfortunately opening the front door just as she was bursting out.

"Sorry!" She grabbed the porch railing to keep from tumbling them both down the brick front steps.

"I rang the doorbell," he said quickly, "but I figured everyone must've been out back. So I was just letting myself in."

"And I was letting myself out—a bit clumsily I must admit."

"Hope?" he said with what looked like a flash of recognition.

She looked into his warm brown eyes with curiosity. "Are you a relative?"

"No. A friend." He flashed a brilliant smile as he extended his hand. "Lewis Garson."

As she told him who she was, she wondered two things. Why did that name sound familiar? And was it just her imagination or could he pass for George Clooney's younger brother?

"It's a pleasure to meet you." His smile remained as he released her hand then stood tall. He appeared to be about six-foot-four or so. His pale blue shirt was neatly pressed and his khaki pants had crisp creases down the front. This guy either had a fastidious wife or an excellent dry cleaners. She wanted to peek at his left hand but felt that was too obvious. And since when did she concern herself with the marital status of male strangers? It must've been all those aunts' and cousins' inquiries over hers. "You don't remember me, do you?" He shoved his hands into his pockets in a slightly dejected way.

She shook her head. "Should I?"

"Probably not." He nodded to the house next door. "Actually, I'm here for your grandmother."

"Oh, I'm sorry. You must not have heard that she passed on."

"I know about that. Actually, I'm Mrs. Bartolli's attorney."

"Oh?"

"Cherry invited me to stop by this evening." He looked slightly unsure. "But it sounds like there's quite a crowd."

"Kind of an unexpected family reunion of my grandmother's relatives."

"Maybe I'll wait to talk to Cherry after the funeral service tomorrow."

"Oh…right…" Hope was curious as to what Nona's attorney wanted to say to Cherry, although it was probably none of her business. "So I assume you're handling my grandmother's estate?" She knew she sounded both stiff and nosy but couldn't help herself.

He simply smiled. "Yes. And I wanted to arrange to meet with the family members after Mrs. Bartolli's service for the reading of the will."

"*All* of the family?" Hope tried to imagine the attorney with all of Nona's relatives gathered together in one room. Certainly he didn't plan to read the will to everyone, did he? As far as Hope knew, Nona didn't really have all that many worldly possessions in the first place. "I mean there are probably a couple hundred relatives. Not that everyone will be here, but I'm guessing there are more than fifty out in Cherry's backyard at the moment." Hope slowly shook her head. "Who knew one little woman could be responsible for so many offspring, eh?"

He smiled. "You remind me of your grandmother."

Now Hope laughed. "Well, other than the fact that I'm about a foot taller than she was or that she was just a bit older than I am, well, I assume the resemblance must be quite striking."

His dark eyes twinkled when he laughed. "I wasn't speaking of stature as much as I was of spirit. You seem to have a lot of your grandmother's spirit in you, Hope."

"Thank you. I will take that as a compliment, and I will get out of your way." She stepped aside to let him pass. "Feel free to go in. They're mostly in the backyard."

"And I'll see you tomorrow?" he asked.

"I'll be at the funeral," she called out as she went down the steps. As she walked next door to Nona's house, she wanted to add that she would, for sure, be looking for him. But then, she wondered about something he'd said...something that suggested she should remember him...but from where? And with those dark good looks and old-fashioned charm, why would she have forgotten him?

Nona's little bungalow was more rundown than Hope remembered. The siding was in need of paint, and some of the shutters looked loose, but it was Nona's beloved flower boxes and garden beds that caught Hope's attention. Weedy and neglected... it seemed to suggest that Nona must not have been in top form these past few weeks. Late May and early June had always been Nona's favorite time of year, and even last year she'd written to Hope about how her various flowers and plants were doing. Hope was tempted to see if the spare key was still stashed under the ceramic frog like it used to be, but she wasn't sure if she really wanted to go inside Nona's house. Perhaps it was better to simply remember it as it once had been. Hope stooped to pull up a milkweed that had forced its way between a crack in the cement walkway. And then she pulled another. And as she pulled the stubborn noxious plants, she found herself remembering.

Nona's house had been Hope's haven while growing up. Faye, more than six years older, had always seemed to live her own carefree life—a life that Hope wasn't old enough to participate in. And Cherry, though only sixteen months younger, had seemed babyish to Hope. Always small for her age, Cherry had been needy and clingy. Plus, she was "so adorable" that people would stop to comment on the curly blond locks and baby blue eyes, making Hope feel invisible, or worse, like the Ugly Duckling.

In Nona's house, Hope felt special. She helped with cooking and gardening and was always spoken to as if she were a grown-up. And although it was never said, Hope always felt that she was Nona's favorite. At least while she lived at home. Once she moved on, Hope assumed that Cherry usurped that title...along with everything else. Somehow Cherry, the spoiled baby, had turned out to be the Cherry on Top. She wound up with everything—Hope's boyfriend, their parents' house, and Nona's love.

Hope felt tears filling her eyes, and she realized that her hands were full of weeds. Here she was in her best courtroom suit, pulling weeds in Nona's yard. She tossed the weeds into the gravel of the driveway then went over to the old separate garage and opened the two side-swinging doors, which Nona never kept locked. Then, she got into Nona's old car. Hope knew the story of the old Rambler well. Not only was it a classic, but it was a Classic. A light blue 1965 Rambler Classic. Grandpa Bartolli, a man Hope had never met since he died shortly before she was born, bought Nona that car "new" for their twentieth wedding anniversary. And Nona had kept it all these years. But because Nona usually walked to town and church, the car still had less than thirty thousand miles on it.

Hope inserted the key, turned it, and presto—the car started. Hope smiled as she put it into reverse. Oh, sure the car was a little clunky and it certainly didn't have all the modern conveniences of her BMW, but it was really a sweet little car. And solid as a rock, too. She wondered what would become of it now. Her best guess was that Cherry would be the one to deal with it as well as everything else. That's probably why Lewis, the good-looking attorney, wanted to speak to her. But if Hope had a double garage, she might even be tempted to ask about buying the old Rambler. But, really, what would be the point? It wasn't as if it were a practical car for the city.

Hope decided to give the car a good run. Hopefully she'd charge up its battery as well as enjoy a sentimental journey. She was surprised at the growth that had taken place in Sisters over the past ten years since she'd been gone. New housing developments, new businesses, a whole new grocery store complex. Really, it was turning into a charming little town. And the shops and restaurants looked busy, too. But then, that had always been the case during summers. And even during the ski season, it wasn't too bad.

As she continued to drive, she discovered a whole new development on the east side of town. A nice looking spa and convention center, restaurant and brewery, hotel and adorable cabins, not to mention a barn-shaped building that appeared to house a theater with four screens and a restaurant, too! Wouldn't they have loved that back in the old days?

She headed out of town now, driving east toward the rodeo grounds. Sisters boasted the "biggest little rodeo" in the world. And it was true, because they awarded the largest cash prizes at the smallest rodeo, luring big-name cowboys from all over the country. Rodeo weekend was always a big event in the small town when she was growing up. How many times had she been in the rodeo parade? Probably not as many times as Cherry, who (thanks to Drew and his family) was actually a rodeo princess when she was a senior in high school.

Drew's family owned Crooked L Ranch, and his dad, Drew Lawson Senior, was on the rodeo board. Plus, he raised some of the best beef around. And horses, too. In fact, that's how Cherry first wangled her way into Drew's world. When she was about fourteen, Cherry begged Hope to take her out to the ranch where she met Drew's mom, an expert horsewoman and barrel racing champion from the fifties. Cherry started taking riding lessons from Mrs. Lawson and the rest, as they say, was history. Whether Cherry planned the whole thing or whether it was just *one of those things* would probably never be clear, but the fact was, Cherry set herself up nicely.

Drew still worked on the family ranch and would own it one day, but Cherry had begged to live in town. She convinced Drew that she would die of loneliness out there in the sticks. And then she'd convinced her dad to sell them the house at a rock-bottom price. And then Avery and Harrison came along and living in town made sense for them. As usual, Cherry got her way. When did she not?

Hope turned the car around in the rodeo grounds. Already the campground looked to be filling up, and rodeo was about ten days away. Not that she had any plans to be here for it. No, those days were long past. Still, she paused, looking longingly at the mountains behind the open stadium. Those had been some good times!

As she drove back to town, she compared her life then to her life now. Were there ever two worlds as different? And if she were being honest—even if only to herself—which world would hold more appeal? If anyone had asked this question ten years ago, she would've said her current life, hands down, was much better. Living in the city, working as an attorney, driving a cool car, wearing fancy clothes, dining in fine restaurants, attending concerts and shows, really, what could've been better than that?

Only now, she wasn't so sure. Something about the sweet simplicity of her hometown was surprisingly appealing. The mountains were gorgeous, the blue sky amazing, the air fresh and clean, the streets less busy, the shops looked interesting and the new developments seemed charming. And yet, what would a corporate attorney do in a town like this?

But did she really want to continue in corporate law? Perhaps that was the biggest question gnawing at her soul. The past several months, she had found herself dragging herself out of bed, wishing she could call in sick, and just plain dreading going to work. Oh, the pay was good and the benefits were great, but the actual work…well, it was lackluster and disappointing and not anything like what she'd imagined her life as an attorney would be like. But then, everyone had to settle…didn't they? Well, everyone except her little sister. Miss Cherry on Top!

As Hope drove back through town, she felt inexplicably tired. Exhausted. So weary she thought she could probably go to bed and sleep for days. But then she would miss the funeral. And wasn't that why she'd come…to say good-bye to Nona?

Hope checked into the hotel, parked the car by her room, and retrieved her bag from the backseat. Even this hotel had been redone. The room was decorated lodge style, including lodge-pole pine furnishings and a rock fireplace. Very warm and inviting. But all she wanted to do at the moment was to sleep and sleep. And hopefully she'd have a better perspective on things—particularly her own life—when she woke up.

But just as she was drifting, caught in that filmy twilight place between waking and sleeping, she thought she heard Nona's voice talking to her. It was as if she were saying: *Just let go, Hope. Let it all go…when you let go, God in His mercy will hold on…let it all go…and He will hold on…just let it all go. Let it go…let go…*

Chapter Four

....

Hope felt unexpectedly refreshed when she woke up in the morning. And she felt something else, too…she felt strangely happy. She stretched lazily in the bed, yawned, and then slowly opened her eyes. But she was surprised to see that she wasn't in her condo bedroom in the city. Instead of her sleek, modern furnishings—espresso-toned wood, stainless steel accents, and glass—she was in a cozy room with warm colors and rustic wood furniture. Oh, yes, the Ponderosa Hotel…Sisters…Nona's funeral. She sat up to look at the clock, worried that she'd slept too late for the nine-thirty service, but was relieved to see that it wasn't even eight yet.

As she showered, she remembered Nona's words—was it really Nona? Or maybe it didn't matter who or what the source was. Whatever the case, as she replayed the "Let Go" mantra in her head, she knew that there was truth and release in those words. For so long, probably since Mom's death, Hope had tried to hold onto every little thing. Her goal had been to control every part of her life, to be in charge, to manage, to direct, to maintain…and to succeed. And yet it seemed impossible. As soon as she reigned in one area another felt like it went slip-sliding away. And in the end, where did all her effort and energy and strife get her? Did it make her happy? Did it bring her peace? Contentment? Fulfillment?

As she dried her hair, she decided it was time to quit thinking about these things. Oh, certainly, there was some wisdom in the

"Let It Go" philosophy, but the truth was, Hope had a career and responsibilities. She had bills to pay and people to please. Letting go might work for some people, but people like Hope probably needed to hold on—and hold on tight.

She brushed her hair back away from her face, wound it around into a smooth French twist, and secured it with bobby pins. Then, she spent her usual five minutes to do some minimal (business-appropriate) makeup. She slipped on her sleeveless "little black dress" and topped it with a sweet little cream-colored lacy cardigan that she'd bought from a boutique in the Pearl District because it had reminded her of one that Nona used to wear. She pushed her feet into a pair of relatively sensible black pumps, although the heels might be a challenge in grass, and finally put on her diamond stud earrings (ones she'd bought for herself, not a gift from some previous lover, although one had offered) and snapped her favorite silver bracelet in place. She picked up her black Gucci bag and gave herself one last check in the mirror. Nona would not be ashamed. Sensibly chic without being ostentatious. Appropriate for a funeral.

Even when Nona was old (or seemed old to Hope) she'd had a good eye for fashion. She respected the classics and was a fan of women like Audrey Hepburn, Leslie Caron, and Jackie O. As a child, Hope hadn't fully appreciated Nona's taste. As an adult, she embraced it.

Hope drove to Nona's church, which wasn't Catholic like one might expect, but rather a small Protestant church that Nona's first husband, Charles Emerson, had belonged to since his parents had moved to this town to start a small lumbermill in the late thirties. Charles had even helped to build the church before being called off to war. And even after his death and Nona's second marriage to

Antonio, an Italian immigrant who had been raised Catholic, Nona
had insisted that the Lutheran church was *familia*. Since Antonio
hadn't been particularly devout after moving away from his family in
San Francisco, he wasn't too sorry to give up Mass anyway. Although
Nona said that she sometimes forced him to go to church with her
for holidays or if they'd had a fight, and she suspected he occasionally
snuck off to confession in his later years. But both Charles and
Antonio had been buried in the cemetery that belonged to the old
church, and it wouldn't be long until Nona's remains would rest
between them.

Hope parked Nona's car then checked her purse to make sure she
had tissues. Not that she expected to break down at the service, but it
was a possibility since her emotions seemed to be playing havoc with
her lately. And, as she recalled, she had sobbed like a baby at her mom's
funeral, although that was to be expected since they were all in shock.
But, if the truth were told, Hope had probably been closer to Nona
than her mother. Not that Hope planned to admit this to anyone. And,
as usual, that thought alone made her feel guilty again. There it was,
the old grief-and-guilt connection—bound together at the hip.

It wasn't quite nine-thirty, but already the church was filling up.
A young man in a bad suit and a nice smile shyly handed Hope a
program. She looked down at the pale pink paper to see what must've
been an old photograph of Nona on the front. But she looked so young
and pretty that Hope almost didn't recognize her. Hope wondered if
Nona had picked it out as one last testament to the tiny streak of vanity
that ran through her since girlhood. But it made Hope smile.

The small church made Hope smile, too. She hadn't been here
since childhood, when she would sit next to Nona in the third pew.

The memory of those happy Sundays filled her with an unexpected warmth now. As a child she'd taken her faith seriously. God had been her best friend. But somehow, that old relationship, like so many others, had slipped away during adulthood.

Hope hadn't asked her sisters to save her a spot with the family, although she'd expected they might. She certainly would do as much for them. But as she made her way down the aisle, it looked as if the first few pews were already packed full. Cherry and Faye were seated next to each other, with Cherry's family to her right, and Monroe, Dad, and Cindy to Faye's left. To balance out the picture, Hope, the middle sister, should've been seated between Cherry and Faye (wouldn't that be how Nona would want it?), but there was no room. And Nona's other numerous relatives were filling up the other pews for several rows.

Hope realized she shouldn't have assumed anything. And she should've set her alarm and gotten up earlier. Really, in her family's eyes, she was probably just a black sheep anyway. Plus, if she didn't hurry to get a seat she might find herself standing in the back since the whole church seemed to be quickly filling up and there were still people milling about looking for seats. Just then someone tapped her on the shoulder, and Hope turned to see a slightly familiar looking woman with short auburn hair.

"Hope?" The woman smiled, revealing a slight gap between her two front teeth.

"*Erica!*" Hope reached out and grabbed her old friend's hand, giving it a comforting squeeze. "What are you doing here?"

"Coming to your grandmother's funeral, of course."

"But all the way from LA?"

"Oh, I don't live there anymore. Didn't you get my last Christmas card?" Then she laughed. "Come to think of it, I didn't send that last one. I meant to."

"You live *here* in Sisters?"

She nodded. "I do."

"Let's sit together," Hope suggested, pointing to a spot not too far from the front.

"But don't you want to sit with your family?"

Hope just shrugged. "It appears to be full up there."

So Erica slid into the last space of the fourth pew and Hope followed, sitting right next to the center aisle. She pushed aside a sense of indignation and turned her attention back to Erica. "What made you move back here?" she asked quietly. The organ music was beginning to play now, and it was probably just minutes until the service would begin.

"I was tired of the fast pace down there."

"But I thought you were working for a TV network or something."

Erica nodded. "I was writing. But I realized I could write anywhere. Plus it seemed like everyone who lived down there kept writing the same thing. I got to thinking if I lived somewhere else I might write about something more unique."

"And is it working?"

Erica grinned. "Oh, yeah. In fact, I just sold my first script."

"Congratulations!"

"We'll see. There's still a long way to go before production begins." Erica looked directly ahead now, up to where the slate blue casket was situated with wreaths and bouquets of flowers all around. "Sorry about your grandmother, Hope," she said quietly. "But she had a good, long life."

Hope nodded. "She did."

"She set a good example on how to grow old gracefully," Erica continued. "I saw her just last week at the post office. As usual, she had walked. But she seemed tired."

Hope nodded again. "I just wish I'd come out here to visit her… you know, one more time before she passed."

Just then the organ music seemed to intensify, the people who had been quietly chatting amongst themselves grew quieter, and old Pastor Murray slowly made his way to the pulpit. Hope was surprised to see he was still around since he'd seemed old to her even twenty years ago. Then, the service began with prayer and there was scripture reading and a short eulogy, which Hope suspected Nona had written herself. It wasn't anything out of the ordinary for an old-fashioned funeral service, but it was sincere and respectful and Nona probably would've appreciated it.

"And now for Madolina Bartolli's favorite hymn." Pastor Murray nodded over to where his wife was preparing to sing. "'In The Garden.' Turn to your programs if you would like to sing along."

IN THE GARDEN

Verse 1
I come to the garden alone,
While the dew is still on the roses;
And the voice I hear,
Falling on my ear,
The Son of God discloses.

Chorus:
And he walks with me
And He talks with me,
And He tells me I am his own;
And the joy we share as we tarry there,
None other has ever known.

Verse 2
He speaks and the sound of His voice
Is so sweet the birds hush their singing;
And the melody that He gave to me
Within my heart is ringing.

Chorus

Verse 3
I'd stay in the garden with Him,
Tho' the night around me be falling,
But He bids me go;
Thro' the voice of woe
His voice to me is calling.

Chorus

Hope opened her program to sing, but seeing the sweet words made her eyes fill with tears so that she was unable to read the words. She simply looked up to the front of the church until they reached the chorus, which she knew by heart.

As they sang the chorus, she couldn't help but notice that her sisters were actually laughing. Laughing! *What on earth was the matter with them?* And didn't they care what their grandmother would think—who laughs at a funeral? She was thankful that she wasn't sitting up there with them. And she was embarrassed for Nona's sake. She exchanged glances with Erica, who seemed equally bewildered by Cherry and Faye's disrespectful behavior. What was wrong with those two?

The service ended, and as the pall bearers carried the blue casket down the aisle, Hope tried to push the aggravation over her sisters' strange behavior away from her. Best to just act cordial, pay her family dues (not that anyone seemed to care), and get out of town as soon as possible. Maybe she could even change her flight to this evening instead of Saturday.

"Are you going to be in Sisters for long?" Erica asked as they were exiting the pew. "Maybe we could get coffee or—"

"Coffee and cookies will be served in the church basement after the interment," an old church-lady friend informed them. Hope couldn't remember the woman's name, but she made a forced smile for her benefit. "Yes, thank you. That will be nice."

"Are you going to the cemetery?" Hope asked Erica.

"Sure." Erica smiled. "Want a ride?"

"Thanks, I'd love one."

As Erica drove in the procession to the cemetery, she updated Hope on the comings and goings of her life, including a divorce that had occurred a couple of years ago. All that Hope recalled of this marriage was getting Christmas cards with photos of the "happy" couple in exotic places like Tahiti or Fiji.

"That was just one more reason it was easy to leave LA behind," Erica said as she parked along the road by the cemetery. "It was one thing being lonely inside of a bad marriage. But going through that whole single thing down there...well, I just didn't have the energy."

"And you think it'll be easier in Sisters?" Hope felt doubtful.

"I've already accumulated a nice circle of friends. That helps."

"You guys weren't married very long," Hope mused as they walked with the processional toward the gravesite area.

"Almost seven years. My mom said that Will got the seven-year itch. I think he'd had it even before we were married."

They joined the others already gathered by the gravesite. This time Hope had no expectations about standing with her family. She figured they wouldn't care one way or another. The burial service was dignified but brief. Nona's casket was laid to rest between her two previous husbands, Charles and Antonio. How the deceased men would've felt about this arrangement would remain a mystery. But as the shiny casket was lowered, Hope suspected that it had been Nona's plan all along. A final prayer was said and some of Nona's surviving children dropped handfuls of dirt into the grave...and then some of the grandchildren, including Cherry and her two children. Hope wanted to push her way through the small crowd and take her place, but convention prevented her. She decided she would return later, for a private moment with her grandmother.

Back at the church, Erica pulled up to the entrance, pausing to dig something out of her purse. "Give me a call, okay?" She handed a slightly rumpled business card to Hope.

"You mean you're not staying for coffee and cookies in the basement?" Hope gave Erica a cheesy smile. The truth was, Hope did not want to go down into the stuffy church basement and chat with old people.

"I'll pass. But, really, if you get the chance, call me. You heard my story already, but we never even got to yours."

Hope nodded as she tucked the card into her Gucci bag. "Thanks for the ride." As she got out of the car, she prepared herself to be polite and social and ladylike. As badly as she wanted to escape with Erica, she would do this one last small thing for Nona's sake. And then she would be free. Or so she would tell herself. Cut the ties that bind and fly home, and nothing would pull her back to this town again.

Chapter Five

....

Hope politely smiled and mingled, pretending to enjoy what was actually some very acidic coffee in a Styrofoam cup. But, as they congregated in the church basement, she did enjoy meeting Nona's old friends, hearing stories of their favorite memories of Nona. Some of them actually remembered Hope from her childhood, but most of them knew Cherry much better. As always, Cherry Bartolli Lawson seemed to be everyone's favorite. Not that they said as much to Hope, but she could see it in their eyes when they spoke of her little sister. Apparently, Cherry was running for Miss Congeniality of Sisters because she volunteered for everything and anything and was often featured in the weekly newspaper. "And she's so photogenic," one woman said. Yes, it seemed that Cherry was still a small-town celebrity. Well, good for her.

"Oh, you were here after all," Faye said to Hope when their paths finally crossed as the crowd in the basement started to thin. "Cherry thought you hadn't made it."

Hope suppressed the urge to say something really mean. "Did Cherry think I'd take time off work, fly in from Portland, and then miss Nona's funeral?"

"She thought maybe you were sick. You know, after you left early last night."

"Oh." Hope made an apologetic smile. "I think I was just tired."

"Well, it's almost over with." Faye sighed. "Nona would've liked it."

Hope wasn't so sure Nona would've liked everything about today. "So what were you and Cherry giggling about?" she asked suddenly. "I could hear you clear back where I was sitting."

"*Giggling?*" Faye looked confused.

"During Nona's favorite hymn. You were both cracking up like twelve-year-olds and I was embarrassed for the family's sake."

Faye smiled as if this was very funny. "Oh, *that*."

"What?" demanded Hope.

Faye giggled now. "Nona's favorite hymn."

"Yes…?" Hope was getting seriously aggravated.

"*And he* walks with me, *and he* talks with me, *and he* tells me I am his own." Now Faye was laughing as if this was the funniest thing in the world.

"What is *wrong* with you?" Hope glanced around to see if anyone was listening to her crazed sister. But mostly it was just family members remaining and they didn't seem to notice.

"*Andy.* Don't you get it? *Andy* walks with me. *Andy* talks with me."

"Huh?"

"Sometimes she sang that song just to be funny. Because *Andy* walked with Nona. *Andy* talked—"

"Oh, *Andy*." A dim light went on as Hope remembered something that Nona had written in her letters, about how she and Andy walked to town together when the weather was nice. "Nona's walking friend. Yes, I remember. But why is that so funny? And, by the way, was Andy here?" Hope glanced around the basement, where it seemed only a few lingering relatives remained. "I would've liked to have met him."

Faye started to laugh harder.

"What is *so* funny?" Hope frowned at her.

"*Andy!*" she sputtered.

Hope just stared. "Yes, but why is that funny? Who is Andy?" Suddenly she imagined some secret lover—perhaps a younger man— even so, what was so terribly humorous about that?

Faye just laughed louder. "*Who* is he?"

Hope held up her hands. What kind of game was this? "Okay, *where* is he?"

"He's at the vet." Faye chortled as she pulled a tissue from her pocket.

"The *vet?*"

"He's—he's being boarded there." Faye was laughing so hard she had tears running down her flushed face.

"*Boarded?*" Hope wasn't sure which one of them was crazy. But now Cherry was coming their way with a curious expression.

"Hope thinks—" Faye grabbed Cherry's arm and continued sputtering. "She—she thinks Andy is a—a *person!*"

Now Cherry was starting to giggle. "Really?"

"*Andy is a dog!*" Faye finally managed to blurt out. But now, both she and Cherry were laughing as if this were the funniest thing they'd ever heard.

"Andy is a *dog?*" Hope nodded, letting this sink in. So Andy wasn't a neighbor, or even a secret lover, but a dog. "Still, it's not that funny."

But it was too late. Both Cherry and Faye were acting like crazy women. Like two drunken sailors, they were now singing the chorus to "In the Garden."

"Andy walks with me. Andy talks with me. Andy tells me I am his own!" And they were howling with laughter.

Hope made her way from them, slipping back up the stairs and into the now quiet church. If her sisters wanted to make fools of themselves, let them. She was not going there. She exited the church, got into the Rambler Classic, and then went to town where she'd seen a florist shop. There, she bought a dozen pink roses (Nona's favorite). Then she got back in the car and drove to the cemetery where all was quiet and the gravesite had already been refilled and the flowers were neatly laid out.

She just stood there looking down at the small sea of flowers then finally took in a long, deep breath. "Oh, Nona," she said aloud. "I'm sorry I missed seeing you before you left. I would've liked to have talked." She laid her bouquet of pink roses near the marble headstone then stepped back. "You were my family, Nona. Maybe you were my only family." Tears were sliding down her cheeks now. She just let them. "I hope I can remember all the things you taught me…all the things you said to me while I was growing up. I'm sure that I'll need them." Then, Hope remembered the words she'd heard last night, just as she'd been falling asleep, words about letting go, about letting God hold onto things. At the time they'd seemed to make sense. Now she wasn't so sure.

"Was that you, Nona?" she whispered nervously. "Were you trying to tell me something?" Just then a breeze rippled through the air, stirring the leaves of the nearby aspen trees. It was a pretty sound, light…airy…free. And something about that sound filled Hope with longing. She bent over and removed one rose from the ones she had just laid down. She held this to her chest as she silently prayed, asking God to guide her…to help her to find her way…and possibly to teach her how to learn to let go. Although she wasn't even sure what it was she needed to let go of.

"Thank you, Nona," she said quietly. "Be at peace. Be at rest. I will always hold you in my heart." Then, she turned and walked away. But as she walked, she sensed that someone was watching her. And as she got closer to her car, she noticed another car—a midsized SUV parked nearby. Probably someone paying respects to someone else, she told herself as she fished the Rambler car keys from her bag. Besides, this was Sisters. No reason to be worried about getting mugged here.

"Sorry to disturb your privacy," called a male voice as a tall figure emerged from the shadows of a stand of Ponderosa pines.

Hope actually jumped, dropping the car keys down on the graveled road.

"And now I've frightened you." He walked toward her and she realized it was the guy from Cherry's front porch last night. Nona's attorney. Or so he had said. Suddenly she wasn't so sure.

Street smart from living in the city for more than a decade, she cautiously stepped back from him now, moving toward the car, and yet fully aware that the keys were still on the ground.

He smiled uncomfortably. "I know…it probably looks like I'm stalking you, Hope. But I'm not. It's just that I saw Mrs. Bartolli's car driving through town and it caught me off guard. And with your hair pinned up like that, well, I didn't recognize you. And for one ridiculous moment, I thought it was Mrs. Bartolli's ghost." He laughed. "And so I followed the car out here." He bent down to pick up her keys, holding them out to her with an outstretched arm as if he was trying to keep his distance. "Remember me?" he said as if he thought she'd gone senile since yesterday. "Lewis Garson."

That's when it hit her. "Lewie Garson," she said slowly.

He chuckled. "Lewie with no Huey or Dewey. I don't even have an Uncle Donald. Although I did go to the U of O, which does make me a duck. Anyway, I gave up the nickname in college."

She smiled in relief. "We went to grade school together."

"And junior high and high school, too. It's just that I kind of blended in with the woodwork during those years."

"Now I remember." She stepped closer and took her keys from him. "You were always shy."

He nodded. "Fortunately, I lost the shyness along with the nickname. Or mostly. I still get an attack of shyness now and then."

"I thought you seemed familiar yesterday, but I just couldn't place you."

"Well, I did change somewhat. My mom said I finally grew into my feet." He pointed down to his shiny brown loafers. "Can you believe they were size thirteen when I was only thirteen, but I was still shorter than most of the girls." He made a face. "Including you."

"I sprouted up fast." She made a face back at him. "And I was taller than most of the boys."

"Not anymore." He stepped closer to her to show that he had a good six inches on her now. And that was with her heels. "Anyway, I'm sorry to have startled you. I don't usually stalk beautiful women in the graveyard like this."

She was speechless now. Had he just called her beautiful?

"As long as I have you here, I might as well remind you that the family will be getting together at Cherry's for the reading of the will."

She sighed. "I doubt that anyone will miss me."

"But you need to be there."

"I'm sure Cherry will see that I get whatever little trinkets Nona may have left to me." Of course, even as she said this, Hope could think of several little mementos she wouldn't mind having. Not that she'd get the chance if Cherry got to them first. Besides, Hope reminded herself, she'd already experienced the most important parts of Nona. She'd gotten those during her childhood.

"You really need to come, Hope." His brown eyes looked sincere and suddenly Hope wondered if this might have more to do with him and her than it had to do with Nona's will. Was he really coming on to her?

"Okay," she said. "I'll be there. What time?"

"Three."

She almost said, *it's a date*, but thankfully did not. "See you at three, then." She smiled brightly then went around to get in the car. She couldn't explain it, but she felt as giddy as a schoolgirl as she started the engine. He had called her beautiful. And when he wasn't watching, she'd glanced at his left ring finger to see that it was bare. Oh, she knew this didn't really mean anything. But there would be no harm in making it to the family meeting at three.

Of course, that was still nearly three hours away. She wished he'd invited her to lunch. She wanted to get to know him better…to gaze into those yummy brown eyes. Instead, she pulled out her cell phone, which she'd turned off for the funeral service and forgotten about since then. She checked for messages, but decided to ignore the work-related ones. Then, she noticed the business card that Erica had given her. Maybe she'd be up for lunch.

"I'd love to," Erica told her. "Why don't you meet me at the new restaurant in Five Pines? It just changed owners again, but I hear it's good." Then she told Hope how to find it, and they agreed to meet there in twenty minutes—not quite enough time to run back to the hotel and change clothes. But when Hope saw that the restaurant, unlike so many in Sisters, was slightly formal, she didn't feel too

LOVE FINDS YOU IN SISTERS, OREGON

out of place in her little black dress. She went ahead and got a table, informing the hostess that a friend was meeting her.

But then, as she was sitting there, she noticed a man that looked a lot like Lewis entering the restaurant. And for a moment, she thought that, perhaps, he was still stalking her. Although, she'd mistakenly parked the Rambler by the wrong building and ended up walking a ways to the restaurant, so he probably didn't know she was here. Even so, she was about to wave to him, or perhaps even go over to the foyer where he seemed to be waiting, when she noticed another familiar face entering the restaurant. It was her own sister Cherry. And she seemed to be alone.

Hope watched curiously as Cherry and Lewis greeted each other—and then embraced. And Hope fought back waves of jealousy as the two of them went through a door that appeared to lead to a lounge. What on earth was going on here?

Just then, Erica arrived, and Hope put on her happy face and pretended that she hadn't just witnessed what was feeling like a very unnerving little tryst. Instead, she began to chatter to Erica about how she was getting a bit disenchanted with corporate law, and how perhaps it was time to move onto some other sort of practice.

"Would you care for wine or anything else before you order?" the petite, dark-haired waitress was asking them politely.

"Yes," Erica said eagerly. She nodded at Hope. "I think we could use a little something, don't you? I suspect your grandmother would recommend a nice red wine if she were here."

Hope glanced over to where she imagined Cherry and Lewis cloistered off in a dark corner of a smoky lounge (even though she knew public smoking had been outlawed in Oregon for some time now), but she envisioned them, head-to-head, sipping martinis, and she said to Erica, "I'll pass." Despite Nona's encouragement that *a little wine was good for one's heart and one's soul,* Hope didn't like to drink.

"I'll have a cabernet sauvignon," Erica began, continuing on to order the soup and salad of the day.

"I'll have iced tea and the soup and salad, too," Hope told the waitress.

"So your career has possibly reached a crossroads," Erica said, "but you haven't mentioned your love life. As I recall you were dating someone rather seriously for quite some time. What happened to that relationship?"

"Curtis…" Hope sighed. "Oh, he's still around…and still interested." In fact, he had called a few days ago and, when she told him she was lonely, he offered to drop everything and come over to keep her company, although she had declined.

"But you're not interested?"

"Not so much. He's a very nice guy. He has a good job and a nice little house by the river. And I believe he sincerely loves me. But something in the relationship just wasn't quite right. And the more he pressured me to get married, the more I began pushing him away. And yet, all the while, I tried to tell myself that he was the one—the real deal. But finally, a few months ago, I got honest with myself. I knew it wasn't working. So I broke it off. But even then, I didn't break up completely. Like a big chicken, I just told him I needed to take a break…to *think* about our relationship."

Just then, the waitress set down their beverages and, after she left, Erica held hers up to make a toast and Hope followed her lead with her tea. "Here's to your grandmother, Madolina Bartolli, a fine independent woman. May we imitate her lead and live life graciously and beautifully and with no regrets."

"Here's to Nona," Hope said simply. "May we make her proud."

They clicked glasses and, as they chatted about old times, Hope tried to divert her eyes from staring at the lounge area, watching to see if the couple ever came out

"So, you said adieu to Curtis," Erica continued. "But you didn't burn your bridge with him."

"Right." Hope nodded and took another sip.

"Maybe that's smart. I've known women who've let a good guy go and then regretted it later. Especially if another woman snatches him up. That old case of sour grapes, you know."

"The thought has occurred to me. But the truth is, I think I'd be happy for Curtis if the right woman came along. He deserves someone who truly loves him."

"How about you?" Erica asked. "What do you deserve?"

Hope sort of laughed. "Well, according to my family, I probably deserve a kick in the pants."

"Why?"

"Because this is the first time I've been home in ten years. Because I wasn't around to see Nona before she died. Things like that."

"Good grief." Erica made a face. "Is your family that dense?"

"What do you mean?"

"I mean, for Pete's sake, we all knew what Drew and Cherry did to you. And right on the heels of your mom's death." Erica shook her head in a sympathetic way. "What did they expect you to do? Run home with open arms?"

"Apparently." Hope sighed and forced her gaze away from the lounge entrance. "I did try to come home once…right after Cherry had Avery. I wanted to play the role of the doting aunt, but it turned into such a farce. I couldn't do it."

"And why should you?"

"Yes, that's sort of what Nona said, too. Oh, she wanted for Cherry and me to be close again, to bury the hatchet and be one big happy family. But Nona understood. She never pushed me."

"The mark of a wise woman. Do not push."

"And so, that made it easier to stay away. And I did."

"I'm sure this is no consolation, and do not say you heard it from me, but I get the impression that Cherry and Drew don't have the happiest marriage."

Hope looked up with interest.

"So you know this already?"

"I have my suspicions." Hope glanced over to the lounge again, wondering how much she should say.

"Well, it's not surprising," Erica continued. "They were so young when they got married. Good grief, Cherry was barely out of high school."

"And Drew wasn't even twenty-one. As I recall, my parents had to sign for Cherry to get married." She sort of laughed. "Can you imagine?"

"To be honest, I'm surprised it lasted this long. But then there are the kids."

Now Hope felt sad. "Yes…the kids."

"That's one thing I was thankful about with Will. No kids." Erica took another sip of wine. "Much simpler that way."

As the waitress delivered their lunch, Hope wondered how much she should say about Cherry. And yet it seemed Erica was already in the loop. "So do you know Lewis Garson?" she ventured after the waitress refilled their water glasses and left.

Erica's eyes lit up. "Oh, yeah. Didn't *he* improve with age?"

Hope just nodded with her eyes on the door to the lounge. "Did you know that he's seeing my sister?"

"Your sister?" Erica looked stunned. "Which one?"

"Cherry, of course."

Erica laughed. "Well, of course. That just figures!"

"How do you mean?"

"That Cherry." Erica just shook her head. "She is a piece of work. And she wins the prize for going after what she wants—and getting it. I mean, seriously, Lewis is about the best-looking, nicest, most available bachelor in town. Why should I be surprised that Cherry would go for him? That girl—she's always getting the brass ring!"

Now Hope felt mad. Not at Erica so much, but partially. Mostly she felt mad at Cherry. Why was she doing this?

"So, do you know this for absolute sure, Hope?"

"I know they're in the lounge together right now."

"No way!" Erica turned around in her seat to look.

"You can't see them. But I saw them arrive. Separately. Then they hugged in the foyer before they slipped off in there." Hope felt slightly catty for telling tales, but on the other hand, she was simply reporting what she'd seen. She was an eyewitness.

"You *are* serious." Erica turned back around. "And you really think they're having some kind of lovers' rendezvous?"

"It sure seems like it. They've been in there the whole time I've been here. Also, Lewis was on his way to Cherry's house last night; he said he wanted to talk with her." Hope paused to remember his words. He had seemed sort of surprised on the porch, but then she'd nearly run him down. But perhaps his reaction was because Cherry had so many people there. Maybe he'd hoped to find her alone. And Cherry had said the barbecue was impromptu.

"You really think they're having a fling?" Erica turned in her seat to look again.

"I don't know what else to think." Hope frowned at the back of her friend's head. "Maybe you should quit staring in case they come out."

Erica turned back around. "Well, I guess I shouldn't be too jealous since I already gave it my best shot to get Lewis's attention." She chuckled. "I even went to the effort of hiring him to draw up a will for me. I dressed to the nines and got my hair and nails done, but that boy was just not biting. I actually wondered if he might be gay because, from what I've heard, he's never been married and no one knows of any past girlfriends. But to be fair, he's only been in a town a couple of years."

Hope's eyes grew wide as the door to the lounge opened. "Don't look now, but I think they're coming out."

"Please, let me look," pleaded Erica.

"No. Okay, here comes Cherry." Hope waited as Cherry exited the building. "And now here comes Lewis." Hope put her head down, trying to be discreet. Then, once Lewis was out the door, she pointed to the window. "Look, you can see Cherry driving away in her red Mustang. And Lewis is getting into his SUV."

"Well, I'll be." Erica slowly shook her head. "I wouldn't have believed it if I hadn't seen it. I can't wait to tell my mom."

"Your mom?"

"Oh, she thinks that Lewis Garson is the best thing since sliced bread. In fact, she's the one who put me up to going after him. Not that his looks weren't enough. But, get this, Lewis goes to her church—it's one of the newer bigger churches in town. She's so convinced he's a nice little church boy and now here he is sneaking around bars with a married woman."

Suddenly Hope felt guilty. "Well…we don't know anything for sure."

"Oh, I'm not saying they're having an actual affair," Erica admitted. "Not yet anyway. But that's usually how these things start. Take it from me, I know."

Hope continued to listen as Erica chattered on about men and women and how hardly anyone was faithful anymore. And while Hope could tell that Erica's perspective comforted her, it only sickened Hope. Plus she felt like a traitor to her sister. Certainly, Cherry didn't deserve Hope's allegiance…and yet, it felt wrong to sit here listening to someone making assumptions about her. And yet, how could Hope argue in Cherry's defense?

Chapter Six

....

Feeling thoroughly exhausted and slightly blindsided, Hope had taken a "little" nap in her hotel room, and after sleeping too long, she quickly changed her clothes and arrived slightly late for the family meeting. Not that she thought anyone would mind or even notice.

"It's about time you got here," Drew said to Hope as he let her into the house. "Everyone is waiting."

"Why are they waiting?"

"Because the lawyer refused to open the will until *everyone* was here." He jerked his thumb toward the great room. "They're all in there."

"I'm sorry I'm late," Hope said as she entered the crowded room. There had to be about forty people in there. She found a spot on the fireplace hearth and sat down, looking at her feet and feeling like an errant child.

"I tried to call you," Cherry said, "but I think you're phone is off."

"The battery was low." Hope looked up at Cherry. She was standing over by the kitchen, wearing a sweet powder blue sundress. Hope tried to imagine how someone who looked so angelic could be such a little devil.

Then Lewis, who was standing nearby and wearing the same dark suit that he'd had on in the cemetery and at the restaurant, cleared his throat as if to get everyone's attention. "As some of you already know, I am Lewis Garson and Mrs. Bartolli's attorney. About a year

ago, Mrs. Bartolli asked me to revise her will. And she appointed
me as her trustee." Now he reached for a legal-sized white envelope.
Carefully opening it, he slid out the document. Hope wasn't surprised
that it wasn't very thick. Nona obviously didn't have a lot of worldly
goods to bestow. Besides, Hope knew Nona had already given a lot
of family heirlooms away. In fact, as a teenager, Hope had helped her
by packaging things up and sending them out one summer. A set of
Dresden china to Aunt Clarita. An old pipe and some photos to Uncle
Bernard. Some crystal to Aunt Belle. Some jewelry to Aunt Amelia.
And so on. Really, there was probably not much more than Nona's
house and car to be disposed of and that, in all likelihood, would go
to Cherry.

"First, Mrs. Bartolli wanted me to read this personal letter from
her." Lewis cleared his throat again. She wondered if he was nervous
to be in front of this many people or if he was nervous over the fact
that Drew was just a few feet away from him. What if Drew had
found out about Cherry and Lewis? Drew had seemed a little cranky
when he'd let her in. She'd assumed it was because she was late. But
what if…

"'Dear Beloved Family,'" the letter began. "'As this letter is being
read, it must be that I have gone on to my new home in heaven. In
that lovely golden place, I will have no need for any worldly goods.
Yet, it is true that I must leave some possessions behind. For we
come empty-handed to this Earth and we leave empty-handed.
Such a relief that is to me. Now, as many of you know, I have
already disbursed family heirlooms that I thought you would find
meaningful. Some were from the Emerson family and some were
for the Bartollis. I hope you will continue to pass them on down to

the next generation. I'm sure you know, and as I've told you before, the most precious gift I could ever bestow on anyone is simply the gift of life. Yet I cannot take credit for even that. The Father above is the giver of that gift. So all I can truly leave behind is the gift of love. To all of you, I leave that gift. My love. As for my other possessions, I have prayed and prayed and I have finally come to the conclusion that my attorney, Mr. Lewis Garson, will now share with you in the content of my last will and testament. Sincerely, Madolina Renata De Rossi Emerson Bartolli.'"

Lewis paused to take a breath then folded the paper back to read the next. "Mrs. Bartolli's will is very simple and straightforward," he told them. "And that actually makes it difficult to contest." He smiled. "Not that I expect anyone to contest it." Then he began to read a list of Nona's belongings, including her house, her furnishings, her car, and her bank account. "And it was Mrs. Bartolli's last wish that all her property would be inherited by her granddaughter Hope Madolina Bartolli." Lewis paused as several people reacted in surprise, then he continued. "However, there's a prerequisite here. And that is that Hope should relocate to Sisters and live in Nona's home for one year and care for Nona's beloved dog Andy."

There were several chortles of laughter, as if this were some kind of a joke. But there were also some gasping sounds as if some family members were shocked at this strange turn of events. And, certainly, Hope was shocked—speechless even. How was this even possible? Why would Nona leave everything to her? Not that it was so much… but it just seemed odd. Especially considering that Nona had many descendents. Wouldn't an even split amongst her children have made more sense?

"I guess that's Nona's way of making sure Andy doesn't get shipped off to the dog pound." Drew laughed as if this was funny.

"I don't understand," Hope managed to say. "Why would Nona—"

"You were always her favorite," Faye shot at her. "Why should you be surprised?"

"Are you sure that's correct?" Cherry questioned the attorney now. "Could there be a more recent copy of Nona's will? Because Hope might've been the favorite when she was growing up, but she moved away…and I'm the one who's been here. I'm the one who was helping Nona. Surely there's a more recent will."

Others began talking now, questioning why everything should go to Hope and making so much noise that Hope couldn't even think. And then Dad began questioning the lawyer about the date of the will and about what happened to Nona's previous attorney. There was clearly some confusion here, and a number of her relatives seemed seriously disturbed. More than that, they seemed angry at Hope. As if it were Hope's personal fault that Nona had written the will like this.

Although Nona's will made no sense, Hope didn't know what to say or do to make anyone feel better. But as she listened to bits and pieces of conversation, it seemed that some of the relatives had gotten the idea that Nona had been quite wealthy, that she'd been sitting on some huge family fortune that was supposed to be inherited by her children. They were all talking as if she'd been some selfish rich widow who squandered away their millions. And the truth was that Nona had lived quite frugally—probably on her social security checks, which couldn't have been much. Hope could still remember counting out the change to her when she did her shopping for her grandmother. Nona was careful not to waste electricity or water, and she tried to grow some of her own vegetables in a tiny greenhouse, which was a challenge in Sisters climate. Finally, Hope couldn't stand it. She had to speak up in defense of her dearly departed grandmother.

"Excuse me," she said loudly, almost as if addressing a loud courtroom. "I want you to know that I'm just as shocked as anyone about this. I can't believe that Nona decided to leave these things to me. I don't understand why she didn't just do an equal split amongst her children."

"That would seem more fair," Aunt Belle said.

"It's all because of that horrid little dog," her husband said bitterly. "That nasty little thing actually bit me once, broke skin, too. I told her she should have the animal put down, and she refused."

"Instead Nona decided to force the dog onto Hope." Faye pointed her finger at Hope with a slight smirk. "That's actually pretty funny. Did Nona really think you'd give up your job in Portland, your swanky condo, and move back to Sisters to live in her rundown house and take care of her dog?"

"But what about the money?" Aunt Clarita demanded. "Is it fair that Hope gets that, too?"

"What money?" Hope asked her. "Some of you are acting as if Nona was rich. And that's ridiculous. Unless she won the lottery recently, which I hadn't heard, Nona was simply a penny-pinching widow who lived in a little house and walked to town to buy her groceries. Good grief, she's had the same old car for close to fifty years."

"Does it say in her will how much money was in her bank account?" Hope's father questioned Lewis. "Because I'm sure there was quite a chunk of change in there and I think we have the right to know."

"It's true," Cherry chimed in. "She did have a hefty bank account."

"How do you know?" Hope challenged her.

"Like I already said, I helped Nona with things," Cherry said defensively. "And I drove her to the bank if there was ice or snow. And while I was there I might've noticed the numbers."

Hope felt confused now. She glanced over at Lewis for help. "Do you want to disclose the amount? Did Nona tell you how to handle this?"

"It's up to you."

Hope held up her hands in a helpless gesture. "Well, I don't want anyone thinking I usurped their inheritance."

"If the shoe fits, wear it," a female voice said from behind her.

"I think we have a right to know how much money's at stake here," Uncle Morty said loudly. "My wife is a direct descendent and—"

"Please," Lewis interrupted. "Squabbling about this will won't do anyone any good." Then he turned to Hope. "Why don't we discuss this privately?"

"Fine," she said a little too sharply. She glanced around. Kids were playing on the trampoline in the backyard. Relatives seemed everywhere else. Finally she nodded toward the front door. "Out there." Then she stood and led the way. But once she was outside, she kept going, marching on over to Nona's yard, where she finally felt she was on safe turf. Lewis was just a few steps behind her. She knew this wasn't really his fault, but the whole thing was so odd. And now it seemed that everyone in her family hated her.

"I'll admit this is a little difficult," he said as he handed her the will. "Your grandmother wanted it read publicly in order to make things less awkward for you."

Hope took the papers, skimming over the details of the house and car and things until she reached the total from checking and savings accounts. Suddenly she felt slightly lightheaded. Not that it was such an enormous figure in some circles, but it was certainly much more than she could've imagined. And she was shocked to find out that Nona had that much money tucked away. Why hadn't she used it for her own needs? Furthermore, why hadn't she split it with everyone? Her aunts were right, that would've been fairer. Why did Nona do it like this?

"Am I reading this figure correctly?" She quietly said the number out loud.

He nodded. "That's right."

"That's nearly a million dollars."

"Right again."

Hope sank down onto the steps of Nona's rickety porch and just stared at the paper. "But why?"

"Why did she have that much money?"

"Yes…and why did she leave it to me?"

He sat down next to her. "She had that much money because your grandfather Antonio Bartolli came from a family with a bit of money. Antonio left it to her, but she mostly left it in the bank, where it sat and accrued interest. You know that your grandmother liked her simple, quiet, frugal life." He smiled and, once again, Hope thought he was awfully handsome—almost suspiciously handsome if that was even possible.

"I know…but I still don't understand."

"Why she lived simply?" He just shrugged. "Can you blame her? She had what she needed. She was content."

"No, I mean why she didn't she just split the money between her children…or her grandchildren? Why did she choose to leave it all to me?"

"Your grandmother had a particular fondness for you, Hope. She spoke of you often. And she worried that you weren't happy… that you'd chosen the wrong life as a result of some of your family's choices."

"Oh…"

"Also, she said you were the most like her late husband, your grandfather, where the money had come from. And in her last year or so, she became convinced that Antonio would want you to have this inheritance. That's why she hired me to change the will."

"So there really was another will?"

He nodded.

"And I suppose some of my family…my father and my sister… might've been privy to this other will?"

"That's a distinct possibility."

"Oh."

"I know this puts you in a predicament."

"I'll say."

"And there is that little prerequisite."

"About living in her house for a year?"

He smiled. "And caring for Andy."

She chuckled now. "Andy. I keep hearing about this guy. When do I get to meet him?"

"He's at the vet's. They have a kennel."

"I'm surprised Cherry didn't want to keep him."

"Harrison has allergies."

"Oh." She peered curiously at Lewis now. "You seem to know my family fairly well."

"Oh, yes." He smiled. "Better than you think."

She wasn't so sure about that. Did he really know everything—like the old problems that had separated sisters?

"So do you want to go in there and face the angry mob?" he asked as he brushed dust off the seat of his suit.

"Not particularly."

"It is up to you whether or not you disclose the actual amount, Hope."

"Right…" She just shook her head.

"Oh, yeah." He reached in his pants pocket and pulled out a set of keys. "You already have the car keys. Here are the keys to the castle." He dropped them in her hand. "And you can come by my office tomorrow, if you want, to sign the agreement."

"The agreement?"

"About the one year."

"Oh…yeah." Hope looked over to Cherry's house—just steps away. Living in Nona's house for a year meant living next to Cherry and Drew as well. Was that even worth a million dollars?

"The money will be held in a trust for that period of time."

"And what if I choose *not* to stay here? Or what if I choose to stay here, but I don't make it for the full year?"

"Why don't you come in to my office tomorrow and we can discuss those details." He glanced over at Cherry's house then down at his watch. "Because I really have to get to another appointment soon."

She wanted to question him, to ask if his appointment was with her baby sister or some other young attractive woman, but then realized it was not only juvenile, but none of her business. "Yes, tomorrow is fine."

"How about ten? We'll go over the paperwork, and then I'll go with you to spring poor Andy." He handed her his card and grinned. "You know how it is being a lawyer, you get put into all sorts of interesting positions."

She could only imagine those interesting positions. Because the truth was, her law practice was nothing like his. And suddenly she was hit with a rush of confusing emotions. On one hand, she felt slightly envious of this small-town attorney who somehow managed to practice law in Sisters. On the other hand, she found herself surprisingly interested in him, almost to the point of distraction—or was it attraction? And, naturally, that bothered her. She had never been one to jump into anything. And certainly not into a relationship with a man she barely knew.

Add to this confusion the fact that Hope had witnessed this man in what seemed like a clandestine meeting with her own sister Cherry. And Cherry was not only Lewis's client's granddaughter, she was married.

Hope watched as Lewis got into his SUV and drove away. What if this thing with Cherry had been going on for some time? Really, how would Hope know? The two of them certainly seemed to be on good terms. But if he'd been seeing Cherry, was it possible that he'd tipped Nona's hand in regard to the will already? And Cherry had obviously been unhappy about it. What if she had some plan to take this inheritance from Hope? After all, there was the one-year clause. What happened if Hope failed to make it that long? Who got Nona's inheritance then? Would Cherry come out on top again?

Hope knew she was being paranoid. Not to mention slightly ridiculous. She stared at Nona's little house and longed to speak to her grandmother. "Why?" she whispered aloud. "Why on earth did you do this, Nona? *Why?*"

Chapter Seven

....

After a restless, almost sleepless, night, Hope awoke early on Friday morning. She put on the same suit she'd worn to fly out here two days ago and carefully packed her other clothes in her one carry-on. Her plane ticket said she was leaving at four forty today. And maybe she was. Really, wouldn't that be the easiest thing to do? This whole other idea—Nona's slightly senile-sounding plan for Hope to transplant her life back in Sisters, inhabit Nona's old house, care for some old dog with the slippery possibility that Hope might inherit a million dollars one year later—well, it was sounding more farfetched and ridiculous all the time.

For starters, there was the money issue. What was Hope going to live on while she remained in Sisters? And who was going to make the payments on her condo and car and everything else? And, if she quit her job like she'd be forced to do, she'd lose benefits like insurance and retirement, and all for what? Seriously, what was the chance that she might make it for a whole year? It was sounding more and more unlikely. Even if, somehow, she did survive a year, there'd be taxes to pay. That near million would dwindle quickly.

Plus, she'd have angry family members to contend with. And living right next door to Drew and Cherry—well, how much was that worth? Really, it was crazy. And it wasn't outside the realm of possibility that Nona hadn't been in her right mind when she'd made these last-minute changes to her will. And, despite Lewis's claim that it would be hard to contest this will, Hope was an attorney. She knew there were ways. Not only that, but even if it were airtight, which was doubtful, anyone contesting the will (like Cherry, for instance) could tie up Nona's funds for years. A lifetime, perhaps. And then lawyers' fees, court fees...well, it would all add up. Hope knew enough about law to know that it could be worthless in the end.

After Hope checked out of the hotel, she drove around town and just wondered...would she be a fool to do this? Or would she be a fool not to? She finally parked in a spot where she had full view of the mountains. The Three Sisters—Faith, Hope, and Charity—still garbed in their white jackets. Hope remembered how her mother would joke about the mountains and their various seasonal outfits. Winter usually saw them wearing full-length fur coats. But, as the days warmed, the Sisters slowly peeled down. They went from short jackets to T-shirts, to tank tops, to string bikinis, and sometimes they stood up there dark and naked for all the world to see. Then, autumn would come with a light snow, and Mom would say they were wearing their chiffon negligees and getting ready to take a long winter's nap.

Hope wondered what her mother would tell her to do right now. She'd probably say, "Go climb a mountain." And, seriously, that wasn't a bad idea. Hope had missed out on those kinds of things in the city. Oh, sure, she worked out in the gym almost daily—telling herself that she was going to go out and hike or bike or do something energetic and outdoorsy on the weekend. But more times than not, she wound up sleeping in on Saturday. Then Sunday came and she'd remember work that needed to be done. And then it would be Monday and back to the grindstone.

She glanced at her watch to see that it was nearly ten already, and she'd already promised herself she wouldn't be late again. She hopped into the old Rambler and drove through town. And, as she drove, she thought of how good it felt to be riding around in Nona's old car. To possibly have a house of her own. And even a dog. Hadn't she always wanted a dog! It might be different to be a grown-up living here. It might even be fun. Having the great outdoors practically in her own backyard. And yet…she knew it all came with a price. But maybe it was too high.

By the time she walked into Lewis's office, which was actually in the downstairs of a very unique building, she couldn't tell if it was old or new, but it was definitely done right with custom touches of what looked like reclaimed wood and metal siding that had an attractive rusty patina. The interior was even better with stained cement floors, oversized pine and glass doors, and oiled bronze hardware. It was a pleasing combination of uptown and rural, and very cool—especially for Sisters. Or the Sisters she remembered anyway.

"This is a very interesting building," she told him when he met her in the small foyer.

"Thanks." He held open the door that led into a smaller office. "I actually live upstairs. Then, I rent out the other offices down here to help offset the expenses. But I can't take the credit for what a great place it is. The architect who designed and built it is local and I happen to think she's a genius because she builds green. My heating bill is amazingly low and most of the materials are recycled or renewable."

"I noticed that the post and beams looked like reclaimed old-growth fir."

He grinned. "It sounds like you know what you're talking about."

"I like architecture and even toyed with the idea of majoring in design in college…but law seemed more substantial."

He chuckled as he pulled out a leather chair for her to sit. "Yes, there will probably always be more demand for lawsuits than homes. Sad, isn't it?"

She nodded and sat down, placing her purse in her lap.

"You look a little overdressed for Sisters," he said as he sat behind a large pine desk. "Not that you don't look lovely."

"Thanks…I guess." She frowned. "When I got up this morning, I had decided to return to Portland, to go back to work, and to forget Nona's harebrained idea."

He folded his hands on his desk and just nodded, as if he were waiting for her to continue.

"And then I drove over to the elk ranch…to look at the mountains." She sighed.

"They look beautiful this morning." He smiled. "I have a pretty good view of them from my apartment upstairs."

She fidgeted with the handle of her purse. "That must be nice."

"So you looked at the mountains…and…?"

"And I felt confused."

He smiled ever so slightly. "That's not the usual reaction that people have when they look at these mountains."

"I mean I felt confused over this decision."

"Do you want to talk about it?"

She leaned back in the chair and exhaled slowly. "Yes, Counselor, I'd like to talk about it. If you have the time, that is."

"I've got nothing but time this morning."

She wondered how it was that a young attorney in Sisters was
doing this well…owning this lovely building…having time to talk.
So many things about this guy made her curious. Yes, and suspicious,
too. And yet Nona had hired him as her lawyer. And Nona had good
sense. Why didn't it all add up?

"You have a puzzled look on your face," he pointed out. "Do you
have questions?"

She forced a smile. Oh, yeah, she had questions. Just not the
kinds of questions one should ask when one barely knows the other.
Or did she?

"I'm sure you're still in shock over how your grandmother
handled her estate."

"I'm shocked that she even had an estate. I mean besides her little
house and car."

"And little dog."

"Yes, her little dog, too. But actually, that was a surprise. How
long did she have him?"

"Just a couple of years. She adopted him from the shelter.
Apparently he'd been abused. But the little guy won her heart and
actually had something to do with her changing her will. Well, that
and a letter that she got from you."

"A letter?"

"Yes. It must've been written more than a year ago. She'd had it for
a while when she came into my office to chat."

Hope felt both confused and exposed now. "Can you explain that
a bit more clearly, *Counselor?*"

He grinned. "If you insist. Although it was *your* letter. I would
think you'd remember." He cleared his throat as if he were stalling.

"Apparently you'd written the letter on your birthday, or there about. And you were not very happy about—"

"That's okay," she said quickly. "I remember the letter now." She glared at him as she recalled the very depressed letter she'd written to her grandmother, trusting that Nona would keep Hope's troubled life to herself. "Did Nona read it to you?"

"No. Not actually. But she did talk freely. Remember we attorneys maintain client confidentiality."

"Yes, of course." Even so it was disturbing to think that Lewis had been privy to one of Hope's most private and depressing moments. She'd written the letter in haste and emotion and never should've sent it. In that letter (written on the eve of her thirty-first birthday—her last day of being thirty) she had confessed to Nona that she was thoroughly disappointed in her life. She was unhappy in love, didn't think she'd ever marry or have children; she hated her job, she didn't even like her condo very much. She was sick of the city noise and smelly air, and to add insult to injury, it had been raining for weeks on end.

Oh, yes, she remembered that night well. And still feeling blue in the morning, she had efficiently dropped Nona's letter in the mail. But later in the day, her friends took her to a birthday lunch, Curtis sent her roses to work then took her to a very swanky dinner, and by the next day, she had totally forgotten the letter. Of course, she was reminded of it when Nona wrote back, begging Hope to take some time off work to come visit her—they would plant perennials together and go through old photos and bake cookies. But Hope immediately wrote back, assuring Nona that everything was just fine—the sun was shining, she had plans to go to the theater on Saturday, and she planned to go hiking on Sunday.

"So your grandmother had a bee in her bonnet…so to speak… and she wanted to do something for her favorite granddaughter."

"Meaning she wanted to turn my life upside down."

He nodded. "Yes, I think she thought it needed to be shaken up. As she put it, you were trapped."

"Trapped?" Hope tried to keep a poker face. The truth was she had felt trapped for years. But didn't everyone?

"And your grandmother wanted to free you from your trap. She said you were like poor little Andy…you needed rescuing."

"I needed rescuing?" Hope felt indignant now. "Of the three Bartolli sisters, I am the only one who's been completely self-sufficient. I'm the only one who hasn't been rescued by someone else. And Nona thought I needed rescuing?"

"She felt you were unhappy, Hope. It was her point of view and motivated by love. How can you fault her for that?"

"No, I suppose I can't. Still, it's a little irksome. I mean both Cherry and Faye got rescued, so to speak, by my parents. Faye was the only daughter to inherit from my mother's old life insurance policy because it had been written before Cherry and I were born and never changed. Yet I'm glad for Faye's sake. She needs that money now that she and Jeff have split up."

"So I heard."

"You seem to hear a lot about our family." She peered at him curiously.

"Your grandmother wasn't just a client, but a friend as well."

"Right. So, anyway, Faye and Dad got the life insurance and Cherry got the house."

"And what did you get?"

Hope considered this. What *did* she get? "Oh, Dad helped me with college some, although I had a pretty good scholarship already, plus I worked and carried a student loan, which is paid off now." She felt a sudden rush of pride. Maybe she was glad that no one had handed her anything. Maybe she didn't want anyone to hand her anything now.

"Quite an accomplishment. And yet you were unhappy?"

She frowned. "Okay, maybe I wasn't completely happy with my life. But who is happy with their life *all* the time? We all have our highs and lows. I think it must balance out eventually."

"Good point." He leaned forward, studying her closely. "So are you happy with your life now?"

"Now?" She took in a deep breath then slowly let it out. "As I mentioned, *now* I feel like my life's been turned upside down by Nona. Really, I don't know what she was thinking." She narrowed her eyes. "Are you sure she was in her right mind?"

He chuckled. "I can't believe you of all people would question her sanity."

"I'll bet my family is questioning it right now. I can only imagine what they've got to say about this strange little setup—and about me. You heard them yesterday. Not that I'm concerned about the Emerson side. Really, this shouldn't involve them. But I'm pretty sure my dad thinks he should get *his* share of his father's money. And I could see Cherry and Drew's reaction. I know they expected to get something after helping with Nona all these years."

"Were they helping Nona or was she helping them?"

Hope considered this.

"Things aren't always what they seem, Hope."

"Yes, I'm aware of that."

"But let's get to the details of your grandmother's will. I'm sure you still have questions—all those what-ifs and what-abouts...right?"

"Right." Hope attempted to get her bearings now. Why hadn't she thought ahead to make a list? She always made lists.

"For starters, I'm trustee and I have my instructions. Your grandmother and I went over it carefully. I think she suspected you might be resistant."

"Really?"

"She said you're a strong-willed woman."

Hope smiled. "I guess it takes one to know one."

"Yes. I have no doubts you and your grandmother are similar. So she asked me to operate as trustee for the duration of the year."

"And can you share the details of your assignment?"

"Not exactly. But I can say that I will do everything possible to help you succeed at this."

"Meaning?"

"Well, I told your grandmother that it might not be easy for you to just uproot your life in Portland. I knew you had a good job, you owned your home, you have financial responsibilities...it's not easy to just let go."

"What?" Hope sat up straighter. "What did you just say?"

"You mean that it might be difficult to give up life in the city?"

"The thing about letting go. You said it wouldn't be easy to just *let go*."

He nodded.

She just sat there running that through her head. Those were the same words she thought she'd heard the night before Nona's funeral. *Let go...let go.*

"I know it's hard to make a move like that. I had to give up a lot when I moved back here."

"Do you mind if I ask *why* you moved back here? I mean it doesn't seem like the easiest place to begin a new law practice."

"That's for sure. My dad passed away about five years ago. And because I'm an only child, I was worried about my mom being alone over here. Especially with the weather, shoveling snow, possibly falling on the ice. In fact, I had her stay with me for a while. I was living in Eugene and I thought she might enjoy it there. But she wasn't really happy and she wanted to come home. She had her friends and her life, and she assured me she'd be just fine. But then she got cancer and she wasn't so fine. I was driving back and forth so much that I finally decided to just make the break. I sold my home, quit my job, and moved over here—lock, stock, and barrel, as my mother would say." His expression grew sad now.

"And you don't have regrets?"

"Not about moving here. It was great being around for Mom. She made it through all her treatments and we really thought she'd beaten it."

"But she hasn't?"

"She died a little more than a year ago."

"I'm sorry."

He nodded sadly. "Yeah, me, too. I still miss her." Now he brightened. "But ironically, it was her death that introduced me to your grandmother."

"How's that?"

"They were friends. And your grandmother came to my mom's memorial service and shortly after that, she made the appointment to see me." He smiled. "Her timing was impeccable."

"How's that?"

"Oh, it was one of those days…I was a little blue…missing my mom…wondering why I'd uprooted my life to move here and then she was gone."

"I can imagine."

"But Mrs. Bartolli said just the right things to cheer me up."

"I can imagine that, too." Hope smiled. "She used to cheer me up all the time. I'm sure I spent more time at her house than I did in my own."

"Speaking of her house…"

"Yes, back to the question. Am I going to do this or not?"

"I understand if you can't make your mind up one hundred percent. But I do need to know if you're absolutely certain that you won't do this. And then the funds will be distributed in another way."

"Amongst my family?"

He just shook his head.

"Really? She didn't have a backup plan that included my family?"

With lips pressed together, he shook his head again.

"So, are you going to tell me?"

"Not until I know your answer."

"My answer?" She wondered what kind of game this was going to be.

"Yes. If you know for certain that you're going to decline your grandmother's proposition, then I can tell you."

"So if I say no, I don't want this—that's it, no second chances, it's over?"

"That's the way your grandmother wanted it. I'm only trying to respect her wishes."

"And I can appreciate that. But it puts me in a tough position."

"Not really. As I said, the estate will not be going to any of your family members, so you really don't have anything to feel guilty about there."

"But you won't tell me where the estate is going?"

"Not until I know your answer."

Hope closed her eyes. The truth was, despite all misgivings, doubts, and worries, she knew the answer. And yet she wasn't sure she could voice the words.

"Do you need more time to think this over?"

She continued to sit there with her eyes closed, breathing evenly and just thinking about Nona—thinking about what her grandmother stood for and what she must've wanted for Hope. "No." She opened her eyes. "I don't think I need any more time. I already made my decision."

He waited expectantly. "And that would be…"

"Yes." Her hand flew to her mouth as if she were surprised by her answer.

"And you're certain of this?"

She nodded with wide eyes. "Oh, trust me, I have my doubts. And I think Nona was slightly crazy to set this up like this. And I think I'm slightly crazy to agree to it. But, yes, I agree." It was the strangest thing, though. As she said the word *yes*, she began to feel a rush of excitement as well as something else she hadn't felt for a long, long time. Hope. She felt hope.

Lewis reached across the table and shook her hand. "Congratulations. I could be wrong, but I think you made the right decision."

"I hope so. And it actually feels right to me. Although I'm surprised to hear myself say that, but it's kind of like I've just opened this door—and I really can't wait to walk through it!" She felt embarrassed now. "Isn't that weird?"

He grinned. "I'm sure some people would think so. But not your grandmother. And I don't either."

As much as she didn't want to, she was thinking more highly of Lewis now. Still, there was that thing with Cherry. And yet Hope realized she might've simply jumped to the wrong conclusion. Like he'd said, things weren't always as they seemed. Perhaps Cherry had legal questions for him—maybe even in regard to Nona's will. Or perhaps they were simply good friends. After all, he'd been friends with Nona. And yet, even as Hope told herself this, she knew it didn't sound quite right.

He was going over some papers and then he slid them across his desk, along with a pen. "Okay, now if you'll just sign some of this paperwork, we will set this thing in motion."

Part of her wanted to question what exactly they were setting in motion, but instead, she focused her attention on what she was signing, carefully reading each word. But it all seemed fairly simple and straightforward. She was agreeing to keep Nona's dog, Andy, and to live in Nona's house for a year as well as to have the use of Nona's car. She couldn't give away the dog or sell or rent the house. And if she changed her mind about any of this, Lewis, the trustee, would switch to Plan B. Also, there was one small clause that proved a pleasant surprise. If she agreed to this arrangement, the trustee (Lewis) would see that she got a monthly stipend for the duration of the year. It wasn't much, but just in case she had trouble setting up a new law practice...or whatever...it should be enough to get her through. If she were frugal and careful.

She handed the signed papers back to him. "So are you ever going to tell me what, exactly, is Plan B? What you would've done if I'd said no today? And, please, don't tell me it would all go to the dog."

He laughed. "You're not far from the truth there."

"Seriously?" She frowned. "It was either me or the dog?"

"Not quite. Your grandmother had selected a number of local charities, but the bulk of her money would go to the Humane Society with a good portion dedicated to dog shelters in the area."

"Oh."

"Speaking of such. I think it's about time we sprung your dog."

"My dog." Hope could barely wrap her mind around this. Not only was she not flying home today, she would soon be giving up her career and condo and everything else in the city. Plus, she was now the owner of a dog. A dog she had never even met.

Chapter Eight
....

Andy turned out to be a Chihuahua mix. With a black-and-white spotted coat and a body that seemed too long for those short legs, he looked up at Hope with big brown eyes that actually melted her heart.

"Hi, Andy," she said softly as she knelt down to pet him. But then he barked and snapped at her like he was going to bite, and she leaped up and looked at the vet. "What's wrong with him?"

The vet just laughed. "Oh, he's a little cranky." She bent down now and spoke to the dog. "Hey, Andy, you don't want to bite the hand that's about to start feeding you." She picked him up and held him for Hope to see. "He just needs to get to know you. The transition of being here has been hard on him. He was so used to your grandmother's attention. I'm afraid he was rather spoiled."

"And I'll bet that being here reminded him of being in the pound before your grandmother rescued him." Lewis scratched Andy behind the ears.

Hope wasn't so sure. "What if Andy doesn't like me?"

"He just needs to get used to you," the vet assured her.

"And once he's back home, he'll probably relax," Lewis said.

"Unless he decides to take a bite out of me."

"Hold your hand like this." The vet held the backside of her hand near Andy's nose so he could sniff and Hope followed suit.

"Hey, Andy," she said softly. "Don't you know that I'm Nona's granddaughter? We're almost related."

Andy looked up at her as if trying to absorb her words and then, to her surprised relief, he sniffed then licked her hand.

"See," Lewis said. "He already likes you."

"Or else he likes the flavor of my hand lotion."

The vet handed Hope the dog. "We have all his records here. He's up to date on his shots and all that. Just so you know, he seems to be about five years old. He's probably a mix of Chihuahua and Jack Russell or some other terrier. He's very smart. And Chihuahuas are social. They need people. They like to be warm, and if well cared for, with a good diet and exercise, they usually enjoy a relatively long life." Then she handed Hope a printed-out page with what appeared to be some instructions about the care and feeding of Andy.

Hope wondered how long of a life Andy could expect to enjoy, but thought it might sound rude to ask. Then the vet left, excusing herself to prep for surgery, and suddenly Hope felt like a brand-new mother. Should she carry Andy in her arms, put him on the leash that the vet had given her, or hand him over to Lewis? "How do you think Andy does in the car?" she asked Lewis as she continued to pet the dog's smooth head.

"He probably hasn't done that as much as walking."

"Right." Hope considered this. "Maybe I should walk him home and then come back to pick up the car later."

Lewis chuckled. "You sound like a nervous parent."

"That's exactly how I feel. I've never owned a dog." She scratched Andy's ear like she'd seen Lewis doing as they exited the vet clinic. He actually seemed to like that, which was reassuring. "I'm curious why Cherry's family didn't let Andy stay at their house after Nona died."

"For one thing, Drew's not particularly fond of the dog. And it seems that Harrison's been having some allergy problems. Cherry thinks it might be animal hair."

"Oh." She hooked the little red leash onto Andy's matching red collar and set him on the ground. He gave himself a little shake then lifted his leg on a shrub by the sidewalk. "Is that okay?" she asked Lewis.

"It's okay for Andy." He grinned. "Not much you can do about it."

"But I've seen people with dogs in the city and they carry around baggies for, well, you know."

"Yes, and if you're on a sidewalk in town, you should probably be prepared, too."

"Right." She walked Andy over to the Rambler now, and he hurried close to sniff at it. When she opened the passenger door, he hopped right in. "Well, he seems to want to ride home," she told Lewis.

"Have fun."

"Thanks," she said with uncertainty.

"By the way, I forgot to mention that your grandmother's house is probably overdue for some maintenance and repairs."

"Oh?"

"Now, don't start getting all worried. I also forgot to mention that, as trustee, I'm allowed to give you what you need to fix the place up."

"Well, thank you."

"Of course, if you don't stay on for the full year, any improvements will simply make it easier to sell the house anyway."

"Right." She opened the driver's door now. "Well, I should probably go before Andy changes his mind."

"Good luck." As Hope drove the few blocks to Nona's house, she wondered if he meant good luck with Andy or with the house.

Maintenance and repairs? Hopefully it wasn't anything too major. No leaky roof or bad plumbing. Surely Nona would've seen to those things.

As it turned out, the roof looked solid and there was no sign of water damage that Hope could see. She and Andy did a complete walk around the house just to check it out. And other than its need for paint and some tightening of shutters and screen doors and whatnot, it seemed fairly sound. And Andy seemed truly happy to be home as he danced around the yard. His tail wagged vigorously, and when they got back to the side door, he was anxious to go in. However, once inside, the house did smell musty. And the kitchen, just the same as it always had been with its forties linoleum, painted cabinets, a stained old sink, and Formica countertop, now appeared antiquated and rundown. And yet it was charming and Hope knew there was potential. The small living room and two bedrooms had been re-carpeted when Hope was in high school, but now the carpet was old and worn. With some suspicious-looking spots which she deduced were related to Andy.

He was sniffing around, too, going from room to room as if on the hunt. And finally he jumped up into the old rose-colored recliner, the same one that Nona had spent most of her evenings in either reading or crocheting or sleeping, and Andy just sat there looking forlorn with his head cocked slightly to one side as if to ask, *Where is she?*

"She's not here, Andy." Hope sighed. "And she's not coming back, either. I'm sorry." She turned on some lights, looking around the room, trying to determine why it seemed so dark. And then she noticed that some kind of storm windows had been installed over Nona's lovely old single-pane, wood windows. Of course, that was the problem. The storm windows were dirty and dingy and probably difficult to clean. And although they might've made the house warmer in winter, they were also blocking the light.

It was time to make a list. And before long, she had made several lists. A to-do list for the house, which included donating some of Nona's old furniture to the Habitat secondhand store that Hope had noticed in town; removing the carpets and storm windows; finding someone to work on the kitchen and bathroom (which was in similar shape to the kitchen); and painting the interior and exterior.

Basically, Hope needed a good handyman. If she were on better terms with Cherry she would ask her. As it was, she half-expected Cherry and Drew to charge over here and accuse her of stealing Nona's fortune from them. Fortunately both their cars were missing from the driveway. Drew was probably at his dad's ranch, and Cherry was probably chauffeuring her children to whatever lesson or practice was on their schedule today. Unless she was having another clandestine meeting with Lewis. And Hope did not want to think about that.

She pulled out the worn card with Erica's phone number on it and called, quickly telling her the news.

"You're kidding!" Erica sounded shocked. "Your grandmother had a million bucks stashed away?"

"Well, not quite. And, like I said, I have to live here for a year to get any of it and there'll be taxes and who knows what else. The house alone is probably going to eat a fair amount. It needs all kinds of work done. In fact, that's why I'm calling."

"You want me to work on your house?"

Hope laughed. "No, but if that's an offer…"

"No. I'm not into that sort of thing."

"Actually, I wondered if you might know of a good handyman, or a painter, or a contractor."

"Hey, do you remember Brian Godwin?"

"Sure, from school. I even went out with him a couple of times before I started dating, well, you know who."

"Yes, your new neighbor."

"Don't remind me."

"That is an interesting twist. I wonder if your grandmother did that on purpose, you know, to help you girls mend your fences."

"Yes…the thought's occurred to me, too. However, I'm afraid that Cherry and Drew probably won't be speaking to me now."

"Oh…because they expected to inherit?"

"That's what I'm thinking. Anyway, back to Brian Godwin. Are you saying he's a handyman now?"

"He's a contractor. And like a lot of other contractors, right now, things are slow. You should give him a call."

"Do you have his number?"

"I probably do somewhere. But just look in the phone book. He's listed."

"Thanks. By the way, I forgot to tell you, I'm now a dog owner."

"Really? What kind?"

"Chihuahua mix." Then she told Erica about why her sisters had been laughing over the old hymn at Nona's funeral.

Erica laughed. "I'm sorry, but that actually is funny."

"I guess."

"Well, I have a dog, too. We can take them on walks together and do play dates at the park, and all sorts of quirky things."

"What kind of dog?"

"She's an adorable Yorkie named Bessie."

"Great, we'll have to get them together." Then Hope thanked her for the tip, dug out Nona's old phone book, found the number, and called Brian. After a brief introduction, he remembered her and offered to come over later in the afternoon.

"Really?" She was shocked. "You can come today?"

"I can for you."

"Well, I really appreciate it."

"See you around four thirty."

"Thanks!" She hung up and looked at her other two lists. One was for groceries, and that could come later. The other was titled *Things Related to Portland*. First on the list was to call the firm and give them a heads-up on this new development in her life. She wasn't expected back in until next Wednesday, but now she wondered whether she'd be back in at all.

"You're quitting?" demanded Hal Winslow. "Just like that? Your grandmother dies and leaves you money and you quit?"

So she explained a bit more.

"Oh?" It sounded like the wheels in his brain were spinning. "I see…you have to stay there to inherit your money. Hmm…can't say as I blame you then."

"I would be willing to work from here," she suggested, "possibly on a retainer or something."

"No, that wouldn't work for us. We need you here or not at all."

"Then I guess it has to be not at all."

"I'd be lying if I didn't say I hate to lose you, Hope."

"Thanks. I'm sorry to break it to you like this. I plan to write an official letter, but I don't have my printer here and—"

LOVE FINDS YOU IN SISTERS, OREGON

"Don't worry about that. I've already got Lydia working on the Birkley account and she's probably just the person to take over Abbington, too."

"So...what do I do then? Just come in and clear out my things?" For some reason, this made her incredibly sad. What if this was all a mistake?

"I guess so. And go by personnel, of course, and sign the appropriate paperwork. Then, make sure you come by my office. I assume you'll want some recommendations...for the future. Unless you're giving up law permanently. Taking up lifestyles of the rich and famous."

She laughed. If only he knew. "Yes, I would appreciate recommendations."

"And we might have some connections for you out there in Central Oregon, too. I'll check around, Hope."

"Thanks, Hal."

"And if you change your mind, you know we'll always be interested. I can't guarantee placement, but you know we'd want to be in the loop."

"Thanks, I appreciate it."

They said good-bye and hung up, and Hope felt like she'd just cut a lifeline. Really, what if this were a mistake? Then she remembered what Lewis had said. If, at any time before the year was up, she changed her mind, the whole agreement would switch to Plan B. She would be off the hook. But she'd also be out of a job. Unless they took her back.

"Stop it!" she told herself, causing poor Andy to jump and then to shiver as if he'd been scolded. "Not you," she said gently as she knelt down. "You are a good dog, Andy. It's me. I'm not a very decisive person today." He looked up with trusting brown eyes. "I'll bet you're hungry. And knowing my Nona, I'll bet she kept treats around here for you." His tail wagged hopefully. "Do you want a treat?" His tail wagged harder.

"Let's check out the kitchen." His little toes tapped on the linoleum as he followed her around the small kitchen. Finally, she located the right cupboard. He had little rawhide chew toys, a box of small Milk-Bones, doggy jerky treats, canned food, and a box of kibble food. "All sorts of good things." She looked down at Andy. "Now the vet said you only eat twice a day, but did you really eat this morning?" She looked at the clock. It was just past noon. "I'll give you another chance," she told him as she filled his little doggy bowl with the kibble food then freshened up his water.

He just looked at the bowl then back at her as if trying to decide.

She backed a few steps away, leaning against the sink. And that seemed to do it. He ducked his head into the bowl, eating eagerly until every bite was gone. She was tempted to refill the bowl but remembered the vet's warning about overfeeding. "That's all until dinner, Andy. Want to come outside with me?"

He seemed to understand, following her out into the backyard where she wanted to take inventory of Nona's flowers and plants. Gardening had always been important to Nona, and Hope had always dreamed of having a small garden herself. In fact, she had kept a number of pots on the terrace of her condo. Pots that would need to be transported back here…along with so many other things. Plus, she needed to list her condo for sale or figure a way to sublet it, in case she needed to go back.

She might not be working nine to five for a while, but she wasn't exactly going to be enjoying a life of leisure. In fact, she suspected that she would be working a lot harder than she'd ever worked before. She only hoped she was truly up for it.

Chapter Nine

....

Nona had trained Andy fairly well because he knew how to stay in his yard. However, he did not know that barking was obnoxious. And every time a passerby came anywhere near their yard, Andy would throw an embarrassing barking fit. And Hope would smile and apologize to the UPS guy or the kid on the bike or whomever was lucky enough to get the onslaught of Andy's tongue-lashing. Fortunately most seemed understanding and as if they were accustomed to Andy's little antics.

As Hope trimmed some overgrown shrubs away from the house—another way to let in more light—she wondered what Andy was saying when he barked so viciously. Was he swearing in dog language? Or simply warning them to keep their distance? But after a while, Andy seemed to tire of playing watchdog and went onto the back porch where a little dog bed was already set up for him. It was a small basket with a pillow in it. He had three of these basket beds, each with a different pillow—a green plaid one on the porch, a yellow gingham one in the living room by the fireplace, and a pink-flowered one in Nona's bedroom. On closer inspection, Hope could see that the pillow covers appeared to be hand sewn. Probably by Nona. Perhaps she took them off and washed them regularly.

"Hi, Aunt Hope!" Avery waved from her yard.

Hope looked up from where she was weeding to see that Cherry's red Mustang was in the driveway now. "Hi, Avery!" Hope stood and smiled. "What's up?"

"Not much. I was over at my friend Lucy's house."

"Oh…" Hope nodded and tried to think of a response. She was glad Avery was talking to her and wouldn't be surprised if she were the only one in the Lawson house who'd be willing to give Hope the time of day. "I'm just doing some weeding here."

"Want any help?"

"Seriously?" Hope was taken aback. "You'd really like to help?"

"Sure." Avery came over, and pulling her hair into a quick ponytail, she tugged a blue band from around her wrist and secured her long, dark hair with it. Just like Hope often did herself. "I used to help Nona in her yard…you know…before."

"Really?"

"Yeah. She was teaching me about flowers and things. But this spring, well, she told me she was slowing down. It seemed like it took all her energy just to walk Andy and stuff. I probably should've come over more to help her in the yard, but I had school and ballet and soccer and…" Her voice dwindled.

Hope put an arm around her shoulders. "Nona understood, Avery. And I know she really loved you. She often wrote about you in her letters. And if you want to help me in the garden or even in the house, I'd be happy to pay you."

Avery's eyes grew wide. "Oh, you don't have to do that."

"But I *want* to." The reason Hope wanted to pay Avery was so that Cherry and Drew wouldn't think she was taking unfair advantage of her niece. "Besides, I'll bet there must be something that you could use a little extra money for."

Avery smiled. "I want a new swimsuit for the Saturday after next. It's Olivia Hanson's birthday, and she's having a pool party, and my old swimsuit looks really yucky and childish. Lucy just got a bikini."

Hope chuckled. "And you probably want one, too."

Avery nodded shyly.

"The Saturday after next, huh? Well, that gives you a whole week to earn the money. Believe me, there's plenty of work around here. Inside and outside. I'm sure I could keep you busy for most of the summer if you liked."

"Cool."

"And you could make a nice little chunk of change by the time school starts."

"When do I start?" She rubbed her hands together eagerly.

"Whenever you want."

"How about now?"

"Now is fine. I'm trying to get the front section done this afternoon," Hope told her. "Do you know where the garden tools are?"

"Yep. And I even know the difference between weeds and flowers. Well, mostly. Sometimes I still have to ask."

"Sometimes I'm not so sure either."

Avery trotted off to the garden shed and returned with both a spade and a pair of dirty pink gloves. Soon they were visiting and weeding together and Hope got the distinct feeling that Nona was looking down and smiling on them. Perhaps this was what she'd had in mind all along when she'd sat down with Lewis to put that whacky will together. Perhaps it wasn't so crazy after all.

"I want to take riding lessons," Avery was telling her as they were about midway down the front flower bed.

"I should think that would be no problem," Hope said. "I've heard that your grandmother Lawson is quite a horsewoman."

"I know. But Mom says I'm not old enough."

"Really?"

"She says I need to be sixteen."

"What does your grandmother say?"

"Poppycock!"

Hope laughed. "Yes, I can imagine Mrs. Lawson saying that."

"Do you *know* her?" Avery's dark eyes grew wide with interest.

"Sure, I know her. She's a nice lady. I like her."

"I like her, too. But Mom hardly ever wants to take me out there. She says it's too far and takes too much time. And Daddy doesn't want to take me out there because he's there all day and he says I would get bored. And then, when he's not working there, he doesn't want to go out because that's what he does every other day. And even when Grandma offers to come to town to get me, Mom makes up some lame reason to keep me from going out there."

"Do you think she's worried you'll get hurt?" Hope paused to watch Avery's reaction.

She nodded soberly. "Yeah. I think that's it."

"I wonder why."

"Didn't you hear about it?"

"What?"

"That girl that got killed on one of Grandma's horses."

"No." Hope shook her head. "What happened?"

"Well, I was only about six when it happened, but I do remember it was a big deal. It was in the newspaper and everyone was talking about it. The girl hadn't been wearing a helmet, and she landed on her head. And people were blaming Grandma, and she felt so bad that she quit teaching riding lessons."

"Oh, that's so sad."

"I know. And it doesn't seem fair that they blame Grandma. Does it?"

"It doesn't seem fair to me. I mean unless there was something wrong with the horse, like he was badly trained or dangerous. And I can't imagine that was the situation. Although, I suppose the girl should've been required to wear a helmet. It's illegal for children to ride a bike without a helmet, and I can't see how a horse should be much different."

"I heard Grandma telling someone once that she had asked that girl to wear a helmet lots of times, but the girl just refused and the parents didn't really care, well, until it was too late. Then they cared."

"Did they sue your grandmother?"

"I don't know. But I don't think so. Still, she quit teaching riding lessons."

"That must've been hard on her." Hope remembered Mrs. Lawson. She loved horses, and she loved teaching kids, not only to ride but how to groom and care for and handle the horses, too. In fact, there was a time when Hope had been starting to learn. But then Cherry got so interested that Hope kind of stepped aside.

"And then Grandma was so happy when I told her I wanted to learn to ride. She said she had just the horse for me. And I really do want to ride, and I know other kids my age who ride and do Four-H Club and all kinds of things. It's just not fair."

"There's a lot in life that doesn't seem fair. It doesn't seem fair that your grandmother isn't teaching lessons anymore. And it doesn't seem fair that people blamed her for the girl's accident."

"And you're a lawyer, too." Avery nodded with satisfaction. "You should know about these kinds of things."

Hope chuckled. "Well, the kind of law I practiced wasn't really like that. But a lot of legal things just boil down to common sense."

"I wish you could talk to Mom."

Hope didn't know how to respond. In a way, she wished she could, too.

"Are you and my mom having a fight?"

Hope stood up slowly, rubbing her back, which was beginning to ache. "No, I don't think we're having a fight. Not that I know of anyway. Why?"

"Because it sounds like she's mad at you. And Dad told her she should talk to you and she said she doesn't want to."

"Oh."

"So it sounded like you were in a fight."

Hope frowned. "Do you think it's okay that you're over here, helping me? I mean I don't want to cause trouble between you and your mom."

"I don't think she really cares." Avery glanced over to her house with an uncertain look.

"But you should probably check with her. And make sure it's okay that I'm hiring you to work over here. I wouldn't want her to sue me or anything." Hope laughed nervously.

"She wouldn't sue you."

"I know. I was joking."

"Do you know why she might be mad at you, though?"

Hope looked over at their house now. It seemed funny to think that was the same house she'd grown up in. And yet it seemed like an entirely different house. The siding had been replaced and was now painted sage green instead of blue. The windows had all been upgraded and the shutters removed. Also the front door was new. Almost everything about it was new and different. Even the landscaping had changed. Some of the big trees had been replaced with smaller ones. And the lawn looked better than ever, and unless Hope was mistaken, they had put in a sprinkler system. "If your mom is mad at me," Hope began slowly, "I'm not totally sure why. But it might be because Nona left this house to me."

"I *knew* she was going to do that."

"You did?"

Avery's brows lifted mysteriously. "But I never told anyone."

"How did you know? Did Nona tell you?"

"Not exactly. But one day she asked if I would like to have Aunt Hope living in her house after she died."

"And what did you say?"

"I said I didn't want her to die."

Hope smiled to herself as she reached for a tall dandelion.

"Then I told her I would like you to live here."

"But you didn't even know me."

"Nona had pictures of you in her house. And you always send me cards and things."

"Yes, but that's not very personal."

"And Nona always told me that I was just like you."

"Ah…" Hope smiled as she brushed a twig out of Avery's hair.

"Maybe Nona knew that I needed you here."

"Being that Nona was one of the wisest women I have ever known, I wouldn't be surprised if she knew that…and a whole lot more."

"So you really are going to stay here?" Avery looked so hopeful.

"I think I am."

Now Avery tossed down her spade and threw her arms around Hope. "I'm so glad!"

Hope ran her hand over Avery's sleek, dark hair. "So am I."

And although Hope knew it was too soon to know whether or not this thing was really going to work, she felt encouraged…and, yes, she felt hopeful.

Chapter Ten

....

"Anyone home?" a male voice called through the opened front door. Naturally this sent Andy into a barking fit.

"Can you quiet him down?" Hope asked Avery as she set the half-filled cardboard box on the bed. They had been emptying Nona's closet, saving a few special old things, but getting most of her clothes ready to be given away.

Hope pushed hair away from her face and hurried to the door. "Hey, Brian." She smiled and opened the screen door. "Come on in."

He shook her hand and grinned. "You're looking real good, Hope. How's life treating you?"

She quickly explained her situation, and how she'd inherited her grandmother's house and wanted to make it a bit more comfortable.

"So you're moving back?" His blue eyes lit up.

"I'm giving it my best shot."

"Well, this town is turning into a pretty nice place to live. A little spendy for some folks, but if you work hard, you can make it."

"So how long have you been a contractor?"

"I had been working in real estate. But the market kind of flattened out. So my dad encouraged me to get my contractor's license and come back to work for his construction company. I worked off and on with him in high school and summers during college. I never thought I'd want to do it full time. But I'm actually kind of enjoying it now. My dad's thinking about retiring in a few years. Maybe sooner if things don't pick up around here. We haven't been overly busy."

"So you think you could do some work for me?"

He pushed a strand of sandy hair away from his forehead and nodded. "I don't see why not."

"I could probably live with it the way it is, but it might be fun to fix it up."

"And with real estate values what they are in this neighborhood, it'll probably be a good investment, too." He glanced at the kitchen and let out a low whistle. "Man, that kitchen looks like it should be gutted."

"Gutted?" Hope looked at the sweet wooden cabinets in alarm.

He patted the doorway wall between the kitchen and living room. "And I think we could take this wall out, too. Put in a beam if it's a support wall to make it a great room." He chuckled. "Guess it'd be a mini great room."

"Oh, I'm not so sure I'd—"

"And you could probably fit an island right here and put in some nice custom cabinets, stainless appliances, and granite countertops, and this—"

"I don't really want to make the place look all modern and contemporary," she told him. "I mean it's not that I don't like that style. In fact, that's what my condo in Portland looks like, and it's great." She gave Brian a hopeful smile. "But I'd sort of like to preserve the integrity of the architecture. The house was built in the forties and, as you know, there aren't that many old houses in Sisters."

He nodded, rubbing his chin. "You're right about that. Thanks to the fires that wiped out some of the good old houses near town. And most of the shepherds' houses have been scrapped. Old homes in Sisters are a bit of a novelty."

"So I'd like to maintain that old charm."

"I'll bet this place has some sentimental value, too. How long did your grandmother live here anyway?"

"Actually, she bought this house after my grandfather died in the mid-seventies. She wanted to be close to our family. Then she lived here right to the end."

He went over to check out an electrical outlet. "We'll need to make sure that it's been rewired. It looks like it has, but if not, you could be in for a real headache."

"Oh."

"And we'll want to check out the plumbing, but I'm guessing that was addressed when the town connected to sewer, so we should be okay there."

"Right…" Hope wondered if she could be biting off more than she wanted.

"So, tell me, what's your plan? What exactly do you want done?" He pulled out a little notebook.

"Well, I thought I could paint the kitchen cabinets. The wood seems solid and I think they fit the house. However, I wish there were a way to fit in a dishwasher. And the countertops and floor need to be replaced. I was wondering about some kind of hardwood running throughout the house. A bigger concern is the windows. I think the wood frames are charming, and I actually like that old wavy glass. But those storm windows are atrocious."

"Maybe we could install some new clad windows, with wood on the inside and a finish that can be painted and handle the weather on the outside. We can get ones that look like your old ones—except for the wavy glass anyway. But you'll have double panes and low-e, which will save on your heating bills. Plus, you can probably get a tax rebate, too."

"Yes," she said eagerly. "That'd be great."

"And I want to update the bathroom." She led him back to the decrepit space. "I actually think it does need to be gutted. Well, except for the claw-foot tub; I'd like to save it. But I want new tile, new sink, new toilet—the works."

"And they make old-fashioned fixtures. I'll give you the name of the plumber and you can go into the shop and look at his catalogues."

"Great."

"I looked at the exterior some, and the roof looks to be in good shape. Other than a few little fixes here and there, you should be okay."

"And I thought I'd try my hand at painting." She grinned. "I helped my dad paint our house when I was a kid. And my niece might want to help."

"That's right," Avery said as she emerged from the bedroom. "And painting sounds like fun." She was carrying Andy and wearing an old velvet hat that looked to be from the forties. "Can I keep this hat, too?"

"Of course." Hope adjusted the beaded veil over her eyes. "It actually looks rather chic on you."

"Hi, Avery," Brian said to her.

"So you two have already met?" Hope eyed Brian curiously.

"Sure. It's a small town. Avery's little brother is on my boy's little league team."

"You have a son?" Hope was surprised.

"Yep. Jack will be nine in August."

"Any other kids?" Hope asked.

"Nope. Just Jack. Leah and me split up when he was only three. Haven't had much time for more kids since then." He winked. "Or women either."

"Oh."

"How about you, Hope? You're not married, are you?"

"No."

"Any boyfriends back in the big city?"

She felt her cheeks growing warm. "Not really. I just broke something off."

Brian grinned, exposing straight teeth that looked extra white against his deeply tanned face. "I'm liking the idea of working for you already."

Hope laughed. "So, will you give me an estimate or something?"

"Sure will. And I'll bring by some window catalogues. And I was thinking about your floors and how you want to keep this house old-fashioned. I have a buddy who's into recycling old buildings. He's got some nice old fir that would look pretty in here."

"Old fir would be fabulous!" Hope had to control herself from hugging him.

"I'll give him a call." He closed his notebook. "And I'll work on an estimate tonight and get back to you tomorrow, if that's okay."

"That'd be great."

He slapped his forehead. "Except I have Jack tomorrow, and he has a little league game at one. But, if it's okay, I could bring him with me in the morning, and you and I could talk this over a bit more."

"Sure, that'd be fine."

"See ya in the morning then." He tipped his head.

Now Hope wasn't naïve. She had a pretty strong suspicion that Brian was giving her special treatment because he was interested in her. And, really, what was wrong with that? For that matter, maybe she was interested in him. He was good-looking and polite. And who wouldn't like having a guy around who was handy with tools. She looked out the window as his turquoise blue pickup pulled out of the driveway. It looked like it was from the sixties and actually looked right at home with her old Rambler. Yes, for all she knew Brian could be a good man to have around.

"I think he likes you," Avery said when she emerged wearing a different hat. This one was burgundy with a pheasant feather in it.

"And I like that hat on you." Hope tweaked the feather. "Are you keeping it, too?"

"Sure, if you don't mind." Avery tilted her chin as if modeling. "But what do you think about Brian? Do you like him, too?"

"I like that he's willing to get right to work on Nona's house."

Avery nodded. "Except it's not Nona's house now, Aunt Hope. It's yours."

Hope considered this. It wouldn't actually feel like her house until the year was up. And who knew if she'd still be here by then? Still, she didn't want to worry Avery with these details. Better to just play along for now.

Hope and Avery had just gotten the bedroom cleared out when they heard Cherry calling. "Avery, are you in here?"

"Yeah, Mom." Avery tossed the last shoe in the box and went out to the living room.

"What are you doing over here?" Cherry's voice sounded irritated.

"Helping Aunt Hope."

"With what?"

"Well, you saw me out there weeding. And then I helped her to pack up Nona's things."

"You packed up Nona's things?" Cherry sounded hurt now.

"And Hope let me keep some—"

"I would've liked to have—"

"We set aside a bunch of things that have sentimental value," Hope said as she emerged with a box. "I planned to invite you and Faye over to pick through."

"After you'd picked through first."

Hope sighed. "They're all laid out on the bed, Cherry. Other than the hats and belts and things that Avery picked, you can take what you like. Honestly, there wasn't that much there. Nona already gave us her jewelry and anything of value."

"Don't forget what Nona used to say—one man's trash is another man's treasure." Cherry marched off to the bedroom, clearly unhappy at being left out. Avery just held up her hands in a helpless gesture, and Hope went outside for some fresh air and to avoid saying something regrettable to her baby sister. Andy followed her around as she paced in the yard. She was pretending to be evaluating what needed to be done out there. But really she was fuming at Cherry.

With an armload of things, Cherry exited the house with Avery behind her. "I gotta go help Mom with dinner," Avery called. "But I'll be back in the morning, okay?"

"Okay!" Hope smiled at Avery. "Thanks for all your help!"

Avery grinned. "No problem!"

Hope and Andy went back inside now. This time she closed the front door. "Well, Andy," she said. "What now?"

He wagged his tail expectantly.

"Let me guess…are you hungry?"

He trotted into the kitchen as if he understood.

"You really are smart, aren't you?" She decided to open one of the dog food tins, spooning some into his dish then topping it off with his kibble food. His tail was really going now. But, like before, he waited for her to back off before he began to eat. And then Hope realized she was hungry, too. She opened Nona's pantry and peeked inside to see a variety of things, including cans of various soups, peaches, pineapple, green beans, corn, tomato sauce, and tomato paste. There were also packages of pasta, and a jar of olive oil, and oatmeal, and few other things.

Next, she looked in the old refrigerator, hoping that nothing had spoiled too badly in the week since Nona had died. She poked around and finally decided to just go ahead and dispose of everything. It would be better to start fresh, and it would be better to have a new refrigerator, too. She suspected this old one wasted electricity. So she got out her notepad and wrote *shop for appliances*. She wondered where one went to shop for appliances—probably outside of Sisters. She would ask Brian for suggestions tomorrow. And she would get groceries tomorrow. As well as some casual working clothes. As she warmed the chicken vegetable soup on the stove, her list grew longer.

She was just about to start eating her soup when Nona's phone rang. Thinking it was probably a solicitor, she answered it with a chilly hello.

"Hope?" It was a woman's voice.

"Yes."

"Sorry to bother you. This is Erica."

"No bother. I just figured it was a sales person."

"I tried your cell, but it—"

"Oh, that's right, I need to charge it."

"Anyway, it's Friday and some of us single girls get together for drinks and laughs and I thought you might like to join us."

"Is food involved?" Hope looked down at the dismal bowl of soup.

"If you like. We meet at the brewery and they make a mean buffalo burger as well as a few other things."

"I'm in. What time?"

"Around six."

Hope looked at the clock to see it was already five thirty. "Sounds good. Hey, are any clothing stores open at night? I need some jeans and working clothes until I get back to Portland."

"The western wear store is open until eight, I think."

"Perfect."

"See you around six then."

Hope hung up and grabbed her purse. With any luck, she could snag some jeans and a couple of shirts and still make it to the brewery by six. "Andy, you be a good boy, okay?" He had already finished his dinner and was snuggled into his living-room bed, looking at her as if he expected her to come and sit in the recliner next to him. "I'll be back in a while," she promised. "You take care of the place, you hear?" Then she rushed out, got into the car, and drove the few blocks to the western wear store. She would've walked, except she was in a hurry.

"Can I help you?" asked an attractive blond woman. She had on Wranglers and cowboy boots, a white western-cut shirt, a tan suede vest, and a lot of silver and turquoise jewelry.

"You look like you're ready for rodeo," Hope said.

"Well, it is next weekend." She pointed to a colorful poster.

"That's right." Hope frowned. "Actually, you can help me. I'm in a hurry, but I need some jeans and shirts. I flew in from the city and only brought city clothes." She motioned down at her now soiled linen pants and shirt. "And it turns out I'm staying longer than I expected and am working to clear out an old house." She waved her hand. "Long story. But I just need a few things to get me by."

Hope wasn't sure if she imagined it, but the woman's eyes seemed to light up. In no time at all, Hope found herself in the changing room, and the woman, whose name was Crystal, carried in one item after the next. And by the time Hope got out of that store, she had spent a big chunk of change, was weighted down with several bags and outfitted in Wranglers and belt, a black pair of Charlie One Horse mules, a white T-shirt topped with a black leather vest, and she even had on silver earrings.

"Look at you," Erica said when Hope located the girls at a pub table in a corner. "You look like you're ready to rodeo, girl!"

Hope laughed. "Crystal at the western store helped me out. Do I look ridiculous?"

"You look hot," a woman with short, highlighted hair told her. "All you need is a good hat."

"And a cowboy," added a thin woman with dark curly hair.

"This is Bobbie," Erica nodded to the short-haired woman, "and Selena," to the curly-haired one. "And this is my old friend Hope."

"You're the one named after the Middle Sister?" asked Selena.

"So you've heard the tale." Hope pulled out a stool and sat down.

"Well, everyone in town already knows South Sister." Bobbie said this in a way that suggested she wasn't overly fond of Cherry.

"Bobbie works for the newspaper," Erica informed Hope.

"Hardly a week goes by but what that sister of yours doesn't make it into the Nugget." Bobbie laughed. "Not that I'm complaining. News is news." She narrowed her eyes at Hope. "In fact, the story of you three sisters all living back in town again might be interesting. Didn't your mom die climbing one of the Sisters mountains?"

"She was on her way to climb," Hope said quietly.

"Which one?" asked Selena.

"Middle Sister."

"Your mountain?" Selena looked sympathetic.

"Well, I don't own the mountain," Hope pointed out. "But, yes, the one I'm named after. That didn't make it any easier on me."

"Well, at least she didn't die *on* the mountain." Bobbie studied Hope. "This really would make a nice human interest story. Would you be willing?"

Hope shrugged. "I guess. I mean if my sisters are."

"Well, we know Cherry would be willing," teased Selena.

"Are your sisters talking to you yet?" asked Erica.

Of course, that got the other women interested. And, without telling everything, Hope filled them in a bit about inheriting her grandmother's house and how not everyone had been too pleased. But as she told them, she realized that she hadn't really seen Faye's response yet. It was possible that Faye would be okay. Hope would give her a call in the morning—maybe even use the newspaper article

LOVE FINDS YOU IN SISTERS, OREGON

as an excuse to touch base with her. Hope knew some people would think it strange to need an excuse to call one's own sister, but then, Hope's sisterly relationships weren't exactly the norm. And judging by Cherry's chilly welcome to the neighborhood, it wouldn't be getting better anytime soon either.

Chapter Eleven

....

"Did I wake you?" Hope asked Faye after the phone rang several times.

"No, not really." But her voice had the roughness of sleep still in it.

"How's it going?" Hope asked cheerfully. "Are you still buying that condo in Pine Meadow?"

"If all goes as planned, I think so."

"I'm staying over at Nona's now."

"Is that weird?"

"Weird?" Hope frowned at the cracked linoleum beneath her bare feet. "How do you mean?"

"I mean because Nona died there. Does it feel weird or creepy? Have you seen any ghosts?"

Hope laughed. "Not yet. But Nona died peacefully in her sleep. I doubt she'd want to come back and haunt me."

"No, being that you were her favorite and all, I guess not."

Hope heard the edge of bitterness in Faye's voice. "Are you mad at me, too?"

"No, of course not."

"Jealous then?"

"Maybe I'm just curious."

"As to why Nona left everything to me?"

"It does make me wonder."

"Want to come over for coffee and talk about it?"

"Maybe. Do you even have coffee over there? As I recall, Nona quit caffeine a few years ago."

"I noticed she only has decaf, and it's instant. But I could run out and—"

"Never mind. I'm staying at Jody's and it's near the Coffee Company anyway. I'll grab us both some. How about a pastry, too?"

So Hope gave Faye her coffee order then took Andy outside to do his business in the backyard. So Faye was staying at Jody's house. Hope had wondered why Faye and Monroe hadn't stayed at Cherry's. But being at an old best friend's house made sense. Faye probably felt more comfortable with Jody than she did with Cherry. And, oddly enough, Hope felt relieved to know this. So maybe Faye and Cherry weren't that close either. Not that it was a surprise, since Faye was nine years older than Cherry and they had never been close. But for some reason, Hope had assumed they were buddy-buddy and she was the odd girl out.

By the time Faye arrived, Hope had dug out several old lawn chairs and a rickety metal table, given them a quick dusting, and set them in the sunshine in the backyard.

"A garden party, I see." Faye set down the coffees and paper bag.

"Monroe's not joining us?" Hope sat down carefully in what appeared to be the weakest chair and hoped that it wouldn't collapse. And before she picked up her coffee, Andy jumped into her lap as if she'd invited him.

"Monroe had already left the house before I got up." Faye took the lid off her coffee, letting the steam escape. "I'm hoping that's a good sign. Maybe he's taken a walk or a bike ride or something outdoorsy. Jody's husband is letting him use his mountain bike while we're here."

"That sounds like fun." Hope mentally added *mountain bike* to her ever-growing list.

"So what's up with you?" Faye asked as she broke off a piece of croissant. "Are you seriously considering staying in Sisters?" Faye laughed in a slightly mean way. "The old lady got you over a barrel, didn't she?"

Something about the way Faye said "old lady" sounded disrespectful, and yet Hope didn't want to question this. She was trying as hard as she could to win Faye's trust again.

"I think Nona sensed by my letters that I wasn't feeling that happy and fulfilled in Portland."

"Really?" Faye looked interested. "I always assumed you had quite the life there."

"I'm sure it could look that way to an outsider. But the truth is I don't enjoy corporate law, and even the city was starting to lose its appeal. I think maybe I really was ready for a change. I just didn't know it."

"So you're really going to do it? You're going to stay on here?"

"I'm going to try."

"But what happens if you fail? I mean does someone else get a chance at the house...and everything?" Faye looked hopeful.

Hope bit her lip.

"I'm sorry to sound nosy, Hope, but she was my grandmother, too. In fact, she was my grandmother first."

Hope just nodded. "Were you and Nona ever close? I mean I don't really remember you being over here much, but then it seemed like you were all grown up and off doing things with your friends...trying to get away from the little kids."

"Well, you and Cherry were a lot younger than me. And Mom was pretty busy with you two for a while. I had to have a life."

"Right…" What Hope wanted to say was that if Faye hadn't taken the time to spend with Nona, was it fair for her to think Nona should leave everything to her just because she was the oldest? And, really, what was fair?

"Listen, I don't want to sound greedy, Hope, but you have to admit that it's odd that Nona left everything to you. I mean what about Cherry? Here she's been, living right next door to Nona all these years and fully expecting to get something out of it."

Hope took a slow swig of her latte as she stroked Andy's smooth coat. Hadn't she read somewhere that petting an animal was supposed to lower one's blood pressure?

"And then there's Monroe and me. Nona didn't realize that I was split up with Jeff. But if she had, would she have offered the house to me? And I was already considering moving back here. Do you see what I'm thinking?"

"I do." Hope nodded. "In fact, I thought those same things. But according to Lewis, the attorney, it's out of my hands. Nona wrote this thing out with him and it's supposedly airtight."

"It's not as if I'd contest the will." Faye took another bite of croissant. "But I do question the fairness of it. And so does Cherry."

"Look, if it were up to me, I'd say how about a three-way split."

"But it will be your money eventually, Hope. I mean if you stay for the full year. What then?"

Hope shrugged. "I don't know. There will be taxes and the expenses of fixing the house. And a year feels a long ways off to me right now."

"Well, for the sake of sisters and family…I hope you'll be fair. And, just so you know, Dad wasn't too with you happy either."

Now this just irked Hope. "You know, it was Nona's decision to do this…not mine. And, as the attorney pointed out because apparently Nona told him, you and Dad got Mom's insurance benefits. Cherry and I didn't. And then Dad practically gave Cherry the house. So maybe Nona felt it was my turn to be on the receiving end."

"But you have it all," Faye protested. "You have a great job, a beautiful condo in the city, a cool car, a boyfriend and—"

"For starters, Curtis and I broke up. And I'm sure everything looked great to you when you visited me a few years ago, but you were only there for one night. You don't know how my life really was. And, like I said, I was feeling pretty disenchanted."

"Well, from the outside looking in, it looked good." Faye stood now.

"Are you leaving?" Hope stood, too, causing Andy to jump down to the grass with what seemed a disgruntled expression, although she wondered if it was possible for an animal to show feelings.

"Yes." Faye's tone was crisp, all business. "I should go check on Monroe. Right now, he's all I've got."

"You've got me," Hope told her.

Faye gave Hope a skeptical look. "So you say."

"You do," Hope protested. "I'm your sister."

Faye looped a strap of her worn-looking purse over her shoulder. "See ya around," she called as she walked away.

Hope looked down at Andy. "I guess you're all I have." He wagged his tail as if this suited him just fine. "I'll bet you'd like a doggy treat, wouldn't you?"

He happily trotted toward the house with her. She knew she'd been spoiling him a bit, giving him treats probably more than she should, but it was still sort of the honeymoon period, and for Nona's sake—as well as Andy's—she wanted to be sure he was happy. And that he liked her.

They had barely gone back in the house when she saw the old turquoise pickup pulling into the driveway. She opened the side door and waved to Brian. He had on a straw cowboy hat, light blue T-shirt, and faded jeans. She watched as he and a slightly built redheaded boy wearing a baseball uniform got out of the truck. Hope smiled at the image—it could've been from a Norman Rockwell painting. Brian waved and called a greeting to her, but the boy lingered back as his dad gently nudged him toward her.

"Hope, I'd like you to meet my best friend Jack. Jack, this is my old friend, Miss Bartolli. If all goes well, I'll be doing some work around her place."

She stuck out her hand. "It's a pleasure to meet you, Jack."

He timidly shook her hand then nodded. "You, too, Miss Bartolli."

"And I hear that you're a friend of my nephew Harrison. Did you know he lives right next door?"

Jack glanced that way and brightened.

"And I'll bet that he's home if you wanted to go say hey." Both the Lawson vehicles were in the driveway so it was a pretty safe bet. In fact, she'd been wondering if Avery was going to come over. Or maybe Cherry was putting her foot down.

"Is that okay?" Jack asked his dad.

"Fine with me. I have some looking around to do here anyway."

And just like that, Jack took off.

"Jack's mom remarried a few years ago. It's a guy who lives a ways out of town, so Jack doesn't get to run next door and play with neighbor kids like we did when we were growing up."

"He seems like a sweet kid."

"Thanks, he's a little shy, but good-hearted."

She held the side door open for him. "Want to come in?"

They went through the enclosed back porch that also served as a laundry room. Then Brian stepped into the kitchen. He shook his head as he patted the side of a wall cabinet. "You sure you don't want to replace these old things?"

"Not unless I replaced them with ones that looked very similar."

"You could get a lot more storage space if you ran them up to the ceiling. And you could have painted cabinets if you like. They do it all. And I have a cabinetmaker friend who's looking for work."

"I'll think about it."

"Cuz what I'm thinking is that if we put in a dishwasher..." He patted the countertop by the sink. "...It should go right here. That means I'll be cutting into this cabinet and I could end up with a big mess of splinters." He nodded over to the wall where the fridge stood. "Also you've got some wasted space there, and it could be filled in some if you decided to go with new cabinets. Now, I don't want to tell you what to do, but in the long run it might be the simpler way to go."

She considered this. "How long does it take to make new cabinets?"

"Being that Rick's not real busy, I'm sure he'd get right on it. Maybe a couple of weeks. It's not a big kitchen."

"And then I wouldn't have to paint them."

He nodded. "That's right. And painting cabinets is not a job for a beginner painter or for the faint at heart. First, you have to remove all the hardware, and then you have to clean and dry them and then sand them and then you still have to paint both the inside and outside at least a couple of times. Even then, it's a trick to make them look good. On top of all that, it's smelly."

"All right." She held up both hands. "I am convinced."

"So what I'm thinking is I should demo this kitchen. But will you miss it much?"

She shrugged. "I can eat out."

"And I'll try to do the bathroom as quick as possible, and I've got the plumber lined up, and I know a good tile guy, but there will be some inconvenience."

"I still have my Portland condo," she said suddenly. "And I need to pack some things up and see about listing it. Maybe I could synchronize that with your work."

He nodded. "That'd be great. Then we could really move in here and get things done."

"So what do I need to do to get the ball rolling?" she asked eagerly.

"You need to take a look at this estimate and if you feel it's fair, sign it." He grinned. "I know you're a lawyer so I'm sure you'll check it out carefully, but I can promise you, you won't find a better deal in town. And you can check out my dad's company, too. All the info and contractor board numbers are there. It's all legit."

"I'm sure it is."

"I wouldn't mess with a friend."

"I appreciate that."

"And I figure if I do a good enough job, I might entice you to go to dinner or something...I mean later on down the line."

"And I might be inclined to go." She smiled. "Thanks for getting this to me so quickly."

"I want to do some more careful measurements now," he said as he pulled out a yellow tape. "The sooner we get the subs scheduled and the demo done and the cabinets being built, the sooner we can put it all back together."

"How long do you think it'll be?"

He scratched his head. "I'd like to say by the end of June since we won't be changing any plumbing or electrical that I can see, but that's probably optimistic. Still, if everyone gets it together, it could happen." He looked around. "And it's a small house and from what I've seen pretty solid. So I'm hopeful."

"Great. I'll read over the contract today, and if it looks good, I'll sign it and get back to you as soon as possible."

"And then I'll get to work." He continued to measure in the kitchen. "And these measurements will make things happen that much quicker."

Andy was barking out in the yard, so Hope excused herself to see who it was this time. Already Nona's house was feeling like Grand Central Station.

"Hey," called Lewis, "I just thought I'd stop by and see how you're doing."

"Oh, I'm glad it's you," she told him as she waved the contract. "I was just going over an estimate for fixing up the house. Is there a certain budget I should be sticking to?"

"As long as the improvements go to the house and you save the receipts, I think you should be fine." He glanced over at the pickup. "Is that Brian's truck?"

She nodded. "He's in there measuring now."

"He and his dad do good work."

"That's what I've heard." She gave him the quick lowdown on her plans and how she even planned to do some of the painting herself, and he said they all sounded like good improvements.

"Just keep me posted and make your check requests a day in advance and we should be good," he said.

"And I'm not pulling out all the stops," she assured him. "I want the house to be solid and nice, but I also want it to look like a forties bungalow." Then she told him about the reclaimed fir floors and having painted cabinets.

"Don't tell me you're having fun," he teased. "And to think we had to twist your arm."

"Well, I've barely begun. But I think it could be fun." She stooped down to pick up Andy. "And he seems to like me."

Lewis patted the dog's head. "I'm not surprised."

"And I gave notice on my job."

He nodded. "Was that hard?"

"It kind of felt like I was burning my bridges...although my boss said they'd consider rehiring me if things don't work out."

"Hopefully things will work out."

"And Faye came by," she said quietly, almost as if she thought Cherry might be in her yard listening. "It sounds like my family is mad at me."

"That's too bad."

"And Faye asked about what I would do with the money after my year is up—that is if I make it a year."

"If you make it a year, it all belongs to you—lock, stock, and barrel."

"So I can do as I please with it."

He simply nodded.

"I mean I'd want to do what Nona would want."

Now he smiled. "Maybe by then you'll know."

"Hope," Brian called from in the house. "You out there?"

"I'll let you get back to it," Lewis told her quickly. "And if you need help painting, I'm pretty handy with a brush. You might not remember that my dad was a painting contractor. So I got plenty of hands-on experience growing up."

She held her finger in the air. "Thank you for telling me, Counselor; I will definitely take you up on the offer." Then she went inside to see that Brian had made her another list.

"I've got more lists," she said as she looked at it.

"I figured you'd want to start ordering your appliances and countertop and all the fun stuff. These are some measurements and whatnot to help you out. And I noted the names of the plumbing place, as well as a good tile shop and a few other places you might want to check out. All but the plumbing place are in Bend."

"Thanks." She held up the contract. "I'll get back to you."

"And I better get Jack some lunch before his ball game. Don't want him fainting out there in right field." He paused by the door. "Hey, you could come to the game, if you want. I mean it's not too exciting, but it's kind of fun in a small-town way."

"It actually does sound fun," she said. "But I think my niece is coming over to help me. We're getting stuff out of here still, and then we're going to start painting."

He tipped his hat. "Maybe another time then." He stepped out the door and, putting his fingers to his lips, let out a shrill whistle. Mere seconds later, Jack came running over.

"Impressive," she said to father and son, waving as the pickup backed out of her driveway, but after the truck was gone, she could see that Lewis's SUV was parked in front of Cherry's house now. And when she looked closer, she saw that Lewis was sitting inside, and Cherry was leaning over on the passenger's side, apparently in deep conversation with him. Feeling like a voyeur, Hope backed away and went inside the house. Still, she wondered what they were talking about. And then she was reminded of the little scene at the restaurant the other day. What were those two up to anyway?

Chapter Twelve

....

Shortly after Brian and Jack left, Avery popped over. Hope put her to work clearing things out of the bathroom while she attacked the spare room. Hope was slowly removing large items that she didn't plan to keep and storing them outside in the driveway until she could get someone to come pick them up next week. Maybe Faye and Cherry would want to look them over first. But slowly the house was emptying.

"Check this out," Hope said as she held out an old fur coat she'd found in the back of the closet. "I'll bet it will fit you."

"Cool." Avery slipped it on. "Ooh, it's really satiny smooth inside."

"But kind of musty smelling, huh?"

Avery ran her hand over a furry sleeve. "But it's so beautiful."

"You want it?"

"Really? I can have it?" Avery looked stunned.

"Why not? You're the only one I know who would be able to fit into it."

"Or my mom."

Hope nodded. "Yes. Cherry would probably fit into it as well. Maybe you two can share it."

"She probably wouldn't like it." Avery rubbed her cheek against the collar.

"You never know." Hope wanted to add that if Cherry thought Hope liked it and wanted it, she would probably like it a lot. "I saw your mom talking to Lewis Garson, Nona's attorney…," she said in what she hoped sounded like a casual way.

"Yeah, Mom and Lewis are old friends. They went to school together."

Hope refrained from pointing out that Cherry had been two grades behind Lewis in high school, and that they probably never exchanged more than two words back then.

"Mom thinks Lewis is uber-smart because he went to college." Avery turned to look at Hope. "Just like you did."

"That's right. We both went to law school. But at different colleges."

"Do you think it's weird that both my mom and dad didn't go to college?"

"Actually, your dad went to community college. A couple of years, I think."

"But then he quit to marry Mom."

"I know." Hope opened the linen closet by the bathroom and pretended to be absorbed by it.

"And you know that he *had* to marry my mom, right?" Avery's voice was quiet, as if she were worried that her parents could be listening from next door.

"What do you mean he *had* to?" Hope kept her back to Avery as she removed a stack of old pillowcases. They had embroidered lace on the edges and were definitely keepers. She sniffed them. *Lavender.* Nona loved lavender.

"You know…because mom was pregnant."

Now Hope turned to Avery, keeping her courtroom face intact. "No…your mom didn't get pregnant until *after* they were married. I remember that you were born more than a year—"

"I don't mean *me*."

Hope calmly smoothed her hand over the soft and well-worn pillowcase on the top of the stack. "I'm confused, Avery. What are you saying?"

Avery took off the fur coat, hung it over her arm, and sighed. "I just thought you already knew...I mean because you're her sister."

"Knew what?"

"About the baby." Avery looked worried now. "Don't tell Mom I told you, okay? She doesn't even know that I know."

"I'm still confused, Avery. What baby?"

"Mom got pregnant during her last year in high school. So Dad *had* to marry her. And then she lost the baby before anyone, well, besides their parents, figured it out."

"She *lost* the baby?" Hope was stunned.

"I mean she had a *miscarriage*. And, don't worry, Aunt Hope, I already know about all the sex stuff. They had a special class in school last month. I didn't even want to go, but Mom signed the permission form, and so I sort of had to. Lucy and I sat together in the back and drew pictures and giggled. But I listened, too."

"Oh." Hope felt the need to sit down.

"I thought you knew."

"Does Aunt Faye know?"

Avery just shrugged.

"Do you think Nona knew?"

Again with the shrug.

Hope didn't know what to say. Or how to react. It was almost too much to take in. Cherry had been pregnant? Drew *had* to marry her? Had they even been in love? Did they regret the marriage?

"Please, don't tell Mom that I told you," Avery said again. "She doesn't even know that I know. I just heard her and Daddy fighting one night a few months ago, and I eavesdropped. I know it was wrong, but I couldn't sleep."

Hope set the pillowcases back in the closet then reached out to hug Avery. "No, of course I won't tell your mom or anyone what you told me. Remember, I'm a lawyer and I know about keeping things quiet. You can trust me."

With the fur coat between them, Avery hugged her back. "Thanks."

They worked quietly together for the rest of the afternoon, but all Hope could think about was what Avery had disclosed to her. Hope actually wanted to talk about it, to hear it played out, and to eventually wrap her head around the whole thing. But she knew she'd respect her promise to Avery. It would remain their secret. Only it would be easier if she didn't know.

Now she actually felt sorry for Drew. Had Cherry trapped him into marrying her? And, if so, why? Just because his family was well-known and respected in the community? Because she wanted to run for Rodeo Queen? But that was crazy. Or was it because Drew had been Hope's…and because Cherry had always wanted what Hope had? And had Cherry really been pregnant at all? Or had she pretended to be so that he'd marry her? Oh, what a can of worms… and one she wished had never been opened!

By the end of the day, the living room was mostly cleared out, and the garage was stacked high with boxes to be picked up. Both bedrooms, the bathroom, and the linen closet had been cleared out and sorted and were nearly empty as well. Hope had put the few things she wished to keep, including the old linens, a couple of silk scarves, a box of old letters, and several books and photos into a plastic crate with her name on it. The other possible keepsakes she had laid out on the spare room bed for Faye and Cherry to sort through later. Hopefully tomorrow, because she wanted to get everything else out of here by Monday or Tuesday so that she and Avery could begin painting the bedrooms.

In the meantime, she would get exterior paint and hopefully start on the outside of the house tomorrow. She had some colors in mind, too—a warm buttery yellow for the body of the house, milky white for the trim and the little picket fence in the front yard, and the flower boxes and doors would be a dark olive green. And then she would plant pink geraniums in the window boxes. In her mind's eye it was perfect.

She hoped to sleep better tonight. With the cleared-out bedroom and fresh sheets that smelled of lavender on the bed, she felt more like this was becoming her own space. And yet Nona was still there, too. Not in a haunting way, but in a comforting way.

The next morning, she slept in a bit later. But when she woke, it was to the shrill sound of the telephone. And when she answered, it was Faye and she sounded frantic.

"What's wrong?" Hope demanded.

"It's Monroe!"

"What?" Hope felt a rush of panic. "Is he okay?"

"I don't know."

"What do you mean you don't know?"

"Have you seen him?" Faye asked.

"No, of course not. What is going on?"

"He's missing."

"Oh…"

"He never came home yesterday. I figured he was just trying to jerk my chain, you know, to let me know he's unhappy. Then it got later and later...and he never came home at all. I called the sheriff's, and they said they'd be looking for him, but they didn't seem too concerned. Apparently fourteen-year-old boys have been known to do this before in this town."

"I'm sorry, Faye."

"I don't know what to do. I thought maybe he'd run to you or Cherry. I mean you are his aunts. But she hasn't seen him either."

"What can I do to help?"

"Just keep a lookout for him. And let me know if you see him."

"I'm going to the hardware store for paint," Hope told her. "I'll drive all around and look for him."

"Thanks. Jody's husband has been all over town."

"Do you think he met someone—you know someone his age, who might've taken him in for the night?"

"I hope it's something like that."

"Keep me posted," Hope told her. "And I'll look and ask around, okay?"

"Thanks." Faye's voice sounded flat and hopeless, and Hope remembered what she'd said just yesterday about how Monroe was all she had. And now he was gone. Hope hurried to dress and tended to Andy and then got in her car. Like she'd promised, she drove all over town. To both parks and even up Three Creeks where high school kids had been known to "camp" in the summer. Of course, "camping" was just another word for partying. Hopefully Monroe hadn't connected with kids like that. But it wouldn't surprise Hope if he had. Still, she wasn't sure she wanted to go snooping around in the woods by herself.

Instead, she drove back through town, watching for teens that she might be able to question. But being it was still early and a Sunday, she figured most of the teens were probably still in bed. Finally she parked at the hardware store and went in to study paint colors. She decided to go with her yellow, white, green color scheme, and while a nice woman was mixing her paints, she went over to the bakery to get something to eat.

A teen was behind the counter and so she figured she'd see if he knew anything about where a runaway kid might be hiding. "My fourteen-year-old nephew is missing," she told the lanky boy as he counted out her change.

"Huh?" He looked confused.

"His name is Monroe," she continued. "And he and his mom are just moving to town so he doesn't really know anyone."

"And he's missing?" the kid asked with what seemed genuine concern.

"Yes. He was gone yesterday, and his mom just figured he was checking out the town, but he never came home last night."

The kid just nodded like he was taking this in. "What's he look like?"

Hope wondered if she had a photo in her purse, but if she did it was probably old. "He's about my height and medium build," she began. "Light brown hair, kind of shaggy long. He probably had on baggy jeans, kind of scruffy, you know."

The kid nodded like he knew the type.

"And I grew up in this town, so I remember how kids used to *camp* up Three Creeks in the summertime."

The kid chuckled as he filled her coffee cup. "Yeah. They still do that. Well, as long as the sheriffs aren't out. They've been coming down hard on camping these last couple years."

"Anyway, I realize he could've made a friend and gone camping."

"Yeah, that's a real possibility." He was putting her quiche on a plate now. "And if that's the case, I wouldn't be too worried. I mean those kids aren't going to hurt anyone or anything. They just like to have a good time."

"Right." She nodded then reached for a pen to write her sister's name and cell phone number on a napkin. "Anyway, if you happen to hear anything..." She wrote Monroe's name and age down, too. "...Could you give this number a call?"

"Sure."

"Thanks." Now she moved out of the line because a couple had just come in. But as she sat down, she kept wondering what else she could do to help. For some reason, she had a feeling that Faye was just sitting in Jody's house—probably paralyzed with fear. And probably afraid to call Monroe's dad, too. Poor Faye.

Hope looked at the numbers in her cell phone and, seeing Lewis's, decided to give him a call. When it went to voicemail, she left a brief message about her missing nephew, and to make it sound less dire she added, "And I plan to start painting the outside of the house today so if your offer's still good, feel free to stop by. Free pizza could be involved." Then, feeling silly and slightly selfish, she hung up and ate her breakfast.

After picking up the paint and miscellaneous supplies, including a painting outfit that consisted of a funny pair of men's work jeans, green rubber flip-flops, and a bright orange T-shirt that said *Do It in Sisters*. She packed everything into her car then cruised around town again, once again hitting both parks and then going over to where the schools and baseball fields were as well. She even toured some of the

newer neighborhoods and was surprised at how much this town
had grown and changed since she'd been a teen. Finally, she went
home and let Andy outside to run. She wanted to start painting but
felt guilty for not doing more to search for Monroe. But what?

She glanced over to Cherry's house to see that both vehicles
were gone. Were they, too, looking for Monroe? Or more likely still
at church. Avery had said she wouldn't be able to come over to help
until afterwards. Hope had been mildly surprised to hear that their
family went to church. But maybe it had been Nona's influence. And
maybe one of these Sundays, Hope might go to church, too.

She decided to call Faye and see if anything had changed. It
would be like Faye to forget to call Hope even if Monroe had made
it safely home.

"No," Faye said dismally. "I haven't heard from him. No one has
seen him. I really don't know what to do."

"Could he have gone home?"

"Home?"

"You know to Seattle…to be with Jeff."

"Oh…"

"Did he have any money? Could he have taken a bus or
hitchhiked?"

"I don't know…"

Hope wanted to reach through the phone line and shake her
sister. "But it's a possibility, right?"

"I suppose."

"Maybe you should call Jeff."

"No."

"But what if Monroe is there right now? Wouldn't you want to know?"

"Jeff would call me."

"Are you sure?"

"Of course he'd call me. That's the responsible thing to do."

"But what if Monroe told his dad that you were moving to Sisters and that you didn't even plan to tell him?"

"Oh…"

"Well, think about it, Faye. I mean Monroe's a kid. But someone's got to be a grown-up."

"Thanks for the little lecture, sis." Faye's old sarcasm was returning. "Coming from someone who doesn't even have kids, well, it's really quite effective."

"I just thought you might want to—" And then Faye hung up on her. Hope wondered who the child really was—Monroe or his mother? She went into the bedroom and changed into her working clothes, tucking the horrible orange T-shirt into the weird-looking jeans, but the waist was so big that she found an old piece of rope to make a belt, tightening it until she looked like a sack of potatoes. "Lovely," she said to the image of herself in the closet door mirror as she slipped on the neon green flip-flops. If her friends could see her now!

Suddenly, Andy was barking again. Someone was at the door. Thinking it might be her long-lost nephew, she made a dash for it, but was surprised to find Lewis standing there, not wearing a suit today, but neatly dressed all the same.

"I got your message," he told her. "Is Monroe still missing?"

She opened the screen door wide enough to let hyper Andy spring out and Lewis in. "No. I was just talking to Faye. I told her she should call her ex in case Monroe went home."

"That's a good idea."

"Not according to my big sister."

"Oh."

"I looked all over town." She shoved her hands into the oversized pockets of her man pants.

"Maybe he's just trying to shake his mom up," Lewis suggested. "Cherry told me he wasn't too thrilled with this move."

Hope frowned. She wanted to ask what else Cherry had told him, and by the way, why was he spending so much time with her married sister in the first place? But she knew that was not her business.

He smiled now. "Your message also said you were painting your house, but I don't see any paint."

"The paint's still in my car. I was so worried about Monroe that it sort of took the wind out of my sails." She held out her arms as if to show off her outfit, which would've been pretty hard to overlook. "But as you can see, I'm still planning on attacking it."

"Since there doesn't seem much you can do for Monroe at the moment, maybe a little house painting would be a good distraction." He pointed to his own attire: neatly pressed gray slacks and a blue and white striped shirt. "I don't know if I can put together a painting getup as classy as yours." He grinned. "That rope belt is a nice hillbilly touch."

"Thanks." She rolled her eyes.

"But I can be ready to work in about half an hour, if you'd like."

Hope nodded. "That'd be great. I'll start getting the paint stuff out."

As she unloaded the car, she thought that Lewis was right. Painting would be a good distraction over worrying about her mixed-up nephew. Although she'd keep her cell phone in her pocket…just in case Faye called.

Poor Monroe, he had looked so lost and lonely at Nona's funeral. Hope had assumed that, like her, he'd been sad to lose a grandmother— rather a great-grandmother. But the truth was, Monroe had probably been sad about losing his home, his dad, his friends...his whole life. How could Faye do that to her own son? Was it simply to punish Jeff? And, if so, it was probably going to come back and bite Faye. Maybe it already had. Hope's best guess was that Monroe was okay, probably on his way to Seattle or maybe even there by now. Still, she felt guilty for not reaching out to him more at Nona's funeral. She already doubted that she was much of a sister, but couldn't she do better as an aunt?

Chapter Thirteen

....

Because the backside of Nona's house got more weather and sun, it also needed more work. Lewis offered to tackle it. He insisted that it needed "prepping," which included some washing, sanding, and, when the siding was dry enough, a coat of primer paint. "And then you can paint it yellow," he told her.

As a result, Hope and Avery were focusing on the front side of the house, which by late afternoon was starting to look pretty good. "You're doing a great job on that window box," Hope told Avery.

"Lewis told me I had to sand it first," Avery explained. "And I think he's right. See how smooth the paint goes on now."

"He's the expert. In fact, I think I should go ask him about this corner of the house where the downspout must've splashed up. I have a feeling it might need some extra attention, too." But when Hope found Lewis in the backyard, he wasn't working, but standing and talking to Cherry over the gate that connected the two yards. It appeared to be an intense conversation, too. Cherry, as usual, looked impeccable with her wavy blond hair flowing over her bare shoulders. She had on a robin's egg blue sundress, which really showed off her tan. But she looked upset, almost on the verge of tears (unless it was an act), and Lewis reached over the gate and put his hand on her shoulder as if to comfort her. Or whatever!

Once again, Hope felt like a voyeur. And yet, she was standing in her own backyard. Feeling guilty and slightly humiliated, she turned and walked away. But as she went around the corner of the house, she grew angry. Was it fair that she couldn't even go about her own business in her own home without feeling guilty for spying on her baby sister? And what was the deal with those two anyway? Maybe she should just throw the cards down on the table and ask. And yet... how would that sound? Of course she would appear to be a nosy, busybody neighbor. And maybe she was, but she didn't have to let the whole world know. Better to just forget about it.

Back at the front of the house, whether it was a mistake or not, she began slapping yellow paint onto the funky place near the downspout. At least it made it look better, and an extra layer of paint probably couldn't hurt anything. Plus, if it needed more attention, she could deal with it later. She was just finishing up and thinking about ordering pizza and calling it a day when Brian's turquoise pickup pulled into her driveway. She tossed down her brush, waved at him, and hurried over.

"Hey, this place is looking great." He nodded to the front of the house. "But I hope you know you'll probably need to redo that window trim after we replace the windows."

"That's okay," she assured him. "It's kind of fun to see it all coming together."

"I got your message."

She nodded. "I went over the contract, and I think it looks good, so I signed it."

"And I already called my buddy about the old-growth fir floor. He's put your name on about one thousand square feet of it. A good thing since another builder was asking about it, too."

"Great. I'll run and get the contract."

Inside the house, she peeked out the bedroom window to see
if Lewis and Cherry were still cloistered over the gate…or perhaps
they'd snuck off to some more private location. But Lewis was back
to work, washing a brush out in the hose. She picked up the contract
from where she'd tossed it on the bed, then on her way out, caught a
glimpse of her image in the mirror. Not only was her outfit atrocious
and spotted with paint, but she'd even managed to get some on her
face. Not that she planned to do anything about it now. She just
laughed and shook her head.

But as she went outside, she couldn't help but mentally compare
herself to Cherry. Why wouldn't someone like Lewis be attracted to
Little Miss Perfect? Well, despite the fact that Cherry was married.
Still, not everyone respected such conventional things as marriage
vows. And not that Hope cared what Lewis or Cherry did anyway.
Why should she? And yet why was she obsessing over it?

Lewis and Brian were talking now. Acting like old buddies,
although she was certain those two probably never spoke to each
other in high school. "Here you go." She handed the paperwork to
Brian with a big smile. "I can't wait to begin."

He smiled back. "I'll be over first thing in the morning."

And then something came over Hope. She knew it was juvenile—
straight out of junior high—but she started to flirt with Brian. "And I
could have coffee for you," she said sweetly, "if you like."

He nodded. "Hey, that'd be great. I'll bet your coffee is way better
than the stuff I grab at Barnie's kiosk."

"I'll bet it is, too," she said in a slightly seductive way. Okay, she
knew this was ridiculous. Especially considering how she probably
looked in her awful orange T-shirt, baggy jeans, and neon green

flip-flops. Not to mention a sloppy ponytail and paint on her face. Seriously, had she lost her senses?

Brian leaned a little closer to her now. "And I like a little cream in my coffee, if that's not too much to ask."

She tilted her head slightly. "And how about some pastry to go with that?"

He chuckled. "I *know* I'm going to like working for you, Hope."

"And I'm going to like having you around, too." Now she turned to Lewis as if she'd just noticed he was standing there watching them. "Hey, I was about to order pizza and call it a day." She turned back to Brian now. "Would you like to join us?" Again, almost against her will, she was turning on the charm.

"I'd love to, but I dropped Jack at a friend's house and promised to pick him up in time to get him home by seven."

She nodded in a coy fashion. "Another time then."

"For sure." He actually tipped his cowboy hat now, grinning like he'd just won the prize pumpkin at the county fair. Of course, in her orange shirt, she probably looked a bit like a pumpkin as she waved good-bye.

"You and Brian seemed to have hit it off." Lewis said this with a question in his voice.

"Oh, yeah." She nodded. "He's great. And he's got some really good ideas for fixing this place up. I can't believe he's going to start tomorrow."

"Sounds like he's made you his number-one priority."

"And that's how I plan to keep it, too." She turned and made a slightly catty smile for Lewis. "Got to keep my contractor happy, don't ya think? Make sure he gets the job done right."

"I guess so." And yet something about his expression looked troubled. And suddenly Hope felt guilty...and silly...and like a big phony. And yet, what was she going to do about it? And why should Lewis care anyway? He obviously had something going on with Cherry. At least that was what it looked like to Hope.

"Are we going to have pizza?" Avery called from where she was finishing up the second window box.

"I'm on it." Hope dug her phone out of her jeans pocket. "What kind do you like?" she asked Lewis, but he was hedging, acting like he needed to go.

"You can't leave before we have pizza," Avery said as she joined them.

"That's right." Hope nodded firmly. Then she made them decide on toppings and called it in, and they all went to work cleaning their brushes and things, getting it all put away.

"Avery!" Cherry yelled from her front porch. "Time to come in for dinner."

"But Aunt Hope's getting pizza," Avery called back.

"I said, come home," Cherry called again.

"But Mom," Avery pleaded.

"Avery!" Cherry called shrilly. She probably didn't realize that Lewis was still around to hear her sounding like a fishwife. Or maybe she didn't care.

"I gotta go," Avery said with disappointment.

"I'm sorry, sweetie." Hope gave her a hug.

"I'll be back tomorrow, okay?"

"Absolutely." Hope stroked Avery's ponytail, giving it a playful flip. "And I have to go to Bend to look at some appliances and things. Do you think your mom would let you come with me?"

Avery brightened. "I'll ask!"

"Great." Hope was relieved to see Avery cheering up.

"And maybe we can stop by Target," she said hopefully. "I mean if you have time."

Hope nodded. "I don't see why not."

Avery nodded eagerly. "That's where Lucy got her swimsuit."

"And it's close to a lot of appliance stores," Lewis offered.

"Sounds like a good plan," Hope agreed.

"Thanks, Aunt Hope!" Avery waved and scurried off.

"What a great kid." Hope watched her trotting up the steps to her house.

"She really is a sweetheart," agreed Lewis.

Now she turned to him. "Do you still want to stay for pizza?"

"Why not?"

"Well, the work party just got reduced by one-third."

"That means more pizza for me." He hungrily rubbed his stomach.

"Which reminds me, I should go feed Andy. Want to come inside?"

"Sure." So they both went in, and while she fed Andy, Lewis went to clean up in the bathroom, emerging and looking as good as new.

"Guess I better clean up, too," she said as she held out her paint-splotched hands. "I hope this comes off." But first, she put out some money on the kitchen table. "Will you take care of the pizza guy if I'm not out when he comes?"

"Be my pleasure. Take your time."

She hurried to the bathroom, scrubbing as fast and hard as she could on her paint spots. Then she took her hair out of the ragged ponytail and made a mad dash to the bedroom, where she quickly changed into her Wranglers and a clean T-shirt. She knew it was silly, especially since she'd heard the pizza arrive, but she even took the time to put on some lip gloss and mascara. And she questioned herself as she did this. Why was she going to this much trouble for a guy who was probably having an affair (or considering it) with her baby sister? On the same token, why had she attempted to make him jealous by flirting with Brian? What was wrong with her?

And when she went to the kitchen, she figured she was getting just what she deserved, because it appeared as if Lewis had left. But Andy was gone, too. As was the pizza. Now this was a bit weird.

"We're out here," Lewis called through the screen door. "You might want a sweater, though…it's cooling off a bit."

"Okay," she called back. Of course the only sweater she could find was the white lacy one that she'd worn to the funeral, but she put it on anyway. Then she went outside to find that Lewis had unearthed an old patio table, which he had set up by the garden along with the old lawn chairs. And he'd even put a red and white checked tablecloth on the table, along with a couple of plates, two glasses of water, and paper towels for napkins. But what really got her attention was the fact that he'd also brought out a pair of Nona's old silver candlestick holders, and the white taper candles were lit.

The scene was actually surprisingly romantic. She wondered if he realized this, or if he'd been simply trying to create a casual outdoor picnic.

"Very nice," she told him as he pulled out a chair for her to sit.

"I try."

He presented the pizza box, actually serving her. She daintily removed a piece and set it on her plate. She was actually speechless— and that was unusual for her.

"June is one of the most beautiful months," he said as he took a couple pieces for himself and then set the pizza box on the small side table that she'd dug out yesterday. "And eating outside on a night like this is too good to pass up, don't you think?"

Just then, Andy jumped onto her lap, and she laughed. "It appears that Sir Andy would agree with you on that." She waited for the little dog to settle down and then took a bite of pizza. "I like to eat outside, too," she admitted. "But my condo in Portland isn't the best setup. My terrace is so tiny I can barely fit one chair and a few potted plants. I guess I won't miss that much."

"But there are other things you'll miss?"

"Probably."

They both ate quietly with only the background noises of crickets, an occasional frog, and what sounded like a mourning dove. And yet, it wasn't the sort of quiet where Hope felt the need to fill in the spaces with words. In a way, it was a companionable silence. Or at least she hoped it was.

"You clean up well." Lewis smiled as he took another piece of pizza.

She looked down at her crocheted sweater. It actually looked pretty in the flickering candlelight. "Thanks."

"Did you hear anything from Faye...in regard to Monroe?"

She shook her head. "I really think he must've gone home. To Seattle, I mean, to be with his dad."

"That makes sense."

"But I would've thought Faye might've called."

"Maybe you should check in with her."

Hope nodded. "Yes. That's probably wise. Faye isn't really good at keeping people informed."

"I kind of get the sense that the three sisters aren't too close." He chuckled. "Kind of like the mountains. Oh, they look close to each other from a distance, but when you're hiking around there, you see how much space is between them."

"That's really true. I've noticed that before, but I never thought about it in respect to my sisters and me."

"Also, the three sisters are volcanic mountains," he pointed out.

"Meaning one of them could erupt."

He shrugged. "Possibly."

"Which sister do you think would erupt first?" She studied him closely now.

"Well, as I'm sure you know, the South Sister, which is also the youngest sister, has had the most volcanic activity. So it's probably most likely."

She wondered if he was talking about the mountain or Cherry now. Perhaps she didn't want to know. Maybe the safest route was to keep the conversation focused on mountains—not sisters. "Did you know that South Sister also has the highest mountain lake in Oregon?"

He nodded. "Teardrop Lake."

"Have you climbed any of them?"

"Only South Sister."

"Yes…well, that's the easiest climb." She was trying very hard not to think about Cherry. They were, after all, talking about the mountains.

"How about you?" he asked.

"What?"

"Have you climbed any of them?"

"Oh…well, yes, of course. I climbed South Sister first. I was sixteen that summer. My mom took our family up there. But Mom and I were the only ones to make it to the top. Mom was disappointed because she really felt that Cherry should've completed the climb, you know, since it was her namesake mountain."

He just nodded, watching her with interested eyes.

"And the next summer, when I was seventeen, Mom and I climbed Middle Sister. That's a harder climb."

"So I've heard. I've been thinking about trying it myself."

"Really? I've actually thought about doing it again, too."

"Maybe we could do it together."

Now Hope knew they were talking about mountains and climbing, but she was thankful for the dim light outside because she was certain her cheeks were flushing. "And I've never climbed North Sister, although my mom and some of her friends had climbed it, and Mom had promised to take me there the summer after I graduated."

"The summer she died?"

Hope nodded then looked down. A lump was growing in her throat.

"Is something wrong?" His voice was so full of compassion that she actually was afraid she really might cry.

"It's just that—" She took a sip of water. "Well, I suppose I still blame myself."

"For your mother's death?"

"Well, yes."

"I know she was planning on climbing Middle Sister that day, but surely that doesn't make you think that—"

"There's more to the story." Hope took another gulp of water.

"Do you want to talk about it?"

"I've never told anyone the whole story."

"You can trust me, Hope."

She looked into his eyes and wondered. "Client confidentiality?" she asked. He nodded. "Okay, I'm going to say this quickly— because I don't want to cry. Mom had asked me to go with her that weekend. She wanted the two of us to climb North Sister together. She had it all planned out and was excited about it. And I told her I didn't want to. Drew had invited me to a barn dance, and I turned Mom down to go to that stupid dance. So, she changed her plans and was supposed to be meeting her friends up there to climb Middle Sister instead."

"Oh, so you think if you'd gone with her, she might not have been in a wreck."

"Seems that way to me."

"But it's not as if you told your mother to go climb Middle Sister."

"No...but she did it because I turned her down."

"That's a heavy load to carry, Hope."

She nodded.

"And, really, you're an intelligent woman; you must know that your mother was an adult and able to make her own choices."

"My head knows that, but sometimes my heart feels differently." Just then, she heard the phone ringing in the house. "Maybe that's about Monroe." She grabbed Andy out of her lap and began to dash toward the house. "Maybe he's okay!"

It did turn out to be Faye, but Monroe was still missing. Not only that but Faye sounded on the edge of hysteria because she had called Jeff and he was furious at her. Hope tried to calm Faye down, but it seemed useless.

"Look," she told her finally. "I'm going to go up to Three Creeks tonight. And I'll look for him, okay? I'll bet that's where he went."

"But why?" Faye demanded. "Why would he go up there? He doesn't even know anyone and—"

"You don't know if he knows anyone or not. I just have a hunch that he could be up there. I'll call you if I find anything out, okay?"

"Okay."

Hope hung up the phone and turned to Lewis, who was putting their dinner party things away. "North Sister is erupting."

He shook his head as he set the dishes in the sink. "Are you really going to drive up to Three Creeks?"

She nodded. "I am."

"Then let me go with you. Better yet, let me drive. At least I have four-wheel drive and a rig that can go off road."

"Do you have a flashlight in—"

"Flashlight, blanket, first-aid kit, flares." He held up his hands. "What can I say? I'm still sort of a nerd."

She patted his cheek. "Nerds come in handy sometimes." Then, grabbing her cell phone and another blanket, just in case, she followed him out to his SUV. "I really appreciate this, Lewis. I know Faye will, too…especially if we find Monroe."

"I've heard it can get a little rough up there," he warned her. "The sheriffs have been cracking down on kids, but that probably just drives them deeper into the forest."

"Did you ever camp up there in high school?" she asked as he headed up Three Creeks Road.

He laughed. "Are you kidding? Remember me? I was the nerd."

"I only went up there one time. Drew thought it would be fun. Turned out he was wrong."

"You know that's the second time you mentioned Drew tonight, and I have to admit that I'd totally forgotten that you two used to date in high school. Being that I was such a nerd and all, I was sort of on the outside of things. But it does strike me as a bit odd that your younger sister married your high school boyfriend."

Hope forced what she hoped was a lighthearted laugh.

"I'm glad you can laugh now, but I imagine it was a little sticky back then."

"It wasn't much fun at the time, but now I'm perfectly fine with it. In fact, it actually feels like I dodged a bullet. I mean Drew's a nice guy, but I'm pretty sure I would've outgrown him eventually. It's just that it was an awkward setup...back then."

"And it's better now?"

She sighed. "Not really."

"I assume that's one of the reasons you stayed away from Sisters so long. The town I mean."

"Yes...Sisters and sisters." She shook her head. "You talk about feeling like an outsider during high school. The truth is after Cherry married Drew, I felt like an outsider in my own family... and in my own town. And since I'm confessing things here, I feel like an outsider at Nona's house, too. It's not easy living next to them." She was about to mention how it was also awkward seeing Cherry and Lewis together, too, but now he was turning off onto a narrow dirt road, which probably led to a "camping" area. And she was feeling more than a little nervous—and she was extremely thankful that she hadn't come up here alone after all. Whether or not Lewis was actually having an affair with Cherry, which boggled her mind more than ever tonight, she was grateful to have him with her now.

Chapter Fourteen
....

Hope wrapped the polar fleece blanket around her shoulders like a cape as she and Lewis walked toward what sounded like a pretty loud party. She could smell smoke from the campfire, and she hoped there wasn't anything more serious than drinking going on here. She'd heard stories about outlaws manufacturing methamphetamines in the National Forest before. And she knew that people like that could be very unfriendly, not to mention unreasonable.

"Hey," Lewis called out in a congenial voice. They were just outside of the firelight, and Hope could see a mix of tents and things and people mingling around. "Mind if we join you?"

"Who are you?" called out a big guy who was standing next to the fire.

"Just friends," Hope called back as she stepped into the firelight so they could see her. "Friends who haven't met yet."

"Come on in," he called to her.

"Thanks." She stepped closer to the fire now, looking around to see if she could spot Monroe. "It's getting cold."

"And we're looking for a friend," Lewis explained. "He's new in town, and we thought maybe he came up here."

"What's his name?" a girl with stringy blond hair asked.

"Monroe," Hope said.

"Hey, Monroe," called out the big guy. "Where you at, buddy?"

Hope felt her spirits soaring. "Is he here?"

159

"Unless there's more than one new Monroe in town."

"Hey, Monroe," the girl called. "Your friends are here!"

Just then a shadowy form emerged from a tent. The way he rubbed his eyes looked like he'd been asleep. "Hey, Monroe, old buddy," Hope said as she went over and threw her arms around her scruffy-looking nephew. "It's been a long time. I heard you were camping up here, and I thought I'd come and hang with you."

"Lucky dog," the guy by the fire said. "I'd offer you guys some beer, but you have to chip into the pot first."

"Here you go," Lewis told him as he handed the guy a bill.

"What are you—"

"What's up?" Hope interrupted him. "You taking off like that and not even inviting me to come, too?"

"Aunt—"

"That's right, Monroe, your aunt is freaking right now. I told her we'd come out and find you. I'd stick around and have a beer, but maybe we should just head back, ya think?"

He shrugged with a confused expression. "Okay."

"We'll take a rain check on that beer," Lewis told the big guy. "You guys have fun and be safe, okay?"

"Okay, dude. Thanks for the donation."

"I think those were grown-ups," the stringy-haired girl said as Lewis and Hope escorted Monroe back toward the dirt path.

"Yeah, whatever. That guy gave us twenty bucks."

"Cool."

"Oh, Monroe." Hope squeezed him in tight a shoulder hug as they followed the beam from Lewis's flashlight. "I'm so glad you're okay. Do you know how worried your mom is right now?"

"She deserves to be worried."

"And she called your dad, and he's all worried, too. Plus he's mad at her."

"Good."

"I know you're unhappy, Monroe. But running away won't help."

"It will if it makes Mom listen to me. She's being so freaking selfish about this whole thing. It's like she's the only one who matters. It makes me sick."

"I know it's hard." Hope sighed. "And if it's any encouragement, I'm on your side."

He turned and looked at her. "You are?"

"Absolutely. I've told Faye several times that I think she's making a mistake."

"Really?"

"You can ask her if you want."

"Thanks, Aunt Hope."

They made it back to Lewis's SUV then he drove them toward town in silence. It was so quiet in the backseat, Hope wondered if Monroe had fallen asleep.

"So where to now?" Lewis asked when they saw the lights in town. "To where Faye is staying—or to your place?"

"Aunt Hope's place," Monroe commanded from the backseat.

"That okay?" Lewis asked her.

"It's fine with me." Of course, even as she said this, she wasn't sure it was so smart. And she knew she had to let Faye know that Monroe was safe. Still, if it helped to keep him with her for one night, who could complain?

"Thanks for your help," Hope told Lewis as she and Monroe got out.

"No problem." He gave her what seemed a genuine smile. "I really feel like I'm part of this family. I don't mind helping."

She just nodded. "I guess this family needs a lot of help."

"Good night."

She told him good night then led Monroe into the house. "Wow, Monroe, you look like you've been rolling in the dirt. How about you take a shower before you hit the hay?"

He sleepily agreed, and she told him to toss his dirty clothes into the hallway and she'd put them in the washer before going to bed. Then, when he was safely in the shower with the water running, Hope called Faye and told her that Monroe was safe and with her.

"Why didn't you bring him here?" Faye demanded.

"Because he wanted to come here. He's in the shower. He's exhausted. Let him get a good—"

"What if he runs away again?"

"He won't run away, Faye."

"How do you know that?"

Hope chuckled. "Because his clothes are all in the washing machine, sopping wet. I won't put them in the dryer until morning. *Okay?*"

"Well...I don't like that you're taking over my affairs...but okay." Then she hung up.

Hope just shook her head. So that was the thanks she got for driving up to Three Creeks in the middle of the night to search and find Faye's long-lost son—a big sisterly scolding. And to think Hope and Lewis had actually been having—what was it exactly? Well, at the very least, it had been a very interesting time. Hope was too tired to think about it as she got ready for bed. But once she was in bed, she wondered…*what exactly was Lewis Garson up to anyway?* A family friend? A romantic interest? Her baby sister's lover? *What?* Fortunately, she was too sleepy to obsess over it much.

Hope had just put Monroe's clothes into the dryer when she heard vehicles pulling up. She looked out to see the turquoise pickup as well as a white van.

"Morning, honey," Brian called cheerfully into the house. "Coffee on?"

"Oh, Brian." She slapped her forehead. "I'm so sorry." Then she gave him the details of how she'd gone up to Three Creeks late last night looking for her MIA teenage nephew. "I totally forgot about coffee."

"Wow, that was brave going up to Three Creeks. I hear it gets wild up there."

"It was a little scary." She hadn't mentioned that Lewis had gone with her. "Anyway, it was so late that I didn't make it to the store."

He waved his hand. "That's okay. Another time. Besides, we're going to start tearing up your kitchen this morning anyway." He nodded to several guys who were climbing out of the van. "The crew's all here—and we're ready to rock and roll."

"Should I leave?"

"Depends on how you like noise."

She shrugged. "I'll try to stay out of the way until Monroe wakes up."

Brian laughed. "I'm guessing he'll be waking up with the first sound of the sledgehammer hitting. Hope he doesn't have a hangover."

"Do you want me to finish emptying the kitchen cabinets?" she asked.

"Unless you want the contents being smashed to bits."

So she grabbed another box, and instead of sorting and sifting like she'd been doing, she simply stacked things into the box. Avery could help her figure it out later. She had barely finished when the crew came in and started to tear into the cabinets. "I can't watch," she told Brian as she backed away.

She went to her room and tried not to feel too terrible at the thought of Nona's old wooden cabinets being destroyed. She wished she'd thought to ask about saving them. Perhaps they could be recycled. But with each crash, smash, and boom, she knew it was too late. She also knew that Monroe was probably thinking that the house was falling down. She tapped on his door and then called in to inform him of the situation. "And your clothes should be dry in about half an hour," she said as she closed the door.

"Aunt Hope?" called Avery through the din of noise. "Where are you?"

"Back here," Hope called. "Welcome to the disaster zone."

"They're tearing up Nona's kitchen," Avery told her with wide eyes.

"It's to put in new cabinets."

"I thought you were keeping the old ones."

Hope sighed. "Brian talked me out of it."

"Oh…" Avery looked as disappointed as Hope was feeling.

"Anyway, Monroe is here and—"

"Monroe is here?" Avery's eyes lit up. "He's okay?"

"Yes." She nodded to the spare room. "He spent the night."

"I'm so glad. I was really praying for him."

Hope smiled. "Seems that God was listening."

"I better go tell Mom. She's pretty worried."

"Didn't Faye call her already?"

"No. Mom still thinks Monroe's missing."

"Then, definitely, you should go and tell her. And I'll take Monroe to breakfast. And when I get back, maybe you and I should just head for Bend. I doubt we'll be able to get much done around here today anyway."

"All right!"

Hope checked her watch. "Around eleven then?"

"Cool. Do you think it would be okay to invite Lucy?"

"It's okay with me."

"Way cool!"

"See ya in a couple hours then."

Hope wasn't sure how much these demo guys planned to do, but to be safe, she removed her personal items from the bathroom, too. Then, hearing the dryer buzzer, she retrieved Monroe's clothes, tossed them in on his bed, and told him to get dressed. "I'm taking us to breakfast as soon as you're ready."

"Good," he called back. "I'm starving!"

Before long, they were sitting in front of their stacks of pancakes, scrambled eggs, and sausage and bacon. Monroe was shoveling it in like he hadn't eaten in days. Maybe he hadn't.

"I *do* understand why you want to go back and live with your dad," Hope was telling him. "All I was saying is that I know your mom needs you, too."

"My mom needs a shrink." He took a bite of bacon then talked as he chewed. "Seriously, the woman is neurotic."

"She's hurting, Monroe. And it probably is making her a little crazy."

"I know." He nodded with a serious expression. "I'm aware of what my dad did to her. And I agree it stinks. But she needs to get over it. I mean she's not the only one who got hurt in this train wreck. But if I can forgive Dad, why can't she? I mean they don't have to stay married. I get that. But if she's going to be flipping crazy all the time, I refuse to live with her."

"What do you mean by crazy?" Hope leaned forward.

"Like I said, she's neurotic. She obsesses over everything. And she sits around doing nothing all day long like she's in a stupor. Even Jody is getting fed up with her."

"Maybe you're right, Monroe."

"Huh?" He looked up from the bite of eggs he was about to eat.

"Maybe she does need to see a professional—a shrink or a counselor or someone who can help her to sort this all out."

"Ya think?"

Hope couldn't tell if he was sarcastic or relieved. Maybe both. "I think you probably know your mom almost better than anyone, Monroe, and if you think she's handing this badly, you're probably right."

He sat a little straighter.

"And I'm trying to understand how she feels. She and your dad had been married a long time, and I remember how in love they were…back in the beginning. I can't even imagine how hurt she must be. That's probably the worst kind of rejection a person can experience. It's heartbreaking."

"She seems more angry than heartbroken."

"A lot of people hide their pain with anger, Monroe. I'm sure you've seen that before."

He nodded as he forked into a pancake. "Maybe so. I might even do it sometimes, too. Kind of a smokescreen, I guess."

"Easier than talking about how you really feel. I think that's what your mom is doing."

"But if she went to a shrink, she could talk about it."

"You're right." Hope picked up her coffee mug.

"And maybe she'd start acting more normal."

"I think she would."

"Will you tell her to get help, Aunt Hope?" he pleaded. "Because even though I said all that stuff about her being neurotic and nuts...I do love her. I mean...she's my mom."

"And she loves you—more than you'll ever know. She told me that you were all she had. Can you imagine how bad she'd be hurting to lose both you and your dad?"

He just shrugged.

"Not that I'm trying to pressure you to stay here in Sisters," she assured him. "I totally respect your choice in this. And it's a lot to ask anyone to leave their home and friends and everything."

"I don't have all that many friends at my old school." He looked surprised that he'd said this. "But don't tell Mom."

"No, I won't. Still, there's your dad and your home and what's familiar to you."

"Don't tell Mom this either, okay?"

She held up her hand as if to pledge.

"Well, I was kinda open to the idea of a fresh start here. But not if my mom's going to be all weird and crazy on me. I cannot handle that. But, if she got help, you know, like we were talking about...well, then I might consider moving here."

"I think I understand."

"But no way am I going to tell Mom that."

"And if your mom thinks you don't want to be here…" Hope was thinking out loud now. "Well, maybe you could use that as a bargaining chip, you know, to get her in to see a counselor."

"But she won't listen to me. She keeps telling me I'm just a kid and that I don't have a vote."

"You do have a vote, Monroe. And in cases of joint custody, like your parents have with you, the judge usually takes the teen's wishes into consideration."

"Meaning I can live where I want?"

"Sort of. It's not quite that simple."

He let out a relieved sigh and leaned back. "Man, I think I'm stuffed." She nodded. "Me, too."

"You don't seem like a mom."

She laughed. "Maybe because I'm not a mom."

"I mean like Cherry and my mom. They talk down to us kids, like they think they're so much smarter. But you talk to me like we're the same."

"We are the same, Monroe. It's just that I've got a few more years on you."

"Would you talk to my mom for me?" His brows arched hopefully.

"I'll talk to her, but you'll have to talk to her, too." She narrowed her eyes at him. "And you have to promise me you won't go running off like you did either."

"If it makes you feel any better, it wasn't much fun. Maybe a little at first. But all those guys up there just want to be drunk all the time. What's the fun in that?"

"Nothing that I can see."

"But I did make a friend and he's not into the drinking thing either. He's the same age as I am, and his folks are divorced, too. His name is Alex, and he plays the guitar. He told me that Sisters has a really cool art and music program."

"That's great, Monroe."

"But don't tell my mom, okay? I don't want her thinking she's going to get her way without getting some help first."

"You have my word."

"And just for the record—without telling Mom—I can't stand my dad's lady friend, and that's enough to make me want to live in Sisters." He grinned. "And it'd be nice having an aunt around, too. Someone who's easy to talk to."

"And it would be nice for me, too. I've missed being around family."

They left the restaurant, and Hope dropped Monroe back at her house to "hang" while she went to talk to Faye. She wasn't sure that she'd be able to convince her opinionated sister about much of anything, but for Monroe's sake, she'd try. And it wouldn't be easy, but she would allow Monroe client-confidant privilege by not disclosing any of his secrets.

Chapter Fifteen

....

"Honestly, Hope, I'd like to know what makes you think you're such an expert on parenting." Faye was pacing back and forth in Jody's living room now, where they'd gone to talk privately. Or sort of.

"I'm not an expert. I'm just telling you what I think is going on. You are hurting, Faye. Everyone around you can see it. And until you get healthy, it's going to be difficult for anyone—including your own son—to be around you."

"Did he say that?"

Hope shook her head. "This isn't about what Monroe did or did not say, Faye. It's about you. You are suffering because Jeff hurt you. As a result you're lashing out at everyone—including me—in an effort to feel better."

Faye sat back down on the sofa again, folding her arms across her front and scowling darkly.

"But is it working?"

"What?"

"The way you're hurting others, pushing them away, saying mean things...is it making you feel any better?"

"What do you know about how I feel, Hope? You go about your carefree little life, doing just as you please, wearing your fancy clothes, inheriting money you don't deserve, coming between your sister and her child. You don't live in my world—you don't know what it's like... so don't tell me how to live my life. And if you don't bring my son home immediately, I will call the sheriff and have him picked up." Then Faye stood and marched back into the room where she was staying.

Hope didn't know what to do, but as she was leaving, Faye's old friend Jody appeared from out of the shadows and followed Hope out. Hopefully not to continue Faye's tongue-lashing, although Hope knew these two friends were thick and went way back.

"Just so you know," Jody said quietly, "I agree with everything you said."

Hope turned and looked at her. "Really?"

Jody nodded. "I've tried to say the same—well, maybe not as well as you just did—but she won't listen." Jody pointed to her own chest. "And I am a parent. I have an eighteen- and a nineteen-year-old— probably had them too soon. Aaron and I were barely out of high school, and I don't recommend it. But I do know a little what I'm talking about, and the way Faye is handling Monroe..." She shook her head. "Well, it's no wonder that kid took off like that. I wouldn't have been a bit surprised if he'd hitched all the way back to Seattle."

"Well, maybe you can talk to her."

"And that bit about calling the sheriff?" Jody rolled her eyes. "She wouldn't even call the sheriff when Monroe was missing. I had to do that."

"Good to know."

"I better get back inside before Faye comes out here and lays into me. She's been a real loose cannon."

"I'll try to get Monroe to come back to her, but I won't promise anything."

"That poor kid might be better off with his dad...at least until Faye gets her act together."

Hope thanked Jody then drove back home. She had no idea how to handle this but decided she would let Monroe call the shots. If he wanted to go home to his dad, and if his dad was willing to have him, Hope would put him on a plane. If he wanted to stick around here, Hope would try to help him do that. Because right now both Monroe and Faye were hurting almost equally, but the difference between the two was that Monroe *wanted* help.

Hope went into the house and told Monroe how it had gone with his mother. Without telling him everything, she was honest. "So, I've decided," she said finally, "that I'll back you in whatever you choose to do. Well, unless it's something dumb like running away."

Monroe looked confused now.

"If you want to go back with your dad, I'll get you a plane ticket. If you want to go back with your mom, I'll drive you over. If you want to stay here—although it's going to be a construction zone, you're more than welcome."

"I'd like to stay here then." He made a weak smile. "Until I figure it out."

"That's fine."

"And I can help work on Nona's house, too."

"Sure, if you want to. That'd be great."

"Do you think they'd let me help tear something out?" He looked hopeful.

She laughed. "I'm sure they'd be happy to let you sling a hammer. I'll let Brian know that you're going to help."

And so, by the time Avery and Lucy arrived, wearing their shopping clothes, Monroe was wielding a hammer and a metal bar and he was tearing the tiles out of the bathroom. "Have fun," Hope called out as she left.

"I like your car," Lucy told Hope as they drove to Bend. "It's cool."

"It was my great-grandma's," Avery told her. "But she hardly ever drove it."

"And I'm getting so used to it, I don't know if I'll want to bring my city car back here or not," Hope admitted.

When they got to Target, Hope started to park, but Avery suggested that she just drop them off at the door. "That way you can go look at appliances while we try on swimsuits. Lowes and Home Depot are both right over there." Avery pointed across the parking lot.

Hope wasn't so sure. "Don't you think I should go in with you?"

"No, that's okay," Avery assured her. "As long as we stay together, it's all right. Mom does it all the time."

"Are you certain?"

"It's true," Lucy backed her up. "My mom does it, too. As long as we stay in one store and stay together, it's fine."

"And we all have our cell phones," Avery reminded her.

"If you're positive." Hope reached for her purse and extracted the amount of money that she'd planned to pay Avery.

"Totally." Avery's eyes lit up as Hope handed her the cash. "Wow, this much?"

"I've been keeping track of your hours; you've earned it."

"Thanks, Aunt Hope." She put the cash in her purse then carefully zipped it.

Hope looked at her watch. "It's close to noon now. How about if I pick you up at one?"

"How about one thirty?" suggested Lucy. "It can take a long time to find the right suit because you can only take six items in at a time."

That actually made sense. "Okay. One thirty. I'll come inside and look for you in the lobby, okay?"

"Okay!" Avery waved and the two girls went into the store.

Hope felt a little guilty, but then she remembered how she used to run all over town by herself at their age. And then, once she was looking at appliances, she put the two girls out of mind. But she did pay attention to the time. At first anyway.

"Wow, I never worked with a woman who could make up her mind so fast," the young sales guy told her.

"Well, I have my measurements, I know what I want, and I want to keep it simple. Just basic white appliances. No big deal." It was only twelve thirty by the time she'd opened an account, which saved her ten percent, and her appliances were paid for and the delivery arranged. Then, seeing a huge selection of colors, she decided to pick up paint samples for the interior of the house. But once a friendly woman started helping her, she quickly nailed down the colors. The woman figured out the amounts and talked her into low-VOS paint and soon began mixing. While she waited, Hope noticed the lighting section and wondered if it might be fun to switch out some of the lights in Nona's house.

But by the time she'd decided on several lights, picked up her paint, and was waiting with her oversized cart in the checkout line, she realized it was already one thirty. The girls would be done and waiting for her. And by the time she was driving back to Target, she was a full fifteen minutes late, and her blood pressure was rising as she imagined those two darling eleven-year-old girls being swooped up by a stranger!

Really, what had she been thinking? Why had she left them there alone? What would Cherry say? Or Lucy's mother? Really, what made Hope think she knew how to do this? What if she'd made a horrible mistake?

But to her great relief, the girls had just finished shopping and actually thought they were the ones who had been late. She didn't even bother to straighten them out. Instead, she offered them lunch. Then, after eating at a Mexican restaurant, the three of them stayed together and looked in a few more shops. Hope was amazed at how much Bend had grown and changed. And, according to the girls, this was just one of the new shopping complexes.

Then, as they pulled into Sisters and Hope was looking forward to being home and putting her feet up, she remembered that Nona's house would no longer look like a home. During her absence, the little house had become a construction site, complete with a bright blue Porta-potty now planted on the front lawn. But at least the trucks were gone and it seemed quiet inside.

Avery and Lucy thanked her for taking them to Bend and to lunch, and then Hope went into the house to begin estimating the damages. Or progress, depending on how one looked at it. The kitchen looked sad and barren. It had been completely gutted. All the carpeting and linoleum were now gone, exposing old wooden floorboards with cracks between them where it looked like spiders and bugs could easily crawl in.

"Monroe?" she called, knocking on his door then opening it to see only the bed in his room, pushed up against a wall, probably to tear out the carpeting.

She checked her room to see that its carpet had also been taken out, and her bed, now shoved in a corner, looked forlorn and lonely.

But the biggest surprise was probably the bathroom. It, too, had been gutted. No shower. No sink. No toilet. Only the claw-foot bathtub remained. Thankfully no one had taken a sledgehammer to that. She tried the faucet and was surprised to see it still worked. So now she had running water (in the tub) and a toilet (in the front yard). Luxurious.

She went outside and called for Monroe, but he didn't appear to be anywhere, and she wondered if he'd gone home to Faye. Or perhaps he'd gone somewhere with Brian. She was tempted to call Faye and check but knew how that could go. If Monroe wasn't with his mom, Faye would blame Hope and wonder if he'd run off again. And if he was with his mom, well, that would be Monroe's choice and he would have to deal with it.

And so, feeling exhausted, Hope kicked off her shoes and took a nap. But when she awoke, she could smell something terrible. It seemed to be coming from the bathroom, and when she went in, she saw a lot of nasty greenish water on the floor. Alarmed, she called Brian but only got voicemail. So she went outside to get some fresh air. As she pacing the yard wondering what to do, Drew pulled up and waved.

She waved back, smiling feebly.

"Nice little toilet facilities you got there," he teased.

"I'm having some work done."

"Everything okay?" His face was shadowed by his cowboy hat as he stood on his side of the yard, but the concern in his voice sounded genuine.

She just held up her hands in a hopeless way. "No…not really."

"What's wrong?" He was walking toward her now. Big, tall cowboy strides, like he was starring in some old western movie, going to come over to help the little lady and make everything all right. She almost laughed.

"Well, they're tearing everything out to replace things in there." She nodded to the house. "Which maybe wasn't such a great idea. So anyway, now the bathroom has this horrible smell and—" Hope stopped talking as a whole new horrible realization hit her. *"Andy!"* she cried.

"Andy's made a bad smell in the bathroom?" Drew looked puzzled.

"No!" She looked around the yard, horrified. "Andy—I've *lost* Andy."

"Oh, well, that's not the end of the world."

"But it is!"

"So what's the deal with your bathroom?"

"It's got a problem," she yelled as she ran around to the backyard, calling for Andy. Then she looked at his bed on the porch, calling and calling for him. Oh, how could she have lost Andy? Dear sweet little Andy. The one precious thing Nona had so wanted Hope to take care of—and not only had she lost him, but she'd totally forgotten about him, too. Hope felt sick—truly sick.

She was walking up and down the sidewalk, literally wringing her hands and still calling for him and thinking the worst, when suddenly Avery popped her head out the front door. "You looking for Andy?"

"Yes!" Hope cried. "Have you seen him?"

"He and Monroe are in the backyard right now."

Hope let out a cry of relief. "Thank God!"

"You want me to tell them to go home?"

"Not unless they want to. It's kind of a wreck over here."

"Okay."

"Thanks, Avery!"

Hope hurried back to her house to find Drew pounding on something in the bathroom. She thought about offering to help but then realized that room was too small for two people. Plus it stank. After about twenty minutes she heard the water running in the tub. Hopefully he wasn't taking a bath. And then he emerged with dripping hands. "I think that should take care of it. Just a cap had popped off. You got a towel anywhere?"

She removed his cowboy hat from where it was hanging on the door handle and reached into the linen closet then handed him a towel. "Thanks so much," she told him. "And I found Andy, too."

He kind of frowned. "Well, I'm not sure that's such good news."

"It is to me. And it turned out he's at your house."

He looked alarmed. "Does Cherry know about this?"

She shrugged. "Avery said Monroe brought him over. They're in the backyard."

"Oh, well, as long as he's not in the house, Cherry shouldn't care." He handed the damp towel to her in exchange for his hat. "So Monroe made it back then?"

She nodded. "He spent last night here."

"Does Faye know about this?"

"Of course."

"Oh, good." He slowly put on his hat, kind of shaking his head, as if trying to grasp something. *"You three sisters…"*

"What?"

"It just boggles my mind."

"What do you mean?"

"I mean how three women couldn't be more different if they tried. I actually find it hard to believe you're all related." He made a funny face. "You sure your mom didn't have more than just *one* husband?"

Hope threw the towel at him. "What a thing to say!"

"It happens."

"You should know."

"What's that supposed to mean?"

Now she turned away from him and went into the kitchen. Or what once had been the kitchen. Would it ever be a kitchen again?

"Seriously, Hope, what did that little comment mean just now?"

"What comment?" she looked innocently at him.

"That I should know. Are you suggesting that I'm not the father of both of my kids?"

"No, not at all." She held up her hands and stepped away from him, bumping into the wall where the refrigerator used to stand. "That's not what I meant."

"Then what did you mean?" He moved closer, putting his face near hers. Not in a threatening way. But not in a comfortable way either.

"Nothing, Drew. I meant nothing."

He sighed and stepped back. "You know, Hope, it's long overdue, but I would like to apologize to you."

"What for?"

"You know what for."

"No, I do not."

"Fine. I'd like to apologize for dating Cherry after you broke up with me."

"Why should you apologize for that?"

"According to some people, it wasn't my smartest move."

"What people?"

"Oh, my mom, for one thing. I remember she threw a hissy fit when I started dating Cherry."

"But I thought she liked Cherry."

"She did. But she did *not* like the idea of me going from one sister to the next."

"She probably could see the writing on the wall." Hope wasn't so sure she wanted to continue this conversation.

"And what do you think the writing said?"

"That you were going to come between two sisters. Seems pretty obvious to me." Hope glanced around the strange-looking room that once was a kitchen. She wondered what Nona would think if she could see it now…if she could see Hope talking to Drew. Surely this hadn't been part of her plan.

"It might seem obvious now. But not back then, not when I was only nineteen and thought I had the world by the tail." He shook his head in a disappointed way.

"So why *did* you start dating Cherry?" Hope couldn't believe she actually said that. But then, there it was—out just hanging in the air. No taking it back.

"You want to know the truth?" He leaned back against the wall where the stove used to stand, crossing one leg over the other the way an old cowboy sometimes would do.

"Do you think I deserve to know the truth?" Hope thought this was his chance to end this conversation, make a run for it, pretend they'd never spoken.

He simply nodded.

"Then I think I can handle the truth."

"Okay then, I'll tell you. I started dating Cherry to make you jealous."

Suddenly Hope wasn't so sure she wanted to know the truth. This wasn't what she'd expected to hear. She figured Drew had gone after Cherry because, well, because Cherry was Cherry. They were in deep waters now, waters she hadn't really meant to jump into.

"Cherry made it easy enough for me. She thought I was all that—I could see it in her eyes. And she was always chasing after me, flirting and turning on the charm. You know how she can be."

"I know."

"And I'll admit it felt good...after being dumped by you."

Hope looked down at the old scarred wood planks on the floor.

"Going after Cherry just seemed like an easy way to get back at you. I wanted to hurt you like you hurt me." He let out a dismal sigh. "I really am sorry about that, Hope."

"I'm sorry, too."

"Kids can be so stupid. And selfish."

"But did you love Cherry? Do you love her now?" For some reason this was important to Hope. Despite everything, and despite some of her feelings toward her little sister, she wanted Drew to love Cherry—or at least to have loved her once.

Drew leaned down and brushed the dust off his jeans as if it were the most important thing in the world.

"Okay, you don't have to answer that."

"You know why we got married, don't you?" He looked back up with curious eyes.

"You mean because she was pregnant?" At least Hope hadn't revealed her source; she didn't say how she knew. She had kept her promise to Avery.

He just nodded.

"But then you stayed together," she said hopefully. "So you guys must've loved each other, right?"

He kind of shrugged. "Love's a funny thing, Hope."

"I guess—but how do you mean?"

"Seems that one person always loves more. And that's always the person who gets hurt most." Then Drew stood up straight, tipped his hat, and walked out of the house. And for no reason she could explain to herself or fully understand, Hope began to cry.

Chapter Sixteen
....

Hope didn't know how Monroe could sleep through the noise of Brian putting down the fir floor this morning. Brian had started in the kitchen around eight, but the noise of his nail gun was like being in the middle of a shooting range. Consequently, Hope had taken Andy outside and was now painting the backside of the house, where Lewis had done all the prep work. She could see how much smoother the paint was going on, thanks to his efforts, but it was slow going working alone. And she wondered where Avery was— probably sleeping in like Monroe. She was trying not to think about her strange conversation with Drew last night. In some ways, it was surreal, and she wondered if it had really happened at all.

At a little before eleven, she put Andy, along with his food and water, into her bedroom. Then she went over to meet Brian's cabinet-making friend Rick. The plan was to pick out cabinets, but when she started looking at all the photos and samples and choices of styles, she began to feel overwhelmed.

"Rick does this to everyone," his wife, Cathy, told Hope while Rick was on the phone. "He's made so many cabinets over the past thirty years that he's pretty much done it all."

"I'll say." Hope closed one of the notebooks.

"Here's what you do," Cathy said quietly. "Just close your eyes and imagine what you'd like to see in your kitchen. Tell me about it, and I'll take notes."

Hope closed her eyes and thought. "Really, all I want are some painted cabinets that look like they're from the forties. Nothing fancy. But not too plain either. And more storage would be nice because it is a small kitchen. But I'm not exactly a gourmet cook, so I really don't need all the bells and whistles. And the appliances I picked out are pretty basic."

"How about these?"

Hope opened her eyes to a page that had been torn from a magazine. It was an old-fashioned–looking kitchen with creamy white cabinets, simple lines, but interesting, and they had what looked like antique-glass cut knobs in a pale shade of green. "Yes," Hope said happily. "Those cabinets would be perfect. Can Rick do that?"

Cathy laughed. "Rick can do anything."

"Well, thank you," Rick said as he rejoined them.

"I found this photo in *Cottage Living*," Cathy explained. "And Hope decided she'd like cabinets like this."

He put on his glasses to study the picture. "Not a problem."

"Now as for the configuration." Cathy had a piece of graph paper where she'd already sketched in the dimensions of the kitchen based on Brian's measurements. She even had the windows and doors and appliances sketched in as well. And based on her suggestions, it wasn't long until they had it completely worked out, including the hardware, which would be the glass cut knobs that Cathy would special order, and the apron sink, also a special order. "But we can get it through our plumber here in town," Cathy told her. "In fact, while we're at this, do you plan on having anything done in your bathroom?"

So Hope explained that it, too, was pretty much gutted. "I thought I'd go with a pedestal sink in there. It might look more old-fashioned."

Cathy nodded. "Old-fashioned, yes, but not much storage there." Then she showed Hope some photos of old-fashioned–looking vanities as well as medicine cabinets that Rick had built, and Hope had to agree they looked perfect.

"Rick can get the bathroom measurements from Brian, and I can order the sink to go with that vanity while I'm ordering the kitchen sink. Do you want me to order anything else while I'm at it?"

Hope grinned. "A toilet would be nice."

Cathy made note of this. "And I assume you want one that doesn't look too modern."

"Absolutely. And I saved my grandmother's claw-foot tub so I won't need to replace that."

"You'll save some money there. But what about the faucet? Do you plan to use it as a shower, too?"

So Hope described the small shower that she wanted to get retiled and how she wanted old-fashioned faucets, too. "But in silver tones instead of brass."

Cathy pulled a catalogue out of a drawer and handed it to her. "Why don't you take a look at these? See if there's something in there that works for you then let me know so I can order them, too, okay?"

"You're really good at this," Hope told Cathy as she was getting ready to leave. "Thanks for all the help."

"She's my right-hand man—I mean woman." Rick winked at his wife. "I couldn't do this without her."

"And what about your countertops and backsplash?" Cathy asked just as Hope thought it was time to go.

"I like what they did in that photo." Hope picked it up to look more closely. "What exactly is that material? Marble?"

"It could be unpolished marble or soapstone. If it were me, I'd go with soapstone."

"Soapstone it will be, then. For both the kitchen and the bath vanity." Hope pointed to the pale green tiles on the backsplash. "Those look like glass."

"That'd be my guess, too."

"Then that's what I'll have in the kitchen. Brian gave me the name of a tile company, and I need to pick out the bathroom tile, too."

"And we know a good tile guy. He's the same one Brian usually uses."

Hope thanked the couple and left. As she drove back home, she felt like things were really coming together. Oh, her house might look like a wreck right now…but in time. Monroe was up when she got back, sitting on the front porch with Andy and wearing an unhappy expression.

"What's up?" she asked as she approached them. Andy bounded happily to her and she picked him up, scratching his ears the way he liked.

"Nothing." Monroe looked down at his shoes.

"Did the nail gun finally get to you?"

"No. My mom's what got to me."

"Your mom?"

He nodded. "She called a little bit ago and said she's on her way over here to pick me up."

"Oh…" Hope sat down on the step next to him.

"Do I have to go with her?"

She considered this. From a legal perspective, he probably did. "Have you spoken to your dad yet?"

"Not yet."

Hope pulled her cell phone out of her bag. "Why don't you call him? Get his take on this."

"Thanks." Monroe took her phone and started to dial. And she decided to give him his privacy by checking on Brian's progress in the house since it was quiet now.

"Wow." She found Brian just going out the back door. "You got a lot of floor down in there."

He nodded. "The kitchen's almost done. I'm going out to grab some lunch." He grinned. "Want to join me?"

"I would, but I think I need to stick around for my nephew's sake." She nodded toward the front yard. "Family problems."

"I wondered about that...heard him talking to what I'm guessing was his mom on the phone. It wasn't a happy conversation."

"No, probably not." Hope frowned down at the kitchen floor. While it was nice to see it getting done, it didn't look nearly as good as she'd expected.

"After it's all down, I'll go over it with a sander and a sealer," he explained as if guessing her thoughts. "And then it'll look like a million bucks."

"Oh." She nodded. "I was wondering."

"See ya then." He tipped his ball cap and headed for his truck, and she went to check on Monroe.

"Dad wants me to come home," Monroe said as he handed her back her phone.

"Do you want to go home?"

He shrugged. "I don't know."

"Do you want to stay with your mom?"

Now he frowned. "Not really. I mean I told her she needs to see a shrink and she went ballistic on me."

Hope could imagine that. "It's okay if you stay here," she told him. "But, as you can see, it's going to be a mess for a while. And the bathroom facilities…well, you know how that goes."

He kind of laughed. "Hey, I'd rather be living in a mess like this and using an outdoor toilet than stuck with my nutty mom."

"Uh, speaking of your mom…" Hope nodded to where Faye's Toyota was rolling down the street toward them.

Monroe swore, then tossing a worried look at Hope, apologized.

"How about if I talk to her first," Hope suggested.

He nodded and, grabbing up Andy, retreated to the house. Meanwhile, Hope braced herself. Taking in a deep breath, she shoved her hands into the pockets of her Wranglers and waited as Faye got out of her car. Faye looked bedraggled and frazzled and like she hadn't washed her hair in days.

"Where's my son?" she asked in a flat voice.

"Inside." Hope smiled. "Could I talk to you?"

"Go ahead and talk." Faye stood on the path, halfway to the house, crossing her arms across her front with a stubborn expression.

"Monroe called his father."

"And?"

"And Jeff wants him to come home."

"So."

"So, maybe it would be good for Monroe to go and stay with him—"

"Look, Hope, I know you *think* you're being helpful. But the truth is you don't really understand the situation."

Hope pressed her lips together and nodded. "Maybe not completely."

"That's right. And you really don't know what's best for my son."

"But I just thought maybe you two could use a little time apart.

You know, so you could focus on getting your condo together and Monroe can have some time to adjust to the idea without being thrown into the middle of—"

"The middle of what?" Faye took a step closer. "Do you think I'm crazy, too? Because Monroe somehow got that idea in his head… suggesting I need to see a shrink. Are you the one who—"

"No, I didn't plant that in his head. But I don't think it's a bad idea to see a counselor. You know that. I already told you that."

"And now you got my son singing the same tune." Faye narrowed her eyes. "Really, Hope, I don't see how you think you can come waltzing back into our lives and expect to take over and tell us all what to do and how to live and—"

"I'm not. All I'm saying is Monroe is having a hard time dealing with—"

"And you think I'm not having a hard time?"

"I know you are, Faye. All I have to do is look at you and I can see you're in pain. But what you don't seem to realize is that you're dragging everyone else into it with you."

"So you're telling me it would be better for Monroe to go home with his dad?" Faye was angry now. Like the mountain about to blow, Hope could hear it in her sister's voice, and she knew she better tread carefully.

"I don't know if that's the best thing, Faye. But I—"

"Because if you think a fourteen-year-old boy with absolutely no supervision and with nothing but time on his hands for a whole summer as well as dozens of ways to get into trouble—maybe even serious trouble—is a good idea, I'd have to say you're the one who needs to get her head examined."

"Maybe he could stay here," Hope suggested. "Just for a—"

"Here?" Faye looked over to the Porta-potty then pushed past Hope and into the house. "Well, now this is a pretty sight, Hope. You're tearing Nona's house to shreds." She pointed to the kitchen. "You don't even have a refrigerator or a sink." Now she went in to the bathroom and just laughed. "You're inviting Monroe to stay in this—"

"I'd rather stay here than with you!" Monroe emerged from the spare room, where Hope was pretty sure he'd been listening to everything. "At least Aunt Hope's not nuts. And she understands—"

"Go get in the car, Monroe." Faye's voice was even now. But cold.

"I'm not a little kid, Mom. You can't make me. Dad said I can come home—"

"Get in the car! Now!"

"I'm not going with you, Mom. And here's a little news flash." Monroe narrowed his eyes. "Jody and Aaron are tired of us staying with them. They won't tell you because they're too nice. But I'll tell you—and I'm not going back there. And if you won't let me stay here with Aunt Hope, I'll go home to be with Dad."

Faye turned to Hope with fury in her eyes. "I hope you're happy now."

Hope didn't know what to say or do. She was clearly over her head. Why had she thought this would work?

"It's not her fault," Monroe told his mom.

"You need help, Faye." Hope tried to keep her voice quiet. "You're not yourself. You're—"

"Quit telling me what I am and what I am not!" Faye shook her fist at Hope. "I *am* Monroe's mother. *You are not!* But since you've already brainwashed him, you go ahead and deal with him. And you will be the one to blame when he winds up in juvenile detention or worse."

"Oh, *Mom!*" Monroe turned away in disgust.

"I'll take care of Monroe." Hope watched her sister storm out. "But, please, Faye, take care of yourself."

Faye shook her fist and swore.

Hope sadly shook her head and closed the door. "North Sister has just erupted."

Monroe chuckled. "How's Middle Sister doing?"

"I'm not too sure." Hope could feel her heart pounding. It was one thing to argue a case in court, but doing it with your sister was entirely different. She didn't know how much of this she could take—or whether or not it was wise to keep Monroe with her like this. Really, what did she have to offer him? Besides no parenting experience, she didn't even have a fully functioning bathroom!

"So, it's really okay then?" He looked hopeful. "I can stay with you?"

She held out her hands in a helpless gesture. "You know what you're getting into."

"I'll help work on the house."

She smiled. "That'd be great."

"And maybe Aunt Cherry will let me use the shower at her house. They have three bathrooms."

Hope was about to correct him, to say they only had two, but then she realized they could have easily put in a third bathroom for all she knew. Not that she'd be welcome to use it. But maybe Monroe would be welcome. And that was worth something. And maybe if Hope really tried, she could mend this thing between Cherry and her. Somehow, hearing what Drew said last night made her realize that they were all hurting over what had happened in the past. Maybe it was time to put some old things to rest.

Chapter Seventeen

....

"Looks like Aunt Cherry's on her way over here." Monroe pointed out the living room window then grimaced. "And it looks like my mom's with her."

Suddenly Hope wanted to run and hide. Really, how much stress could one woman take? Unless, perhaps, Cherry planned to handle this in a mature manner. Maybe she would be objective and reasonable about the situation. After all, Monroe had spent part of the day at her house yesterday. Maybe Cherry could see his side, too. Perhaps she'd even talked some sense into Faye. Faye might be willing to listen to Cherry since she was a mom, too.

There was a loud knocking on the front door, and before Hope could open it, both Cherry and Faye let themselves in. Cherry just stood there looking around as if she were in shock. "It's true," she finally said. "You *are* tearing the place down."

Hope sighed. "No, I'm not tearing it down. I'm just getting some work done. I'll admit it doesn't look great now."

"Where are Nona's things?" Cherry frowned at the mostly empty room. "Did you throw *everything* away?"

"No, of course not. I set aside the things I thought you and Faye might want to look through. It's all out in the garage and driveway."

"I thought maybe you were having a yard sale." Cherry turned up her nose, confirming Hope's suspicion that little Miss Perfect didn't enjoy living next to such a messy-looking place—even though it was temporary.

"You can go through everything if you want. I set aside a couple of boxes that I thought you might want to—"

"That's not why we came over," Cherry said.

"Oh?"

"Faye told me that you are interfering with Monroe."

"Interfering?" Hope glanced at Monroe now. She wanted to tell him to go outside and play but knew he was too old. And yet, she didn't want him to be in the middle of this sisterly feud either. She didn't want him to think it was his fault, since it wasn't.

"Faye wants Monroe to go home with her."

"Home?" Monroe stepped forward. "Mom doesn't even have a home."

"You know what I mean," Cherry said pleasantly. "Your mom is between houses at the moment." She glared at Hope now. "And maybe if you hadn't torn Nona's house to pieces, she and Monroe could stay here until the condo is ready."

"But I—"

"And it really doesn't seem right for an outsider to come between a mother and her child, Hope. I would think you, as a lawyer, would know better."

Part of Hope knew that Cherry was right…and yet what could she do? Should she force Monroe to go with his mom? Was that really the best thing for anyone?

"Aunt Hope is just trying to help me," Monroe protested.

"You keep out of this," Faye told him. "This is between Hope and us."

Monroe blasted out of the house, swearing even more loudly than his mom had.

"See," Faye pointed to the door, "this is what happens when people butt into other people's affairs."

Hope just stared at Faye. Really, what was the point of responding?

"And while we're on that subject," Cherry continued in a calm but chilly voice, "I would like to ask you to stop interfering with my family, too."

"What?" Hope turned to Cherry. "What are you talking about?"

"For starters, there's Avery. I thought it would be okay for her to come over and help you in the yard from time to time, but it seems you are determined to make her into your slave, and I will have to—"

"My slave?" Hope felt her hands balling into fists. "I have hired Avery to—"

"Oh, yes, the matter of money and shopping and—"

"Avery told me that you gave her permission to go to Bend with me yesterday."

"But I did not give her permission to buy that skanky little excuse for a bathing suit."

"But I—"

"Yes, I don't expect you to understand these things, Hope. You're *not* a mother, so how could you understand? In fact, that is precisely our point. You are not a mother, and yet you insist on interfering with our children."

"I'm their aunt."

"And you are an interfering aunt who seems set to turn our children against us. Do you know that Avery and I had a terrible fight last night? And all because of you."

"But why?"

LOVE FINDS YOU IN SISTERS, OREGON

"Because Avery thinks you're her new best friend and that you think it's okay for her to go around practically naked and you understand her and—"

"I never even saw the swimsuit she bought, I only—"

"And that is precisely my point. You let her pick out something without even knowing whether or not it was appropriate for her age. Maybe you think it's okay to turn an eleven-year-old into a tramp, but I will put my foot down. Because I am her mother."

"I'm sorry, Cherry." Hope was sincere in her apology. "I honestly never dreamed Avery would get something that wasn't appropriate. She seems like such a mature girl that I—"

"She is a child!"

"I said I'm sorry, Cherry."

"Well, Avery is grounded from coming over here. And if she tries to sneak over, I would appreciate it if you sent her home."

Hope didn't know what to say.

"And, while we're talking about my family, I would appreciate it if you kept your hands off my husband, too."

Both Faye and Hope looked equally shocked by this.

"What?" Hope stared at Cherry in disbelief.

"I know Drew was over here last night. Some excuse of helping with your plumbing, which is really pathetic, if you ask me."

"He did help with my plumbing. A cap had come off and—"

"Whatever." Cherry waved her hand. "But Drew stayed over here for quite a while, and I saw you two talking in the kitchen— or what *used* to be the kitchen. And then he acted funny when he came home. And I have a pretty good idea about what was going on over here."

"Nothing was going on over here." Hope just shook her head. "But maybe your mind works differently than mine."

Cherry stepped closer to Hope now, looking up at her with a furrowed brow. "And just so you know, I saw you on Sunday night, too. Out in the backyard with Lewis, eating by candlelight like you're making a move on him. Like you think he's interested in you."

"Wow, I'm surprised you even have time to be such a super mother, *Charity*." Their mom had always resorted to full names when she was irritated. "You're so busy spying on me." Hope knew it was a childish thing to say. But this whole conversation was just getting more and more absurd.

"That's not all I know about you," Cherry shot back. "What about your contractor Brian Godwin? I overheard his son telling Harrison that you and Brian have something going on, too. It's like you can't get enough men!"

"That's crazy!"

"What is it with you, Hope?" Cherry shook her finger under Hope's nose. "You making up for the fact that you lost one man by going after everything in pants?"

"Maybe you're like that hussy my husband's been sleeping with," Faye said suddenly. "She's that type."

"I always knew you were selfish, Hope." Cherry's chin was trembling like she was on the verge of tears. "You never wanted to share any of your clothes or your time or anything with me. You hogged all of Nona's attention, and now you even hogged her house. I thought maybe you'd grown up, but it's plain to see I was wrong."

Hope felt like she was about to explode—or erupt. Instead she sucked in a quick breath. "*Fine.* I see how my two sisters feel about me. Now I will thank you both to leave my house." She spoke as evenly as she could, but she could feel her hands shaking. "Feel free to take any of Nona's things that are outside. And then do not come back here uninvited again."

"Big surprise there," Cherry told Faye.

Hope turned her back on them and then, feeling as if the room was tipping sideways, she went into her bedroom and loudly closed the door. Her heart was pounding so hard that she wondered if it was possible for an otherwise healthy thirty-two-year-old woman to suffer a heart attack. She sat down on the bed and attempted to breathe deeply. Then she flopped back and gave in. If she died right now, it would be because her sisters had killed her. She felt hot, angry tears sliding along the sides of her face and down the back of her neck.

Hope woke up later to the feeling of something wet licking her cheek. She opened her eyes to see Andy standing on her bed and Monroe in the doorway. "Sorry to disturb you, Aunt Hope," he said quietly. "Are you okay?"

She sat up and put Andy in her lap. "I guess."

"I heard them tearing into you."

"They're really mad at me. I'm not totally sure why." She looked around the barren room. "But I know it has a lot to do with this house—and the fact that Nona left it to me."

"They're just jealous."

She pushed the hair away from her face. "I can't say that I blame them. I'd be jealous, too."

"Why *did* Nona give everything to you?"

"I think she felt that Faye and Cherry had already gotten their inheritance." Then she explained about her mom's insurance policy that went to Faye, and how Cherry had practically been given the family home. "I think Nona felt a little sorry for me." Hope kind of laughed. "I also think she hoped that her gift would bring the three Bartolli sisters back together. Although it seems like it's just driving us further apart."

"Well, my mom's not thinking real clear these days," Monroe said slowly, "but I'm not sure what's gotten into Aunt Cherry. I never saw her act like that before."

"I think it's me." Hope set Andy down and stood up. She wanted to say she thought it was a mistake for her to be here in Sisters—that her presence was rocking everyone's boat. But then, where did that put Monroe? Especially since it seemed that, at least for the time being, he was her responsibility.

She went out to the living room and wished that she'd never started the wheels turning on this remodel. Really, what had she been thinking? "Has Brian been around?" she asked Monroe.

"He showed up while the fireworks show was still going on."

"You mean while we were all fighting?"

"Yeah. I tried to explain to him that my mom was nuts. He said he'd come by later."

"I wouldn't blame him if he never came back at all." Hope set the phone back on the small table she'd kept in the living room. "Except that we have a contract."

"I've been doing some painting outside." Monroe smiled proudly. "It's kinda fun."

"Really, you like painting?"

"Yeah. It's something you can do to take your mind off of other things."

"I'll pay you for your time, Monroe."

"You don't have to—"

"I was doing that for Avery," Hope insisted. "I will do it for you, too."

"Sounds like Avery won't be coming back."

"Yes. Cherry is certain that I corrupted her."

Monroe went back out to paint, and Hope started pacing inside. She wondered if there was some way to put the brakes on everything. She would tell Lewis she'd changed her mind, call to see if she could get her job back, and book a flight to Portland for tomorrow. She wasn't sure about Monroe. But maybe she'd book him a flight to Portland as well. And then, after a day or two, she could send him on to Seattle and let his dad figure it out. Really, what more could she do? Like her sisters had both clearly said, she was not a mom. She was in over her head. And she wanted out! The sooner the better.

"Hey, Hope," called Brian from the back porch. "You around?"

"In here," she called back.

"So, I'm guessing *Family Feud* is over." He grinned.

"Sorry you had to hear that."

"And I thought *my* sisters were bad." He shook his head. "But there are only two of them. I guess having three girls in a family complicates things even more."

"I'll say." Hope pressed her hands to her cheeks. "I'm so frustrated that I'm thinking about jumping ship."

"What do you mean?"

"I mean going back to Portland…getting back my job…having my own life again…pretending I'm an orphan. That's what I feel like doing."

He frowned. "What about this house?"

"Oh, the house still needs to be finished, Brian. We still have a contract and, believe me, you'll get paid. But I'm just not sure I can take living in the same town as my sisters. Especially with one of them right next door."

"That's a tough one."

Hope faked a confident smile for him. "But you don't need to worry about this. In fact, it'll probably blow over soon. Just keep up the good work, and I'll try to keep the family fights to a minimum." Then she told him about picking out the cabinets and how she was going to look at some glass tile for the backsplash. "In fact, I might do some looking in Portland. I have to go back there to take care of some things anyway. I might just stay a few days."

He brightened. "That's not a bad idea. Especially considering the shape your house is in. Now what about those bathroom tiles? You sure you don't want to go with the plain white subway tiles?" Brian had suggested this earlier, saying his tile man had gotten a great deal on a bunch of them, but she had said she wanted to think about it.

"I think the white subway tiles would be perfect," she told him. The truth was she no longer cared. As long as it looked good and would appeal to a buyer. Because, as far as she was concerned, Nona's house would be going on the market before the end of summer anyway. And the Humane Society and the other charities would all be a little better off.

"I'll let him know first thing."

"Thanks, Brian." She gave him a sincere smile. "What would I do without you?"

"And don't worry about a thing while you're gone. I've got your cell phone number, and I'll call you if any major decisions come up."

"And maybe I should hire a painting contractor, too." She remembered her plan to paint the inside of the house and realized that would be impossible if she returned to work and her old life in Portland.

"That would probably speed things up." He rubbed his chin. "Although this is the busy time of year for painters. It might be a challenge, but I'll see who I can dig up."

"Thanks. And I'll mark the paint cans accordingly and leave it on the back porch." As she said this, she felt sad. She had been excited to see the paint colors in the rooms. To watch as the whole thing unfolded. But plans change. And right now the only plan that made much sense was a getaway plan.

She went to her bedroom to call the law firm. She spoke to Hal's assistant and asked her to leave a message about Hope's change of plans.

"Wow, that was quick," Becca told her. "We barely had time to miss you."

"It's probably best that I figured it out before Hal hired someone else."

"He's barely started to look at résumés. But I have a feeling he'll be relieved to hear that you've changed your mind."

"I hope so. I'm going to try to get a flight out of here tomorrow. And I'll come by the firm on Thursday."

"I'll let him know."

"Thanks." Hope hung up and wondered how she was going to break this news to Monroe. Just then, she noticed Andy's little bed on the floor next to hers and remembered the feel of his warm tongue on her cheek earlier. And in that moment, she decided that no matter where she lived, even in the city, Andy was going with her. He was her dog. And hopefully he'd be allowed on the flight. She'd seen dogs in carrying cases on flights before. It had to be okay.

Outside, Monroe was finishing up the backside of the house where she'd been working earlier. "Want to take a lunch break?" she asked. "A late lunch anyway?"

He nodded and set down his brush. "Yeah, I'm starving."

"Why don't we walk," she suggested as she leashed up Andy. "The deli's only three blocks away." Then, as they walked, she told him that she needed to go to Portland. She knew she wasn't being totally honest, but it seemed the easiest way to do this.

"I have to take care of things there," she explained. "I plan on taking Andy with me, and I thought maybe you'd want to come, too. I have a spare room in my condo." She laughed. "And it actually has things like indoor plumbing and a kitchen."

"Wow, all the comforts of home," he teased.

"I'm going to try to book a flight for tomorrow. Or I might even drive, although I'd rather leave the Rambler here. Maybe drive my BMW back."

"Sure, I'd be glad to go to Portland," he said eagerly. "If you really want me."

"And I was thinking I could get you a ticket to fly up to Seattle, you know, for a few days to see your dad and maybe pick up some of your things...since you probably didn't bring everything you wanted when you and your mom came down for the funeral."

"Really? You'd do that for me?"

"Sure. You're my nephew. Why not?"

"I would like to get some video games and a few other things. And it might be cool to see my dad...you know, to talk things out with him."

"All right, then," she said as they reached the deli. "I'll book us both a flight."

So as they were sitting outside waiting for their lunch, she called the airlines. But the best they could offer was to fly standby. "What are the chances of getting two standby seats?" she asked the agent.

"Not that great."

"Hang on for a minute," Hope told her. She quickly explained the situation to Monroe, saying that it was summer travel season and a last-minute booking. "I may not even get a seat to Portland, but I'm willing to try. Should I ask her about getting you a flight to Seattle instead? That might be easier."

He shrugged. "I guess."

"Then you could get your stuff together there, and either stay with me in Portland for a few days or come straight back here."

He nodded. "Yeah. That makes sense."

So she inquired about Seattle and actually booked him a seat. "Round trip?" the agent asked. "Yes," Hope told her. "But open-ended. On both tickets, please." Then she gave her Visa number, wrote down a confirmation, and hung up just as their food arrived. "We're set," she told him as she picked up her fork. "Your flight's a little before seven in the morning and mine's about half an hour later. We'll have to leave the house around five to get to the airport on time. Can you let your parents know?"

"I'll call my dad." Monroe frowned. "But I don't know about Mom."

"She'd probably hang up if I called her."

"How about I call her when I get to Seattle?" He looked hopeful.

"That's fine with me." She forked her salad. "And call me, too. Remember what your mom said, I'm responsible for you."

"Okay." He nodded. "I'll call you first."

They made small talk as they ate, but every word seemed to cut into her. She could feel how much Monroe trusted her. But it was bittersweet. And she hated to think how he'd react when he discovered that she was actually running away from Sisters—not so unlike what he'd done while hiding out at Three Creeks. What would he say when he found out that she had no intention of coming back here to live—ever? Would he ever forgive her? Would he take Faye and Cherry's side, proclaiming her selfish? And, if he did, would that help to bring him and his mom back together? She could only hope.

She tried to push these thoughts away as they walked home. The truth was, she cared deeply about Monroe, but she could not rescue him. And when she considered what a mess she'd managed to make of everything—and in such a short amount of time—well, it seemed fairly obvious that she could barely take care of herself.

Chapter Eighteen

....

"I need to run some errands," she told Monroe when they got back to the house. "Do you mind if Andy hangs here with you?"

"That's fine. I plan to keep painting. I want to finish up this whole side before dark."

"Great!" She tried to appear excited, as if she planned to come back here and enjoy the results of all the hard work that was going into renovating Nona's old house.

As she drove through town, she attempted to rehearse the speech she planned to give to Lewis—her big farewell. But as she parked her car and walked up to his office, her smooth words seemed to slip away.

"Hey." He grinned as he opened the door for her to come inside. "Didn't expect to see you today. To what do I owe this pleasure?"

"Have you got a few minutes?"

His brows lifted. "Sure. Something wrong?"

"Just everything."

Once they were behind closed doors, the words came tumbling out. And so did the tears. Oh, she knew she probably sounded like a drama queen, and it would be a wonder if he could even make sense of her blubbering. But she just continued to let it go, pausing only to accept the tissues offered to her and to blow her nose.

"I'm sorry," she finally said. "But this whole thing has turned me into a real basket case."

"I'm sorry, too." He pressed his lips together and shook his head.

"And usually I'm not one to give up. In fact, I've always considered myself a fighter. But I cannot stay here and fight with my sisters. I don't even think Nona would've wanted that."

"No, I don't think so either."

"So Brian will continue working on the renovations until it's done. I've picked most of the things out, and I don't even care about the rest. Just as long as the house will appeal to a buyer. But I am going to keep Andy. I hope that he'll be happy in Portland. And it'll get me out to walk more regularly." She sniffed. "Besides…I think I need him."

"That would make your grandmother happy." But Lewis frowned.

"But you think she wouldn't be pleased that I'm giving up?"

"I'm sure she didn't expect it to be this hard."

"So you think I'm doing the right thing?" Hope studied his expression.

He didn't answer.

"I just can't take it. I mean I've only been in town for a little over a week, and yet it feels like a year. And it feels like the hardest year of my life. And that's including the year my mom died…the same year that Cherry and Drew got together. I might've been unhappy, and I might've been weighed down with guilt. But that was nothing compared to everyone in my family hating me."

"Your niece and nephew don't hate you."

"Not yet. But they will. If I don't do it myself, their moms will see to it."

"What about your dad? Is he mad at you, too?"

Hope considered this. "I haven't actually talked to him. But that's not a good sign either. My best guess is he thinks he should've inherited some of Nona's money. And he probably blames me for that, too."

"Poor Hope."

"I don't want you to feel sorry for me." She stood now. "I just want you to help unravel the mess I made. Put the wheels in motion toward Plan B now. As you can see Plan A has left the station."

He just nodded, but his eyes were sad.

She wanted to say something more. But, really, what more was there?

"I wish you'd give it a little more time," he said as he stood. "A little more thought."

She didn't want to start crying again. How could she expect him to understand? Did he know how lucky he was to be an only child? Sure, she wished it had gone differently, too. For a short while she imagined herself remaining in Sisters and being perfectly happy here. Happier than she'd ever been in her whole life. Happier than she had a right to be. But it was clearly not going to happen. Faith and Charity had seen to that!

"I can see how hurt you are, Hope." He put his hand on her elbow as they both walked outside, standing on the sidewalk in the sunshine. "But I honestly don't see how running away will make you feel better."

"You know what they say…" She forced lightness into her voice. "If you can't take the heat, get out of the kitchen."

"And if you can't take the sisters, get out of Sisters?"

She smiled. "I guess so."

"But they'll still be your sisters."

"But at least they'll be a hundred and sixty miles away."

He reached out and touched her cheek. "I'd be lying if I said I'm okay with this, Hope."

She didn't know what to say. Just the feeling of his hand on her cheek, his eyes looking directly into hers…it made her feel slightly weak in the knees.

"And the whole while you've been talking about how horrible things have been, I've been selfishly sitting there trying to devise some scheme that would force you to stay."

She was still speechless, not to mention slightly faint.

"But if a million bucks and a house can't entice you to stick around…well, I don't know what could." He reached over and pushed a strand of hair from her forehead, and for one startling moment, she expected him to kiss her. But he didn't. His hand slid away from her cheek, and he let out a long sigh. "I'm going to miss you, Hope. I barely got to know you, and yet I know I'm going to miss you."

She attempted a smile. "And my little dog, too?"

He nodded. "Yes. And your little dog, too."

She swallowed against the lump in her throat. "I'm going to miss you, too, Lewis. And I really appreciate all you did. You tried to make it work. Nona would've appreciated that."

He shrugged. "I hope so."

Right then, she had the strongest impulse to just grab him by the side of the face and kiss him. But, to her relief, she suppressed that urge. Instead, she told him good-bye and hurried to the old Rambler. But as soon as she was driving away, she felt like she'd just made the biggest mistake of her life. In fact, it felt as if a piece of her—was it her heart?—had been left behind.

"Don't be ridiculous," she told herself as she braked at the stop sign and waited for the traffic to pass. And what about Cherry? With her own two eyes, she'd seen the two of them together. And not just once, either. And she'd heard the familiar ring of jealousy in Cherry's voice when she accused Hope of putting the move on Lewis. *Don't be a fool*, she told herself. The only safe route was the one that would get her straight out of town.

And if she were smart, and lucky, she would never have to come back here again. She would handle the rest of the house renovating from a distance, making her apologies by phone. Still, as she drove through town, she wondered why it was she was crying again. Maybe she was just hormonal. And hurt. But in time she'd get over it. Hadn't she gotten over it before?

Morning came early the next day—especially after barely sleeping all night. Thankfully, she was all packed and ready to go. She'd gotten a little traveling case for Andy at the pet store yesterday, and had even packed some of his favorite things in her own bag. She'd have to get him a new bed in Portland. And Monroe, as before, was traveling light. She'd listened to him talking to his dad the evening before, and she could tell by the sound of Monroe's voice that he was eager to see his dad. And that brought a little comfort.

"You kids ready?" Erica asked sleepily when Hope opened the door.

"You don't know how much I appreciate this," she told Erica.

"No problem. I love getting up before the sun." Erica yawned. "But I understand your concern about leaving that sweet Rambler at the airport. Bobbie left her little red Karmann Ghia there once and came back to find a big dent on the driver's side door."

"And old cars cost more to fix," Monroe said from the backseat.

Hope hadn't told Erica that she didn't plan to return. She didn't want to go through the story another time.

"So will you be back in time for rodeo?" Erica asked as they were unloading their things in front of the terminal.

"I don't think so."

"Too bad. I'm having a rodeo picnic on Sunday, and I'd hoped you could come."

Hope gave her a phony-feeling smile. "Well, if I can make, you know I will."

Erica hugged her. "Travel safe and let me know when you get back."

"Thanks for the ride."

Erica feigned another yawn. "Now, it's back home. I can hear my bed calling."

Hope checked her bag, and they got their boarding passes, then they went through security, getting inside the gate just as the flight to Seattle began to board. Hope reached out and hugged Monroe. "You are such a great kid," she told him.

"And you're a great aunt." He laughed. "Well, not my great aunt."

"Be sure to call me when you get there," she reminded him.

"For sure. Thanks for everything, Aunt Hope!" He waved then hurried out the door. And he was barely out of sight when she realized how sad she felt to part with him. And she wondered if he'd ever speak to her again. Certainly not with the kind of trust she'd seen in his eyes these past few days. For that matter, Avery would probably feel the same as her cousin. Thanks to Avery's grounded status, Hope had been unable to see her niece…unable to say good-bye. But Cherry was probably already at work trying to turn Avery against her, too. Really, leaving was the only thing to do.

Hope sat down and placed Andy's carrying case on her lap. He was whining, and she knew that she'd pushed him out of his comfort zone, too. But what could she do about it? Take him to the pound and force him to start over with a new owner? She didn't think so. Besides, she needed him. "It's okay," she said soothingly. "Lucky for you, it's not a long flight."

Hope was grateful for the noisy, bumpy plane trip this time. It helped to muffle the sounds of Andy's whining. She was tempted to take him out and hold him on her lap, but she didn't think the flight attendant would appreciate it.

"We're almost there," she told him as she carried him down to baggage claim. Of course she still needed to ride the Max or get a cab. And then, without really thinking it through, she hit her speed dial button for Curtis. And just like that he answered.

"Hope?" he said cheerfully. "What's up?"

"I'm at the airport," she told him nervously. "And I have a dog with me. Just a little dog. But I was going to ride the Max and I thought—"

"Why don't I come get you?"

"I shouldn't have called," she apologized. "It was just an impulse."

"Sometimes impulses are good. And in your case, it was a lucky impulse. I'm only a couple of miles from PDX right now."

"Seriously?"

"Absolutely."

"I'm on my way to baggage claim—"

"I bet I'll beat you to passenger pick-up."

"You're on." She began walking faster.

"Loser buys dinner?"

"You got it." Okay, she had no idea why she'd agreed to that. Maybe it was just the sound of a friendly voice. The offer of a ride.

The excitement of being back in a town where two sisters weren't ready to drive you out with a loaded shotgun.

"I win," Curtis told her as he opened the trunk and placed her carry-on inside.

"I am eternally grateful," she told him.

He leaned over to peek in Andy's carrying case. Of course, Andy barked in a snippy way.

"He sounds like a brat," she said as she opened the door and hooked Andy's leash onto him so he could walk around and stretch his legs. "But once you get to know him, he's rather charming."

Curtis chuckled as Andy lifted his leg on a lamppost. "Charming."

"Anyway, he was my grandmother's dog," she said as she picked him up and got into the car. "She left him to me in her will."

Curtis laughed. "And did this grandmother even like you?"

"It was Nona," she reminded him.

"Oh, yes, Nona the wonderful." He frowned. "I'm sorry. I didn't know she'd died. But I also didn't know that you'd quit your job and left town."

"So how did you find out?"

"I ran into Marty."

She nodded. Marty was a mutual friend, and an attorney at the same firm.

"Did Marty tell you that I was returning…to beg for my old job back?"

"No." He glanced curiously at her then back to the road as he merged into the left lane. "Are you?"

"I am."

"So the whole going-home thing didn't work out for you?"

"Not so well."

"What made you think that it would?" His mouth twisted. "I mean you always seemed to want to stay away from there—what made that change?"

So she told him a shortened version of Nona's will.

"Are you serious? You gave up a million dollars?"

"Well, that was before taxes. And before fixing up the house. And I'd already sort of decided that if I'd made it for the full year, I would share it with my sisters, which only shows how out of my mind I must've been."

"But that's a lot of money, Hope. It seems like a pretty good trade-off for just one year of your life. And, from what I hear, Sisters is a cool little town. Lots of people are trying to buy property there. And you were handed a house? And you just walked away?"

"You sound like you want me to go back." She stared indignantly at him. "I thought, of all people, you might be glad to see me come home."

He laughed. "Depends on why you came home…and if this is home."

She wasn't sure she wanted to answer him now.

"Sorry," he told her. "I am glad to see you back. But I'm slightly flabbergasted that you gave up all that money. You're a good attorney, but I don't think you make that kind of money."

"I don't. But I decided my sanity was more valuable than a fat bank account."

"Sisters was making you lose your mind?"

"My sisters in Sisters were."

"Oh."

Hope changed the direction of the conversation to him, a subject he was comfortable with, and she pretended to be hugely interested.

And finally he was pulling up to her condo. "Want help with your bags?" he asked as he set the carry-on down for her.

"Thanks, I can get it." She balanced her purse and Andy's carrying case while holding onto the leash and still managed to pull her carry-on behind her.

"And what about that bet?" he called.

"Bet?"

"Loser buys dinner."

"Oh, yeah," she called over her shoulder. "How about if I fix it at my place. That way Andy won't be left home alone on his first night in the big city."

"I like the sound of that."

"Sevenish?"

"Sounds great."

Great, she thought as she pushed the elevator button. Now she was stuck fixing dinner for her ex. Such was the expense of taking a free ride. She had barely dropped her things in her condo when Andy began sniffing around and whining. She suspected he needed another chance to "stretch his legs."

"Okay," she told him as she picked up her mailbox key. "Let's go back down." Of course, once she was down there, she realized she'd forgotten to bring a plastic disposal bag with her.

An older woman who was on the condo board gave Hope a withering glance, and Hope pretended not to notice. "Oh, dear," she said to Andy. "I forgot your baggie, we'll have to go back up and get it." Then, knowing full well that Mrs. Hobbs would check later to see if Andy's little calling card was still there, Hope rode the elevator once again and dug out a baggie, returned back down, and cleaned it up.

Then, she realized she'd forgotten her mailbox key. About a dozen rides up and down the elevator later (or so it seemed), Hope finally felt like she was ready to sit down and sort out her mail, but she'd only opened one envelope when Andy decided he needed to go outside again.

Perhaps city living with a dog wasn't quite what she'd imagined it to be!

Chapter Nineteen
....

"My apologies for dinner," she told Curtis as she rinsed the scorched bottom of the saucepan. "I can usually do marinara sauce with my eyes closed."

"I think your dog is a distraction."

She didn't like how he said *your dog*, and she suspected he didn't like Andy. It probably hadn't helped that Andy had relieved himself on Curtis's shoe when they'd taken him down for yet another potty break before dinner. She still couldn't understand why Andy would do something like that. Well, except that perhaps he didn't like Curtis. And some people thought dogs were a good judge of character. Or maybe Nona had a secret communication line to Andy.

"Earth to Hope?" Curtis was peering curiously at her.

"What?" She set the pan in the sink to soak.

"I was talking to you, but you were on another planet."

She nodded. "Yes, I think I was."

"Which planet was it?"

"The Nona planet."

His expression softened. "You really miss her, don't you?"

"Yes." She dried her hands, giving him her full attention. "Now what were you saying while I was spacing?"

"Just that your little dog, sweet as he is..." Curtis made a face at where Andy was curled up on the makeshift bed of a feather pillow and blanket, "might pose some challenges for you."

"He's just not used to all this," she defended. "First, he's lost his beloved Nona, then I go in and tear up his happy home, then I throw him in a box and force him to fly to the city. And now he's got to get used to condo living."

"My point. Condo living with a dog could be tricky, Hope." Curtis nodded over to the growing pile of pink slips that she'd set by the phone. "What about those?"

"They weren't all for Andy." She frowned. All the years she'd lived here, she'd never gotten one pink slip. Today she had three. "One of those came while I was gone…because I'd forgotten to stop my mail and it had overflowed my box."

"But the other two belong to Sir Andrew."

"No." She shook her head. "They belong to me. I didn't have a doggy-do bag when he did his business earlier today, which of course busybody Hobbs had to witness. But I will explain that to the management tomorrow, because I *did* pick it up later. And the other one is simply that I need to pay a pet deposit, which I will also explain." Still it irked her that she was being penalized so quickly.

"You're missing my point."

She frowned at him. "What is your point?"

"That a condo isn't a very pet-friendly place."

"Andy seems perfectly happy now." She smiled at the sleeping dog.

"Because he's worn out from going up and down the elevator seventeen times in the last three hours."

"You're counting?"

"No. What I'm saying is that Andy would be much happier in a real house, with a real lawn, and with someone to be home with him during the day to take him for walks." Curtis smiled, and Hope felt confused.

"You want to adopt my dog?" It was true that Curtis's house did have a lawn, and since he worked from his home he would be around to keep Andy company, and he might even make a good parent, except for one thing—she was not parting with Andy.

"I want to adopt both you and your dog, Hope."

"Oh…"

"You wanted to take a break," he began. "So we took a break. Then, you thought you were going to quit your job, quit the city, and move back home…but then you realized that was a mistake. Now here you are again…and here we are together…and I don't think it was a coincidence that you called me from the airport or that I just happened to be nearby."

"What then?"

"Fate."

"Oh…"

"Think about it, Hope. It makes sense. It's like all the pieces of the puzzle are here. You and me and Andy. We could make it work."

She placed her palms on the breakfast bar between them and, leaning over, looked directly into his face then smiled. "You are a persistent guy."

He smiled back. "My dad always told me persistence paid off."

She wondered. "Well, you asked me to think about it, right?"

He nodded cautiously.

"So I will. And if you don't mind, I'd like to call it a night. Like Andy, I'm exhausted."

"I'm kind of beat, too," he said as he came around and into the kitchen. He was about to make what she knew was an attempt to kiss her. But she lowered her chin and, instead, he planted a kiss on her forehead. "I'll call you tomorrow, Hope. Get some rest."

She followed him to the door. "You, too." She gave him a tired smile as he went out, then she locked the deadbolt and leaned against the door, releasing a deep sigh. She knew she could do much worse than Curtis Phillips. And she knew lots of women who would beat down the door to get to a guy like that. But she also knew, perhaps now more than ever before, that he was not the one.

"*Why not?*" she exclaimed out loud, causing Andy's little head to pop up and look at her with startled brown eyes. "It's okay," she said quietly, going over to the couch next to where she'd arranged his bed. "I'm just being the crazy lady, talking to herself. You can go back to sleep now." She stroked his smooth coat and continued to ponder this aggravating situation. On one hand, the trip to Sisters could've been just what she needed to decide that everything she wanted was right here in the city. It could've been that final nudge to make her want to settle down with Curtis, live in his house by the river, work at the firm…settle down. Or maybe just settle.

Instead, her visit to Sisters had stirred something up. And her encounters with Nona's handsome attorney, though relatively few, had left her with a deep, unsatisfied longing—and something else too. *Hope.* Hope had finally found hope. And yet, thanks to her sisters—her sisters in Sisters—that hope had been dashed.

She quietly stood now, pacing around her condo, and like a dog chasing its tail, her thoughts ran in circles. Stay here and settle with a man who loved her and wanted to care for her and, consequently, avoid painful family conflicts and chaos…or return to Sisters where nothing was certain except for painful family conflicts and chaos. The smart choice seemed obvious.

Hope looked around her orderly home, which, unlike the construction site at Nona's house, had a place for everything and everything was neatly in its place. Her white chenille sofa, her plum club chair and ottoman, her oriental rug...all fit beautifully. The lamps and tables were perfection. And her well-outfitted kitchen, with its sleek stainless state-of-the-art appliances, cherry cabinets, and granite, was any cook's dream. Well, except for hers tonight. And even Curtis's slightly less modern house was far more convenient and much larger than Nona's old bungalow would ever be. And it was by the river. Really, the choice should be easy. Why wasn't it?

She continued to compare the two completely different worlds. Weighing the pros and cons of here and there. Here there was no angry little sister next door, about to burst in here and shatter Hope's peace with wild accusations. Here there was no ex-boyfriend/brother-in-law ready to come over and dump his problems in her lap. And here there was no brokenhearted and slightly neurotic older sister to show up and blame Hope for all her troubles.

But there was also no eleven-year-old niece with her big brown eyes, her honest questions, and her frank confessions—her neediness and her helpful heart. There was also no insecure adolescent nephew, a boy who had trusted her implicitly and, like he'd promised, called her to say he'd made it safely home and perhaps would stay a week or so. Monroe still had no idea that she was not going back.

There were other things missing here as well—the small-town charm...her old friend Erica...the mountains. And, of course, there was Lewis. Or there was the illusion of Lewis. She really didn't know who he truly was. She didn't understand the link between him and Cherry. Although, she found it hard to believe that someone like

Lewis would chose such a compromising relationship. Still, she hadn't asked him. Perhaps because she hadn't wanted to know the answer... couldn't bear to think of history repeating itself. Only this time—if she let it—it would hurt far more.

She got ready for bed, luxuriating in her marble-encased steam shower, toweling dry with Egyptian cotton, applying expensive lavender lotion, pulling on her best silk pajamas, and finally sliding into fine percale sheets and resting her head on a down pillow—a far cry from the rustic conditions she'd just escaped. Yes, she sleepily told herself, this was the life she wanted...this was exactly what she needed.

But three hours later, as she sat wide awake, staring blankly out the window at the city lights, she was not so sure.

Chapter Twenty
....

By morning, she was thoroughly confused. And unhappy. Not to mention tired from her sleepless night. She pulled on her sweats and leashed Andy, who'd been dancing around by the door. But as they exited the elevator, fully equipped with a plastic bag, she wondered how she could possibly settle for such a confined life. The air was already warm, and the smells of the city felt thick and heavy...and slightly suffocating. The sounds were the usual city noises—engines revving, tires squealing, the occasional horn honking, busses grinding by as they transported people to jobs and wherever.

Hope grimaced as she plucked Andy's still-warm deposit into the plastic bag then hurried to drop this in the handy trash receptacle. How did people live like this? Already Curtis's offer of "adopting" Hope and Andy had become more appealing. Because, despite Hope's initial delight at being back in her condo with *all the comforts of home*, she no longer felt so comfortable—or at home.

Back in her unit, she fed Andy his breakfast and hurried to get dressed for the office. She had told Becca she was coming in, and she planned to stick to her word. What she'd say when she got there was a mystery. "You be good," she told Andy as she reached for her bag. "I'll only be gone a few hours. Then we'll take a walk." Naturally, at the mention of the word *walk*, he was ready to go, standing by the door and wagging his tail hopefully.

"Not now, Andy." She shook her finger at him. "Later. Go back to your bed. At least one of us should get some rest." He just sat and stared at her. And then she left. As she drove to the office, she thought Curtis was right. Having a dog in the city, in her condo, was not going to be easy. Not for her or Andy. And it was probably a mistake.

"I hear you want to come back," Hal said when she stopped by his spacious corner office to see if he had a minute.

"I thought I did."

He motioned to a large leather chair opposite him. "But now you're not so sure?"

"I'm confused." She glanced at the Remington prints hanging on his walls. Hal, though a successful lawyer, was really more of a cowboy at heart.

He just nodded. "Well, I've started reviewing some résumés. None as impressive as yours."

"Thanks." She gave him a weak smile.

"Still, I can't keep your job open forever."

"I know. And I really thought I was coming back here to resume my old life. I was sure of it."

"You don't like it in Sisters?" His brow creased with curiosity. "Lynnette's been nagging for years to get some property there. She loves the mountains, the trees, the lakes, the charming little town. She thinks it's heavenly." He chuckled. "And I have to admit I'm inclined to agree."

"It is heavenly." Hope sighed.

"But you don't want to live there?"

"I thought I didn't when I left. Everything just felt too hard—like it wasn't worth it. Now that I'm back here, I'm not so sure."

He frowned now. "Were you running away from something?"

She kind of laughed. "Just my own family."

He grinned. "Family can be a royal pain—this I know from experience. But I don't think running away improves things much."

"Being there didn't seem to help either."

"You gave up awfully quickly, Hope. I never thought of you as a quitter before. You used to have more fight in you."

His words startled her, and she wasn't sure how to respond.

"Did I say something to offend you?"

"No, it's just that someone else—an attorney in Sisters—said almost the same thing to me."

His brows arched with interest. "An attorney in Sisters? Someone you're involved with, perhaps?"

"Just a friend," she said quickly. "He was my grandmother's attorney."

Now Hal smiled. "Your face betrays your words, Hope."

She just shook her head. "You've always been good at reading people, haven't you?"

"I have a reputation for getting the best jurors." He pointed his finger at her. "And I'm guessing this Sister's attorney has sparked a little something in you. Am I wrong?"

"Probably not. But that doesn't mean that it's right, either."

"Now, I'm no expert on matters of the heart—although Lynnette and I have been married for close to forty years—but I think you need to go back to Sisters, Hope. I think you need to finish up what you started there. And if you give it your all and it still doesn't work out, then you come back here and we'll talk about your job. Not that I'll be holding it for you. Sometimes you have to give something up to find something better."

She nodded then stood, sticking out her hand to shake. "Thanks, Hal. And in case I never told you before, you are one of the wisest men I know."

He chuckled. "Hey, isn't the Sisters Rodeo right around the corner?"

"This weekend."

He shook his head. "One of these years, Lynnette and I will have to make it over for that again. We used to go, back in our younger days."

"Thanks for taking the time to—"

"You just listen to your heart, Hope. And if I were you, I'd get back there in time for rodeo."

She shrugged. "I'm not even sure I'm going back."

He just grinned. "I'm pretty sure you are." Then he waved her away. "Sorry to end this, but I need to brief for a settlement I'm trying to put to rest."

"Thanks!" She closed his door then was stopped by Becca on her way out.

"So, are you coming back to work?"

"Not today," Hope admitted.

"Next week?"

"I'm not sure."

"Oh?" Becca cocked her head to one side. "Are you thinking about going back to Sisters?"

"I really don't know."

"Well, I've heard it's not such a great place."

"Really?"

"My older sister lived there for a while. She taught at the high school." Becca frowned. "She hated it."

"Hated it?"

"She said it was a horrible place for single people. Especially women."

"Really? Why was that?"

"Not much to do. Hardly any available men. Not good ones anyway. And even then, she said unless you hung out in bars, there was no way to meet them."

"Oh?"

"She couldn't wait to get out of there."

"How long ago was this?"

"The early nineties."

"What's your sister's name?" Hope asked. "I lived there then."

"Lois Barton."

Hope suppressed the urge to laugh now. "Miss Mink is your sister?"

"Did you know her?"

Hope nodded with a poker face. "I had her for English." She did not add that Miss Barton was not particularly well liked by her students and that it was no surprise she never met a "good man," since she was such a stick-in-the-mud.

"So you're probably smart not to go back there," Becca said knowingly as her phone buzzed. "I don't blame you one bit."

Hope nodded and waved as Becca answered the phone. Then she went to the supply room to get a box and on to her office, which to her relief no one had touched, and she began to empty her desk. Several old friends popped in, asking her if this was the real deal or if she would be back again next week. To all inquiries, she simply told them the truth—that she didn't know. But as she rode the elevator down, she wondered if it was really for the last time.

Andy was barking as she came down the hallway to her condo unit. And there in front of her door was her fourth pink slip.

Balancing the box in one hand, she picked it up to see that she'd been cited for barking this time. Well, that would be hard to argue her way out of. She unlocked the door, scolded Andy, and then dropped the box of office things on the counter. "What am I going to do with you?" she asked Andy. "With us, for that matter?"

She changed out of her business clothes then, as promised, took Andy for a walk. But she could tell he wasn't enjoying the traffic and noises and exhaust fumes any more than she was, and after twenty minutes, they were both back in the condo. She was pacing, and he was watching. "I know how you must've felt yesterday," she told him, "trapped in your little carry case and not knowing where you were bound."

She did feel confined—almost as if she were in prison. Even though, unlike poor Andy, she had the freedom of choice, she didn't know what to choose. Despite Hal's encouragement, she sure wasn't ready to go back to Sisters. The mere idea of facing her sisters was overwhelming—especially before she completely made up her mind about what she was doing. And, as much as she wanted to see Lewis, she had no idea what she'd tell him either. It shook her to the core to feel so totally flaky, miserably indecisive, and thoroughly confused. This was not her normal take-charge self.

She sat down and tried to remember what she'd felt Nona telling her that day, shortly before the funeral service—something about letting go. Well, it seemed that she had let go all right. And look what happened. Now she was left dangling—or maybe she was freefalling. But when—and how—would she land?

The ringing of the phone rescued her, but to her dismay it was Curtis. "How's it going?"

"Not well."

"Not well in what sort of way?"

So she filled him in about packing up her office, finding another pink slip, and her general state of dazed and confused.

"So you're going back to Sisters?" he asked sadly.

"I don't know. But not today, for sure. And yet I don't want to be here in Portland either. Any more pink slips and I'll probably get the book thrown at me."

"Come and stay here with me," he offered.

"Thanks. But I need to figure this out, Curtis. I don't see that happening at your house when you're there to distract me. And I'm on needles and pins here in the condo. And I can't go back to Sisters and think. I need to—"

"Go use my folks' beach cabin," he suggested.

"Really?"

"Sure. I don't think anyone's there this week. Hang on and I'll check the calendar."

She held her breath as she waited. The beach cabin would be perfect. She'd only been there once when Curtis's sister and husband were there, but she knew Curtis managed the beach house for his parents, and it was out of the way and quiet and—

"It's free until the weekend after next," he told her. "That's nine days."

"Really? Could I stay there that whole time?"

"I'm penciling your name in as we speak. It's yours for the taking."

Now she wondered if this wasn't setting herself up. "And I'll be there by myself, right? Just Andy and me?"

"Meaning, am I secretly planning to come over and crash in on you?"

"Well, the thought occurred to me."

"I will leave you to yourself, Hope. And maybe you'll think about me while you're there."

"You can count on that."

"And while you're there, you'll see the model clipper ship I built as a boy and the shells I collected...and you'll be thinking—"

"Okay, okay," she told him. "I get the hint. But I can't promise that being in your family's beach house is going to persuade me one way or another. I just need some peace and quiet."

"Nothing but peace and quiet there," he assured her. "And the key is hidden under the old captain sculpture by the front door. It's pretty heavy, but if you tilt it slightly you can kick the key loose with your foot."

"Thank you so much, Curtis."

"Just promise to think of me while you're there."

"I will."

"And call if you need anything. There's a list of helpful notes by the door. I'm sure you'll be fine."

So they said good-bye, and Hope immediately began gathering up her things and tossing them into a bag. It wasn't long before she and Andy were on their way to the beach...where hopefully she could sort things out and make some decisions. She imagined herself going to a neutral place—like Switzerland—where the only influences would be the sound of the sea and her own heart.

Chapter Twenty-one

....

The first few days at the beach were blissfully quiet and peaceful. And mostly she just walked the beach with Andy, read from Curtis's mom's collection of novels, shopped at the nearby market, cooked simple meals, chopped firewood for the fires she built in the big rock fireplace each night, and sat on the deck just looking out at the surf.

Oh, she was fully aware that she was in avoidance mode. And always in the back of her mind was this nagging sensation that she had some thinking to do. But mostly she was just plain tired. Mostly she just wanted to turn down the noise in her brain and simply relax. She was on vacation.

And she kept her promise to Curtis. She did look at the clipper ship he'd built, wondering how a boy of only nine (she knew this because his mother had written it on a slip of paper taped to the stand) could put together something so intricate. Perhaps even then he knew he wanted to be an architect. And she admired his shell collection, not just randomly thrown into a dusty basket but laid out neatly under glass with each shell identified with its Latin name.

And she chuckled over the numerous old photos of him and his sister Christy as kids. Someone had enlarged them into black and white and neatly framed and hung them. Probably Curtis's mom, since she was clever like that. And Hope wondered about the scruffy black dog in some of the pictures then missing later on. She studied the photos of his parents with their contented smiles and well-adjusted lives. So amazingly normal.

The Phillips family had always been her ideal—just the sort of family she could imagine being a part of—so vastly different from her own. But when she tried to imagine herself married to Curtis, since she knew that was his ultimate goal, she always thought of Lewis.

And finally, this made her mad. She got so mad, she dialed Lewis's phone number and was ready to question him on what he'd been up to with Cherry and why he insisted on ruining Hope's life by making her so miserable. But before he answered, she hung up. And then she turned her phone off just in case he had caller ID and attempted to call back.

As the weekend came and went, she pushed thoughts of Sisters out of her mind. She knew she was missing the rodeo parade, which she'd always loved, as well as the rodeo, as well as Erica's rodeo barbecue. But she told herself she didn't care. She blocked out what was happening—or not happening in the renovation process at Nona's house. But finally on Monday, she called Erica.

"Hey, where are you?" Erica demanded. "I thought you were coming back for rodeo."

"I told you I wasn't sure. And right now I'm at the beach."

"The beach?"

"To do some thinking."

"Must be a tough life."

Hope attempted a laugh. "So how are things in good old Sisters?

Did the rodeo tourists burn anything down this year?"

Now Erica laughed. "No, the sheriffs try to keep things down to a pretty low roar anymore. But remember that year when they started to burn the picnic tables at the park?"

"Yeah, that was crazy. So how was your barbecue?"

"Fun. And guess who was here?"

"I haven't the slightest."

"Your baby sister's love interest."

Hope's chest tightened at this, but she decided to play dumb. "Love interest?"

"You know, your grandmother's handsome attorney."

"Oh, Lewis." Hope tried to sound nonchalant. "What was he doing there?"

"He's friends with Bobbie. She invited him."

"Oh?"

"Poor Bobbie, she's had a crush on Lewis ever since she interviewed him for the paper."

"She interviewed him…for what?"

"Oh, I think he was heading up a Habitat project. Either that or Bobbie just made something up for an excuse to spend time with him."

"So, is Lewis interested in Bobbie?" Again, Hope tried to sound disinterested.

"It's hard to say, but I have to hand it to Bobbie. The girl's got guts. She cornered him about your sister Cherry."

"How did Bobbie know about that?"

"I'm sure some little bird told her."

"A little bird named Erica?"

"This is a small town, Hope. Things get around."

"So anyway, did he have a response for Bobbie?" Hope could feel her heart in her throat now. She wasn't sure she even wanted to hear the answer.

"All he said was that he would never get involved with a married woman and if he'd been seen meeting with Cherry it was strictly business. Or something like that."

"Strictly business in a restaurant lounge?"

"I don't know, but Bobbie seemed satisfied. In fact, she offered to join Habitat for the next building project. She's never slung a hammer in her life, but she said she'd be willing to learn to spend more time with him."

"She told him that?"

"Oh, I don't know. That's what she told me."

Hope knew she needed to be careful. "Speaking of Habitat houses, I wonder how mine's coming."

"I'm surprised you're not back here checking on it, Hope. Do you have any idea how many things can go wrong in a remodel left to itself? I learned that the hard way down in California. But, seriously, you should be around to make sure it's okay."

"I just can't right now."

"Oh, yeah, that's right…you're too busy being a beach bum. Let me guess, it's time for you to turn over in the sun. Hope you're using your sunscreen."

"For your information it's foggy today."

Erica laughed. "It still sounds lovely."

"Would you do me a big favor?"

"What?"

"Would you go and check on my house for me?"

"I guess I could do that."

"And, don't forget, Brian Godwin is working there. And he's a pretty cool guy, too." Hope had no idea why she said this. It probably sounded as if she were using Brian to bait Erica.

"From what I hear, there's something going on between you and Brian."

"Who told you that?" Hope imagined Cherry out there spreading rumors.

"I can't even remember. But you know those jungle drums."

"Well, it's not true. Brian is a great guy and a hard worker, but we're really just friends."

"So far anyway."

"Honestly, Erica. That's all there is to it."

"So you're saying that should I, say, go over there and flirt my head off at Brian, you would be just fine with it?"

"I swear, I would."

Erica just laughed. "Okay, I'll go and check on your house, Hope. Want me to call you back with a full report?"

"Sure, I'd love that."

"And if Brian and I decide to run down to Reno, you want to hear about that, too?"

"Sure, Erica. In fact, let me know and I'll come and dance at your wedding."

Erica laughed harder now. "You better hurry back to Sisters, Hope. I think I need you around for the laughs."

"I'm working on it," Hope told her.

And really, wasn't that what she was doing? She *was* working on it…trying to figure it all out. It was just that these things took time. But this newsflash about Bobbie and Lewis and how she'd questioned him about Cherry, well, that sounded positive. Of course, what was Lewis going to say to Bobbie? Did she expect him to answer, yes, as a matter of fact, he *was* having an affair with a married woman? And not just any married woman, mind you, but the one who made it into the newspaper regularly, the one who'd married into one of the old ranching families, the one who almost everyone in town seemed to love? Not likely.

Hope walked and thought and even prayed. Then she thought and walked and prayed some more. And the whole while, Andy stayed close to her side—just like he'd always done with Nona. Maybe even while Nona was rethinking her will, trying to make a plan to help Hope. But in the end, it was up to Hope. And now she remembered the impression she'd had before—the sense that Nona was telling her to let go…and to trust God. And as Hope walked and considered all these things, that is exactly what she did. She let go. And she trusted God to hold on. This was, she decided, what Nona would call faith. Like stepping from the known into the unknown. And, Hope realized, it was a relief to let go. It was exhilarating to trust God. And to think that, after all these years, He was still there for her…still ready to be her best friend. More than ever, she needed that.

So, by the end of the week, two things seemed perfectly clear. She no longer wanted to live in Portland. And she did not want to marry

Curtis. She firmly believed what she'd suspected before—Curtis deserved someone who truly loved him, not someone who was using him as an escape route, someone who was willing to settle. Just being here in his family's beach house helped to convince her of this. And that's what she gently told him on Friday morning. To her surprise, he took it well.

"I kind of knew this was coming," he admitted. "But I'm glad you took the time to really think it over and to come to a firm decision."

"Some really wonderful woman is going to thank me for letting you go someday," she assured him. "And you will, too. I know it."

"I'll have to take your word for that."

"I'll clean the cabin up before I leave tomorrow," she told him. "I've chopped and stacked all the firewood."

He chuckled. "Wow, you must've been struggling over this really hard."

"I was." She didn't admit that the struggle wasn't completely over him, or even completely over yet. But she did tell him that, in her own way, she would always love him and she would always appreciate her friendship with him. "But I know it's over."

"I know that, too. I've heard of couples breaking up and trying to be *just* friends, but it never seems to work. And I know it wouldn't for us."

"Take care, Curtis."

"You, too. I hope you find what you're looking for."

"Thanks. Me, too—for both of us."

Later that day, Monroe called and left a message, saying that he was ready to return to Sisters, asking if it was okay if he stayed with her again. As she called him back, she knew she was sealing her fate—

really letting go. "I'm going to put my condo up for sale," she told her nephew. "So I need to pack some things up and clear some things out. Do you think you'd want to come to Portland to help?"

"Sure!"

"Would your dad mind?"

"I doubt it. He thinks you're the sane one in the family." Then Monroe laughed and told her about how both Cherry and Faye had called his dad, trying to convince him that Hope was not to be trusted. "But he didn't believe them."

"You should be able to get your flight changed pretty easily. There are more flights from Seattle to Portland than to Redmond. And then we'll just drive to Sisters together."

"Sounds good. I'll ask Dad to help me with the ticket."

They decided that Monday would be soon enough for him to arrive. Hope didn't tell him she was at the beach...or that she'd only just decided to return to Sisters. But she was glad Monroe was coming, and glad that she'd have to stick to her decision now. No backing out. To seal the deal even more, she called her Realtor friend Natalia and asked her about listing her condo.

"Of course I'd love to list it. I haven't had anything in that side of town for ages. I might even have a buyer for you."

"Seriously? Already?"

"I have an older couple who want to downsize. Their home closes in a couple of weeks. We've been looking."

"That's fantastic."

"When can I come over?"

So Hope explained that she wasn't even home. "I'll be there

tomorrow afternoon. But you might want to wait until Monday."

"Are you kidding? How about five tomorrow? Will you be home by then?"

So it was agreed, and Hope spent the next morning cleaning the cabin. Her goal was to leave it better than she'd found it. And she also left Curtis's mom a note saying what a wonderful man she'd raised, and how much Hope respected their whole family, and that it hadn't been easy to walk away, but that it was over. And then she and Andy left.

She got home before four and, worried that she needed to straighten her house for Natalia, ran around dusting, taking out the trash, and even picking pieces of lint from the furniture. But, really, the place was immaculate. Natalia thought so, too. "So how soon can we begin showing it?" she asked after they'd settled on the price and Hope read and signed the contract.

"My nephew is coming on Monday," Hope explained. "He's going to help me pack up some things. Like the kitchen and whatnot. All those small things that take time to pack and that I'll need in Sisters once my house is done."

"But you'll leave your furniture here, won't you?" Natalia looked worried. "It's always easier to show a house that's staged, and this place looks just about perfect as is. Although a little clearing of clutter and personal things won't matter."

"I'll leave the large pieces until my house in Sisters is ready," Hope told her. "That's probably weeks away...or longer."

Natalia nodded. "Well, I have a feeling this place will sell quickly. This is a desirable neighborhood without many listings. And we've priced it well."

Hope took in a steadying breath, realizing that she really was cutting her ties here. If her condo sold that quickly, there would be no turning back. "Good…I guess that's good."

"Of course it's good. And lucky you!"

"What?"

"Moving to Sisters!"

"Oh, yes…well, I hope you're right."

"So, what if I wanted to bring the Tylers by tomorrow?" Natalia asked eagerly. "Before your nephew gets here and you start making messes with packing. Would that be okay?"

"I suppose so. Maybe you could do it earlier in the day. I thought I could get some boxes and start packing tomorrow."

"Is one early enough? These are church people."

"One is fine."

"And be sure to have the doggy gear cleared out. It smells just fine in here, but sometimes a buyer sees dog things and gets concerned."

Hope nodded. "Okay. I can do that."

"Thank you so much for this listing! You won't be sorry, I promise." Natalia joyfully hugged Hope then left.

"Oh, Andy," Hope told him, "the wheels of progress are turning now." But his tail just wagged happily, and she wondered if he understood what was going on. "Do you want to go home to Sisters?" she asked. He ran to the door and waited for her like he thought it was time.

"Well, not now, silly." She got his leash and a plastic baggie. "But we could take a walk." Then, as she strolled him around the condo's lawns, she began humming to herself and finally singing out loud the old hymn that Nona had loved.

"*Andy* walks with me. *Andy* talks with me. *Andy* tells me I am his own." Suddenly Hope stopped walking and started to giggle like a crazy woman. *She got it*. She understood why Cherry and Faye had laughed so hard at Nona's funeral. It really was that funny. Or at least it seemed that funny to her at the moment. But then she noticed Mrs. Hobbs watching her with a suspicious expression.

So Hope just waved and continued to walk, and continued singing the old hymn to her happy little dog. So what if Mrs. Hobbs reported her to the condo committee for singing on the condo lawns. Before long, Hope wouldn't live here anymore.

Chapter Twenty-two

....

On Sunday Hope was antsy to start packing and wished she hadn't
told Natalia that she could show her place. On the other hand,
maybe this older couple *would* want to buy her condo. Of course that
seemed nothing short of miraculous. But just in case, Hope decided
to do some de-cluttering and to put her energy into making her unit
sparkle and shine. She even ran out and bought lemons to put in a
pretty bowl on the counter and a gorgeous bouquet of irises to set on
the dining room table. Then she rounded up all of Andy's things and
ran them down to her car. Then she rounded up Andy, which wasn't
difficult, and set out to find a dog-friendly café with outdoor seating.

By the time she picked up packing crates and got back to the
condo, the only sign that someone had been there was Natalia's
business card. So, assuming the coast was clear, she started to empty
out the bathroom cabinet. And instead of feeling gloomy about the
prospects of leaving her condo and jumping off into the black abyss
(otherwise known as her sisters in Sisters) she felt only a happy
anticipation. She wasn't even too troubled by the phone call from
Erica a few days ago, reporting that there was no sign of anything
going on at Nona's house. No trucks, no Brian, nothing. Just a pile of
old furniture and things out by the garage.

"Are you having a yard sale?" Erica had asked. So Hope had
explained that those things were supposed to have been picked up
by someone, and Erica had mentioned that Hope was lucky not to

have any CC and Rs in her neighborhood. "I'd be in deep doo-doo if I did that where I live," Erica had joked. Of course Hope was aware that, where Cherry was concerned, she probably already was in deep doo-doo herself. But then Cherry could've called to have those things removed if they were troubling her.

Hope wondered how Cherry and Faye were doing, and if they had even noticed her hasty departure. Of course Monroe or his dad would've been in communication with Faye, so she probably had an idea of what was up. Still, it seemed a little odd that neither of them had called. But then, that's how it had always been between the three of them, at least in adulthood. They were disconnected. Almost totally disconnected. And, to be fair, Hope was as much to blame as any of them.

Monroe's flight from Seattle arrived shortly before noon on Monday. She took him for some lunch at McDonald's (his choice) and listened as he filled her in on his situation. "Dad wants me to live with him in Seattle. At least that's what he says. And that's what he's telling my mom. But I heard them on the phone, arguing as usual, and it sounds like it has more to do with paying child support than him really wanting me. He thinks if I stay with him, it'll save him money." Monroe's fist was clenched. "I just wish I could divorce both of them."

Hope sort of laughed. "Yeah, I see your point. But you have to realize they're both in a really tough spot right now."

"A tough spot that they got themselves into, don't you think?"

She nodded. "It's certainly not your fault."

He looked down at the remains of his Big Mac.

"You don't think it's your fault, do you, Monroe?"

He shrugged then picked up a fry, slowly dipping it in ketchup.

"Monroe, no matter what you think, it is not your fault." She was using her attorney voice now. "You do understand that, don't you?"

"I don't know. I think I might be partly to blame." He looked up at her with sad brown eyes. "I mean I didn't exactly make it easy for them. Sometimes they fought over me—I mean like what was the best way to parent me, you know?"

"I know a lot of parents struggle with that, Monroe. But it's not the kids' fault."

"Well, they didn't agree on much. Dad's pretty easygoing about stuff. Like he'd tell mom to lighten up, or that he'd been like me as a kid. And Mom was like the heavy, you know. Kind of like she thinks she has to control me or I'll go out and smoke crack and shoot somebody."

Hope smiled. "I doubt she thinks that. But she loves you, Monroe, and she seems to be a worrier."

"Isn't it funny that her name is really Faith."

"What do you mean?"

"I mean, even though she calls herself a Christian, she worries about everything. She always expects the worst. That doesn't seem like faith to me."

Hope considered this. "That's interesting. To be honest, I don't think my name fits me too well either. At least it hasn't in the past. Anyone who knew me well would not have described me as hopeful. And yet I feel more hopeful than ever now."

"How about Aunt Cherry?" Monroe continued the game. "I know her real name is Charity, but I'm not sure exactly what that means. I guess that she's always giving and helping others. According to Mom, she does a lot of volunteering so maybe her name fits."

LOVE FINDS YOU IN SISTERS, OREGON

"Maybe…but I remember Nona telling me about our names once. She said they were taken from a place in the Bible. I don't know it by heart, but it was something like this: 'Faith, hope, and charity, abide these three, but the greatest of these is charity.'" Hope made a face. "At the time I was a kid and I didn't really like hearing that Charity was the greatest of us three girls. Especially considering she was the youngest and, in my opinion, pretty spoiled. But then Nona told me what the scripture really meant."

"What did it mean?"

"The best I can remember—and I should probably look up the verse—but Nona said that charity was actually another word for love. And, of course, the Bible wasn't talking about us three girls or even the Sisters Mountains. But what it meant was that love was the most important thing of all."

Monroe had a thoughtful look. "Yeah, that makes sense."

"Unfortunately, there hasn't been a lot of love between my sisters and me."

"So Faith, my mom, hasn't been very faithful. And you, Hope, until recently, haven't been very hopeful. And Aunt Charity might be good at volunteering and stuff, but I don't think she's been very loving. Not to you anyway. I've heard her talk."

"Ironic, isn't it." Hope shook her head. "I wonder what our mom would think."

"I'm glad my name doesn't mean anything."

"Of course, it means something," Hope told him. "Monroe was my mom's maiden name."

"Sure, there's that…yeah. But it doesn't really mean anything else." She smiled at him. "Well, why don't you make it mean something then?"

Hope thought about their conversation as she and Monroe unloaded the contents of cabinets and closets, carefully filling the plastic crates she'd purchased and clearly marking each one so that once she was able to unpack them, it might not be too confusing. When that would be was anyone's guess.

On Tuesday she called about renting a U-Haul truck. Her plan was to pack and move as much as she could without making her place look barren—so that Natalia would be happy while showing it. And she and Monroe would transport this to Sisters. Then, eventually, when her condo sold or Nona's house was finished, she would fly out, make arrangements with movers, and then drive her car back to Sisters. She knew it was an optimistic plan, but it felt good to be hopeful. She wanted to live up to her name.

By Thursday afternoon, she and Monroe had loaded the last of the crates into the rented truck. And since she'd get another pink slip if she left it parked there all night, she decided it was time to pack up the dog and just go.

"I've never driven a truck like this," she confessed to Monroe.

"Oh, it's not that big," he assured her as she pulled out of the parking lot. "You'll do fine."

"Too bad you're not old enough to drive." She looked both ways, checked her rearview mirrors, and then cautiously turned left onto the busy street.

"I turn fifteen next month," he told her.

"That's right. July fifth. You were almost a firecracker baby."

"I tell my friends that Fourth of July fireworks are just my birthday eve celebration."

"That's a good one."

"Mom probably won't let me get my permit, though. She'll probably assume that I'll get in a wreck or run over someone."

"Give her time, Monroe. Going through this divorce has stretched her in ways she probably doesn't even know yet. Maybe eventually it'll help her to grow."

"If it doesn't, I'm heading back to Seattle."

"So you never told me exactly how it went with your dad. I know he wants custody of you, but why did he let you come back?"

"Mom convinced him that I'd get into serious trouble being unsupervised, as she calls it, for the whole summer."

"Oh…"

"And I told Dad that I wanted to give Sisters another try. I called Alex while I was home, and we talked a lot. He seems like a good guy. He's going to teach me some guitar chords, and he told me about the music program at the high school. He says it's pretty cool."

"And there's a lot to do in Sisters," Hope assured him as she cautiously entered the freeway. "Hiking, lakes to explore, horses if you're into that, mountain biking—"

"I want a mountain bike. I rode Aaron's a few times. There are some cool trails around town."

"I want a mountain bike, too," she admitted. And then she realized that would be a perfect birthday present for Monroe. Maybe even an early present so that he'd have a way to get around. Hopefully Faye wouldn't object. Hope remembered the adage "sometimes it's easier to beg forgiveness than to ask permission." Maybe that's what she'd do with the bike situation. Besides, last time she'd spoken to her older sister, Faye had told Hope that she was responsible for Monroe now. So, really, how could she complain? And she would make sure that Monroe had a helmet.

Hope stopped at the café in Marion Forks for dinner. Monroe had never been there before, and he seemed to enjoy all the hunting and fishing paraphernalia there. He even got into a conversation with a fisherman while he was walking Andy down by the river. And, as Hope continued the drive up the mountain, Monroe talked enthusiastically about learning how to fish. "I saw a fly fishing shop in town," he told her. "Maybe I'll go and check it out."

She wanted to say, "See, there *is* a lot to do in Sisters." But that sounded so parental that she decided to hold her tongue. "I've always wanted to learn to fly fish, too," she said instead. "Maybe we can take a class or something."

Monroe continued to chat pleasantly, and as they got closer to Sisters, she realized how thankful she was for his company. And his cheerfulness was like the antidote to her old fears and concerns about returning to the same place she'd gone running from a little more than two weeks ago.

"Look how much snow has melted from the mountains," he said as they drove over the pass.

She glanced briefly and nodded. "My mom would say that the Sisters were wearing their summer frocks now."

"Is it too early to go hiking up there?"

"It might be—for beginners anyway. But it's close."

"Maybe by my birthday?" he asked hopefully.

"It's a possibility. As long as the weather stays warm."

"Have you even been to Hoodoo?" he asked as they passed the ski resort.

"Oh, yeah, lots of times. It's where I learned to ski. Back then it was pretty small with only a few lifts, but I hear they've really improved it. I'd like to check it out this winter."

"Me, too," he said eagerly. "I want to learn to snowboard."

She laughed. "For a guy who was dragging his heels about Sisters, you seem to have a lot of things you'd like to do."

"I think I was dragging my heels more about living with my mom," he said quietly.

"Oh, yeah…" She nodded. "I kind of forgot that."

"But as long as you're around, I'm not so worried."

She nodded slowly, telling herself not to feel pressured by his trust in her. He was only being honest. Besides, didn't she plan to become a full-time resident in Sisters? Wasn't she cutting all ties to Portland? Really, there was no turning back now…was there?

And then, just as the sky became pink with the sunset, they were rolling into town. "I have no idea what condition the house will be in," she confessed as she reduced her speed. "I had a friend check on it and she said it looked as if nothing was being done."

"But Brian wouldn't stop working on it, would he?"

"I don't know." She had wondered if her being there had been an incentive to Brian. And just thinking that made her feel guilty because she remembered when she had shamelessly flirted with him simply to get Lewis's attention. Almost as if she'd been imitating her baby sister, and that was really humiliating to think about.

But now, even if it meant slowing down the remodel, she should make it clear to Brian that theirs was simply a business relationship. Unless he wanted to be friends. That would be fine, too. She felt uneasy as she turned down her street. Hopefully Cherry wouldn't be outside or looking out her kitchen window when this big hulk of truck parked in front of Nona's house. Although, she did want to talk to Cherry eventually. She wanted to make an attempt at amends. She just didn't want to do it tonight. For that reason, she came up to her house from the other direction, quietly pulling up and turning off the engine.

"Trying to sneak into your house?" Monroe teased.

"Sort of. I don't want to disturb Cherry and her family."

"And you probably don't want to be disturbed by her either."

She gave him a wry look. "Yeah, you're probably right. Let's get out quietly, okay? Just get what you need for tonight. And we'll unload tomorrow." She reached for Andy, who was trembling with excitement, as if he knew he was home. "No, please, do not bark," she warned him as she let him out of the truck. Thankfully, he just made a beeline for the front grass, relieving himself on his favorite lilac bush, then rolling in the grass as if to say he was happy to be home.

"Look at that," Monroe whispered to Hope as they went around to the door that led into the back porch and kitchen. "Looks like your windows have arrived."

Hope looked at the neat stacks of plastic-wrapped bundles. "I think you're right." She felt a surge of hope as she pulled open the screen door then unlocked the other door. Andy burst into the porch ahead of her. She turned on the light to see that things looked pretty much the same in there. Washer, dryer, as well as some paint cans and tools and things, sitting neatly on a piece of plastic on the counter next to the washer.

Hope opened the door to the kitchen, bracing herself for the state of deconstruction that she'd left behind, but was pleased to see that things had changed. She turned on the light switch to see that the old-fashioned chrome and glass chandelier had been hung in the kitchen. But also the lower cabinets, the appliances, and the sink were in place. Although the soapstone countertop and upper cabinets were still missing, it was encouraging to see this much. "Wow," she said as she ran her hand over the smooth surface of the cabinets. "These are nice."

"Check out the floor," Monroe exclaimed.

She looked down as Andy trotted around, curiously sniffing everything. "That is gorgeous!" She knelt down to run her hand over the wood grain.

"They turned out nice, huh?"

"Much better than I expected."

"Looks like someone's been painting, too," Monroe said as he went ahead of her into the living room. He turned the light on there, and Hope noticed that the new chandelier had been installed there as well. She was glad she'd taken time to mark the light boxes with their final destinations. Also the furnishings she'd had piled in one corner were now neatly arranged. Maybe not to her liking, but at least a person could sit down on the old sofa or the wooden rocker now.

"Is this the right color?" Monroe asked as he looked at the celery green paint.

"It is." She nodded in amazement. "Do you think it looks okay?"

"Yeah. It's nice with the wood floors." He went ahead to look in the spare room now. "It's painted in here, too. Cool color, Aunt Hope."

She had picked out a darker green for the spare room. Almost an olive. "You like it?" she asked as she peeked in. "Not too dark?"

"I think it's great."

"And it's good with the floors, too." She noticed that the bed was centered on the back wall again, with the end table she'd saved in place as well. "I wonder if Brian did all this."

"Man, he must've been one busy guy then." Monroe had moved onto the bathroom now. "Check this out, Aunt Hope."

She went in to see that tile work was in process. And a toilet was already in place. "Wow, indoor plumbing!" she exclaimed as she tried a flush.

"And the shower's nearly done," Monroe told her. "It looks nice."

"And someone painted in here, too," she said in wonder.

"Another great color."

"Kind of a robin's egg blue..." She ran her hand over the sleek white tile.

"The sink's not in yet," Monroe observed, "but at least you have the one in the kitchen."

She just nodded, trying to take it all in. Then she went to peek in her bedroom. And it, too, was painted, the same robin's egg blue as the bathroom. It made a pretty contrast with the beautiful wood floors. And her bed, like the other one, had been centered on the back wall, with one end table next to it.

"This place is starting to look like a real house," Monroe said as they went back to the living room.

"It gives me hope." She sat down on the rocker and just stared in wonder.

"Aunt Hope has hope," Monroe teased. "Maybe you can start a trend with your sisters."

"Wouldn't that be something?" And Hope really did feel hopeful as she rocked in the chair. Her little house was really starting to fall into place. Not only had she misjudged Brian—worrying that he'd abandoned the project—she now owed him a great big thank you. Maybe she'd get up early enough to locate her coffeemaker and grinder from the back of the U-haul and greet him with a hot cup of coffee when he arrived in the morning.

Chapter Twenty-three

First thing in the morning, after a really good night's rest, Hope took Andy out back to do his business. Then, hoping to distract him, gave him his food—canned food, which was a special treat. Feeling like a thief, she quietly slipped out of the house and into the back of the U-Haul. It wasn't even seven, and though she knew it was juvenile— not to mention paranoid—she didn't want to be spotted by her baby sister just yet. And she did want to make coffee. A small gesture, perhaps, but Brian deserved it for all his hard work. Fortunately, it wasn't long before she located the appropriate plastic crate, thanks to her "labeling fetish," as Brian called it, and she snuck back into the house without disturbing any of the neighbors.

"Good boy," she told Andy as she came inside. "You didn't even find anything to bark at while I was gone." Then she set up her coffeemaker on top of the dryer in the laundry room, since there was no countertop in the kitchen, and proceeded to grind and make coffee. Remembering that Brian took cream, she decided to make a fast run to the market. And to ensure Andy's silence, she took him as well. It took only about five minutes to get there, on foot, and by seven thirty she was back in her house with not only cream, but some fresh fruit, yogurt, and pastries as well.

She dug around until she found some of Nona's plates and things, and she set these up in the laundry room as well. Not exactly luxurious, but somewhat tempting, she hoped. Then she poured herself a cup of coffee and went into the living room to sit in the rocker and to admire the floors and the walls by daylight. She was actually relieved not to have to do the painting, and she knew she never could've done such a great job. That Brian! How did he manage to do it? She leaned back and imagined how nicely her white chenille couch and plum chair and ottoman would go in here. As well as her oriental carpet and other things. She couldn't wait to make this house her home.

Of course, now she wished she'd hired real movers and brought the rest of her things to Sisters as well. She was just envisioning how she would arrange the living room when she heard what sounded like someone at the back door. Assuming it was Brian, she hurried out to greet him, but when she looked out she was surprised to see it was Lewis instead.

"Oh…" Slightly stunned, she stood there with a coffee cup in one hand and the screen door in the other, realizing she hadn't even brushed her teeth yet. "It's you."

His brow creased slightly. "I was actually hoping it was you in here. But you seem disappointed to see me. Should I leave?"

"Of course not. Come in. I just thought it was Brian."

Lewis stepped into the laundry room, taking in the homey scene of coffee and goodies. "It looks like you were expecting company."

"That was for Brian." Even as she said this, she had a feeling it sounded wrong…not like she'd meant it.

He just nodded, but his eyes seemed troubled.

"But, please," she said nervously, "help yourself. I got way more than enough."

He shoved his hands into his jeans pockets now. "That's okay. I already had something to eat."

"Have you seen the house?" she said eagerly, hoping to move the conversation in another direction.

"Do you like it?"

"I absolutely love it." She set down her coffee cup and opened the kitchen door. "Come in and see it."

So he followed her in, and she took him from room to room, except the spare room where Monroe was still sleeping, and showed him how wonderful everything looked.

"I like the wall colors you chose," he told her.

"Thanks. I can't believe how well they look with the floors. I'm just so pleased."

He made a puzzled frown now. "So, I see that U-Haul out there. Does that mean you've changed your mind?"

Suddenly she remembered that this wasn't just Lewis (her friend and, hopefully, something more someday if she was lucky), but he was also the trustee of Nona's estate. The attorney in her realized she should've informed him of her intentions before coming back here like this, blasting into the house and acting as if she still owned it. For all she knew, he could've sold the house by now. Especially considering her state of mind the last time they'd talked. She'd adamantly pulled the plug on the whole thing, told him it was over, and then run like a whipped dog back to Portland.

"Uh, yes," she stammered. "I guess I should have let you know that I changed my mind."

He nodded somberly. "That would've been nice."

Just then she noticed a turquoise blue pickup pulling over. "Wow, this place is getting pretty busy this morning," she said. "I wonder if I should move the truck so Brian will have a place to—"

"That's okay," Lewis said quickly. "I'll move my SUV out of the driveway."

"Thanks." She gave him what felt like a weak smile.

She watched as Lewis backed out and Brian pulled in. The two smiled, waved, and exchanged some words, then Lewis just kept on driving down the street.

"I hear you have breakfast ready for me," Brian told her as he came into the laundry room with his tool belt in hand. "So you finally kept your promise."

She waved her hand toward the mini feast. "Help yourself. And I have to say I'm really impressed at the house. It looks fantastic. You've done wonders."

"You can be thankful for some good subs." He set his tool belt down then picked up a chocolate-glazed donut. "And the tile guy should be here soon. I came early to do some quick tweaks to that shower before he finishes tiling. Hopefully he'll get the tile up today and start grouting tomorrow. Then, if we can get the plumber in as planned, you should be able to take a shower by Monday night. How's that sound?"

"That's wonderful!" She had already poured his coffee and was adding cream. "Say when."

"That's good." He took the cup and grinned. "I had no idea you were so domestic."

"It's just my way of saying thanks." She wondered how she could gently hint that this was just a working relationship without offending him.

Brian finished his donut and, with coffee still in hand, picked up his tool belt. "If I want to get that done before the tile guy gets here,

I better get moving. Thanks for the treats, Hope."

"You're welcome. Thanks for the great work!" She went over to the kitchen window and looked out, hoping that perhaps Lewis had returned or was going to, but the street was quiet and void of traffic. She wished she had handled that differently. But she'd been so surprised to see him. Especially so early in the morning. She wondered what he had been doing here. Was it possible that he really did intend to sell the place? Maybe there was a Realtor's sign out there right now—perhaps she hadn't noticed it.

She went out with Andy on her heels and checked out the front yard but saw no for sale sign. However, she did notice that the exterior painting had been finished as well. It looked great, but she was a little disappointed since she'd imagined that she and Monroe would complete it together. Still, there would be plenty else to do. That is if she got to stay here…if Lewis hadn't put the wheels in motion for Plan B.

She was just going back into the house when Andy started to bark like a wild thing. Thinking it was probably the plumber, she turned to call her dog and was surprised to see Cherry striding purposefully toward her. Hope couldn't read Cherry's expression but decided to take the high road and just smile. "Hey, neighbor," she called out in a friendly tone.

"What are you doing here?" Cherry's voice was flat.

"It's so nice to know you're glad to see me," Hope said sarcastically. "Thanks for the warm welcome."

"I heard you'd gone back to Portland—for good." Cherry remained about ten feet away from Hope with her arms folded across her front.

"I had." Hope studied Cherry. How had her baby sister attained this information? No one else knew that she'd gone for good. Even Monroe, who might've told Faye, had assumed Hope had only been going to the city for a short while. "Who told you that anyway?"

Cherry gave her what seemed a sassy little shrug, but said nothing.

Hope took a couple steps closer. "No, really, Cherry, *who* told you that?"

"Lewis." She made a half smile.

"Why did Lewis tell you that?"

Again with the little shrug. "What difference does it make?"

Hope felt a rush of panic now. What if Cherry and Lewis really were lovers? What if Lewis was in some kind of scheme with her? And what if the house was already sold? Or worse than that, what if it wasn't? Would Hope have the guts to remain in Sisters, to just calmly sit by as history repeated itself? This whole scenario seemed impossible…and yet….

"I'm just curious as to why Lewis told you that." Hope tried to sound light, but she could feel the pulse in her temples now. She was sure her cheeks were flushing.

"Lewis and I are friends." Cherry said this in a way that insinuated more. "He keeps me informed. What more can I say?"

"Why does he keep you informed?" Hope put on her courtroom persona.

"Because, like I said, we're friends. We talk. And he knows that I live next to Nona's house, so naturally he understands how I'd like to be in the loop. Which is more than I can say for my own sister."

A legal term was running through Hope's mind now. *Attorney-client privilege*. It seemed to her that Lewis had broken her confidence by sharing her information with anyone. Even if Cherry was Hope's sister, Lewis knew their relationship was rocky at best. How dare he tell her about Hope's personal affairs?

"Don't get mad, Hope." The way Cherry said this sounded like a juvenile taunt. The kind of thing she used to spout after borrowing Hope's favorite cashmere sweater then leaving it soiled and trashed in the bottom of the dirty clothes hamper.

Hope took in a slow, deep breath. *The high road*, she reminded herself; she had planned to take the high road. "I'm not mad," she said quietly. "Just a little disappointed."

"It's no big deal," Cherry said lightly. "You shouldn't be offended if Lewis talks to me. We were friends long before you came back home."

"Right…" Hope was backing away now. She didn't know if she could trust herself to remain on the high road much longer.

"Besides, I was curious," Cherry continued. Hope could tell her baby sister was switching gears now because her features softened and her voice grew slightly higher. "I just wanted to know what would become of Nona's estate after you backed out."

"And did Lewis tell you that, too?"

"He said I should talk to you." Cherry came closer now, even smiled. "So here I am. Want to talk?"

"Yes. Sometime we should talk, Cherry." Hope pressed her lips together and nodded. "Just not right now."

"What's wrong with now?" Cherry's lower lip jutted ever so slightly.

"I've just got a million things to do at the moment." Hope forced a smile. "How about later today, okay?"

Cherry was clearly disappointed. "Okay. If I'm not too busy, that is."

"Sure. If you're not too busy."

"We have a Habitat house we're finishing up," she said importantly. "The dedication is tomorrow, and I want to get some curtains hung."

Hope nodded. She remembered what Erica had said…how Bobbie had been teasing, saying she wanted to start volunteering with Habitat in order to spend time with Lewis. Yes, it was all starting to add up now. Or so it seemed. Still, Hope had difficulty believing Lewis would get seriously involved with a married woman. Even so, she was irked at him for talking to Cherry. How dare he disclose her personal affairs to anyone?

She put Andy back in the house, got her purse, and then told herself to remain calm as she drove over to Lewis's office. But once there, she knocked loudly on the door.

"Come in," he said with a curious expression.

"I want to talk to you," she declared.

He nodded, pointing to a chair.

Ignoring the chair, Hope jumped right in. "Cherry just informed me that you told her everything."

"Everything about what?" He frowned.

"About me. The things I told you when I thought I was leaving Sisters for good. Things said privately. Then you went and told her the whole thing."

"I only said that you were—"

"What about attorney-client privilege?" she demanded.

"Technically, I'm not your attorney," he said calmly. "Your grandmother hired me. But I do represent—"

"*Technically*. So I tell you something in confidence—*as my friend*—and you go around blabbing it to everyone in town?"

"I didn't tell anyone else. And I only told Cherry because she asked and I explained—"

"So you admit it, you *did* tell her?"

"Am I on the witness stand now?"

Hope sank down in the chair like a deflated balloon. This was not how she'd planned to handle this.

"I'm sorry this upset you," he said as he leaned back on his desk. "Cherry asked me where you'd gone. I told her Portland. It didn't seem that was any violation of your trust. She *is* your sister."

"My sister who hates me."

"That's a little harsh."

Hope stared up at him. "Do you really *know* her?"

"Sure. I've known her for quite a while. She goes to my church and—"

"I mean do you *really* know her?"

He held up his hands. "Look, I don't want to get in the middle of a sisterly quarrel here."

"No, I expect you wouldn't." Hope stood now.

"And, honestly, I'm sorry if you feel I divulged too—"

"From now on I would appreciate it if anything I said to you in private would be kept private. When I told you those things—all that stuff about me—it was because I trusted you, Lewis. To tell Cherry was—"

"I only told her you'd gone to Portland, Hope." His tone was firm, as if addressing a judge or a jury—no longer a friend. "After more than one week passed, she wanted to know if you'd gone for good, and I told her she would have to talk to you about that. I don't see how I can be blamed if she drew her own conclusions."

"No, I suppose not." Hope reached for the door.

"For that matter, I believed you had left for good—that's what you'd told me you were doing. When I didn't hear from you, I assumed that you'd returned to your job and your life."

"Yes, I'm sorry about that. I should have informed you that I'd changed my mind. But, as you mentioned, you are not my attorney."

"But I do manage your grandmother's estate and that makes me—"

"I said I'm sorry, Lewis. I realize I was at fault. I can only hope you haven't sold my house in my absence—or moved onto Plan B and completely erased me from Nona's will, because I'm sure *she* would've understood."

He looked angry and hurt now. As if her words cut deeply. Yet, there was a part of her that didn't care. Hadn't he hurt her as well? Perhaps it was the simplest way to end this thing—whatever this thing was, which was probably nothing more than her imagination anyway.

"I'm sorry to have bothered you, Counselor." She opened the door.

"Don't be like—"

"I'm sure you have other more important matters to attend to. *Real* clients."

"Hope…" His eyes looked concerned. And perhaps sad.

But not nearly as sad as she felt. And if she didn't make a run for it, she would be crying in front of him. She did not want to do that again. "Thanks for your time, Mr. Garson."

Hope told herself she was driving to the grocery store, where she would purchase food and supplies for her and Monroe, but she drove past the store and back around…finally pulling over by the elk ranch, where she parked and got out of the car. Standing there with clenched fist, she stared at the mountains. Her mother used to say, "I look to the mountains from whence cometh my strength." Then, later on, when Hope said these words to Nona one day, her grandmother finished what turned out to be a Bible verse, saying, "I look to the mountains. From whence cometh my strength? My strength comes from the Lord who created the heavens and the earth." And Hope had been surprised.

Today she looked at the mountains…but she prayed that God would give her strength. Then, breathing deeply, she let go of these things. And she told herself that she had acted childishly, emotionally, stupidly. And if Lewis never spoke to her again, she deserved it. He had probably been perfectly honest with her—that he had only told Cherry that Hope was in Portland. And, naturally, Cherry had pestered him and most likely drawn her own conclusions. But what still irked Hope, what rankled her beyond all else, was that Lewis and Cherry were "friends." And as badly as she wanted to let this go, she just couldn't.

It wasn't her imagination that she'd seen Lewis in intimate conversations with Cherry. And more than once. And yet she'd tried to believe it was nothing. She'd wanted to believe that Lewis was above something like that. But what if Cherry and Lewis really were involved? What if Hope had been wrong? It wouldn't be the first time now, would it?

Lewis had told Hope to talk to Cherry. And that is what she was going to do. But first, she would cool off and get groceries. And when she talked to Cherry, she would be in control. She would not turn into an emotional basket case. She would simply get to the bottom of this thing. And then she would get on with her life. And she wouldn't let Cherry or Lewis drive her out of Sisters—even if she had to fight for her right to Nona's house in court. And she would put in her one year. After that…well, who knew? But she was not going to run again. Not this time.

Chapter Twenty-four

....

It took until Saturday morning for Hope to feel calm enough to approach her sister. She had used the excuse of unloading the truck, telling herself that she'd save a few bucks if she turned it back in before the weekend. She'd avoided looking toward Cherry's house as she moved the car to the street and the U-Haul into the driveway where Monroe helped her to cart the crates into the garage. And even then, she took her time, meticulously arranging the boxes so that she could easily find things as she needed them. Just before five, she had returned the truck to the rental place, walking back slowly through town. She had been in no hurry to confront Cherry. And on Saturday morning, she still wasn't. But some unpleasant tasks, like taking out the trash, simply had to be done.

"Oh?" Cherry answered the door with a surprised expression. "What do *you* want?"

"To talk." Hope glanced behind Cherry to see if anyone else was around. She'd seen Drew loading the kids in his SUV a few minutes ago, and she had assumed Cherry was alone. "Is now a good time?"

Cherry frowned at her watch. "Well, I was just getting myself ready."

"You're fixing yourself up to go *work* on the Habitat house?" Hope could hear the accusation in her voice and knew she needed to back off a little.

"Actually, we're *dedicating* the house today. The ceremony is at ten thirty. Then we get our pictures taken for the newspaper. So, naturally, I want to look nice."

"*Naturally.*" Hope told herself to watch it—to take it down a few notches. So she attempted a smile. "But it's only eight thirty. And I noticed Drew and the kids just left."

"They're going out to his folks' ranch." Cherry said this as if it were a bad thing. And Hope remembered about the helmetless girl.

"To ride?" Hope asked hesitantly.

"Hopefully not. But they're going to discuss it. They all know that I'm dead set against it. But do you think anyone listens to me? Certainly not my husband."

"You're worried about your kids getting hurt?" Hope softened.

Cherry nodded with a furrowed brow. "Did you hear about that girl?"

"Avery told me. But I remember watching Mrs. Lawson giving lessons, and she was always so careful. And you took lessons from her and you were okay."

"I know."

"So maybe Mrs. Lawson just needs another chance. It must've been hard on her having that taken away from her."

"What about me? Don't you think it's hard on me to have my kids endangered like that?" She glared defiantly at Hope. "But, of course, you'd take their side."

"I don't think Drew or the grandparents will do anything to put your kids in danger."

Cherry had gone into the kitchen. Although uninvited, Hope had followed. "Anyway, that's not what you came over to talk about," Cherry snipped as she turned off the coffeepot.

Without waiting for an invitation, Hope sat down on one of the massive metal barstools. They appeared to have been hand-forged and were actually quite handsome. "You've really done a great job on this old house."

"Thanks." Cherry perched on a stool opposite her, watching Hope like a cat might watch its prey.

"First of all, in answer to your question, yes, I have come back to Sisters to live. I quit my job, my condo is for sale, and I plan to live in Nona's house." She almost added for at least one year, but stopped there. Cherry did not need to know everything.

"Oh…" Cherry looked truly disappointed and this both irked and hurt.

"I'm sorry if you're not happy about this. But we can both agree to keep a safe distance if that helps."

"But you don't really *want* to be here," Cherry said suddenly. "We all know you hate it here. You're only staying to get Nona's inheritance."

"That's not true."

Cherry rolled her eyes.

Hope bit her lip and waited.

"So, fine, you're going to live in Sisters. Or so you think." Cherry made a sly grin. "Just wait until winter. You might change your mind."

"And if I do…" Hope studied Cherry's face. "What do you think that means?"

Cherry just shrugged.

"No, seriously, Cherry. What do you think happens if I don't make it a year?"

"Obviously, you lose Nona's house…and her money."

"And?" Hope waited.

"And, well, I can only assume that either Faye or I might get it. Or maybe both of us."

"That's a big assumption."

"Or Daddy. I suppose he might get some, too."

"You're wrong on all accounts."

Cherry looked genuinely shocked.

"Do you want to know who gets it—gets everything if I don't stay here?"

Cherry just nodded.

"The Humane Society gets most. The local dog shelter gets a nice chunk of change. And several of Nona's other favorite charities get the rest. Including your beloved Habitat for Humanity, which I happen to feel is quite nice. In fact, if I make it for the whole year, which does remain to be seen, I plan to share portions of Nona's money with all those causes anyway. So, there you go, mystery solved."

"That's so unfair!" Cherry slapped her hand on the granite countertop.

"Why? It was Nona's money. The reason it's called a will is because it was her *will* that her estate be handled like this."

"What if we contest it?"

"*We?*" Hope just laughed.

"Fine. I should've known you wouldn't help me."

"Why should you *need* help, Cherry?"

She didn't answer, just sat there pouting.

"Now that I've answered your question, Cherry, I have a question for you."

"What?" She narrowed her eyes like she probably had no intention of answering.

"What is going on between you and Lewis Garson?" Hope watched her sister closely.

"We're friends." Cherry got a catty little smile. "Like I already told you."

"I think you're more than just friends."

"What if we are?" Cherry leaned forward. "Would that make you insanely jealous?"

This time Hope just shrugged.

"It would, wouldn't it? Admit it."

"Mostly it would make me sad."

"Why?"

"Because *you are married*, Cherry. Remember?"

"I won't be for long."

"*What?*"

"I want out."

Hope was too stunned to respond.

"Don't you go judging me."

"I'm not. I'm just surprised."

"Well, don't be. Lots of people get divorced. Look at Faye. And Drew isn't the man I thought he was when I married him. I just didn't know that then. But now I know what I want."

"And that would be Lewis?"

Cherry looked like the proverbial kid caught with her hand in the cookie jar. "Yes, if you must know, it is Lewis. He and I are so much better suited to each other than Drew and I will ever be."

"What about your children?"

"They'll be fine. Good grief, half of their friends have parents who've divorced and remarried."

"So that's your plan?" Hope was amazed at how calmly she was taking this…at least on the outside. "Divorce Drew and marry Lewis. Just like that?"

"Well, if you must know, I had hoped to inherit Nona's little house when she passed. I was going to move out of here and into there. Or else make Drew move into there. I hadn't really figured all the details out yet. And then with her money, I would buy myself some time and maybe even have some fun or travel or whatever—because you know I never got to do those things, not like you did. And then after the divorce was final and a respectable amount of time had gone by, then Lewis and I could get married. But only after I'd done some things I want to do." Cherry looked at Hope as if this had been the most sensible plan in the world. Then she frowned. "But then you came along and ruined everything."

"By inheriting Nona's estate, you mean?"

"Yes. And moving back here. And don't think I haven't noticed that you've been flirting with Lewis as well. I'm sure you're only doing that to get back at me."

"To get back at you?"

"Because of Drew."

Hope drew in a quick breath then simply nodded. "I see."

"And don't you see how Drew and I were way too young to get married back then? What a mistake it was?" Cherry's big blue eyes got bigger, the expression she used when appealing to someone's sympathies. "And if only I'd had family around at the time—someone who cared a whit about me, they would've told me that I was making a big mistake. They would've warned me. But instead, I just blundered right into it. And look where it got me."

Hope heard the accusation, but it was unbelievable. "Are you saying I should've said or done something to stop you?"

"Well, Mom was dead. Dad was checked out and missing her.

Faye lived in Seattle. And Nona didn't say much. You were the closest one to me. Yes, maybe you should've said something, Hope."

"That is absurd."

"Why is that absurd? You were older than me. You were the sensible—"

"I wasn't even two years older than you, Charity. And I was only eighteen when you and Drew started dating. And that wasn't exactly a comfortable situation for me. Little sister steals big sister's boyfriend, and big sister is supposed to step in and say they shouldn't get married. Get real."

"Your EX boyfriend, Hope. Don't forget, you broke up with Drew, remember?"

"Yes. My ex-boyfriend that you swooped in and grabbed the moment I was gone. Even if I was done with that relationship, you put me in an awkward position. And if you honestly think I could've stormed into town and put my foot down, well, you need a serious reality check. Besides that you were..." Hope stopped herself.

"What?" Cherry narrowed her eyes. "I was *what*?"

"You know what."

"Who told you that?"

"Does it matter?"

"Drew told you, didn't he?"

"He might've mentioned something." There was no way Hope was going to bring Avery into this mess. Besides, Drew *had* mentioned it.

"It figures. Probably that night he was over there supposedly helping with your plumbing problems, right? But really, he was pouring out his heart, saying what a horrible wife I am and how he wishes he never married me. *Right?*"

"I'll admit he seemed unhappy. But that's not what he said. Besides, you're the one who just admitted that you want out of your marriage. That you and Lewis are having an…well, whatever it is that's going on between you two." Hope stood up. She had heard enough. More than enough.

"You mean Lewis didn't tell you what's going on?" Cherry stood, too.

"He told me to talk to you. And now I have."

"But you're going to go back and talk to him now, aren't you?" Cherry had come around to the other side of the counter and was actually standing in front of Hope as though she was trying to block her from leaving, which was perfectly ridiculous, considering Hope was about eight inches taller than her baby sister.

"Would that bother you, Charity?"

Cherry seemed to be considering this. "Maybe not."

"So, there you have it. Nothing to worry about."

"Don't tell him I said that, please." Cherry was pleading now, almost desperate. "That bit about leaving Drew for Lewis. Please, don't tell him that, Hope. I was just getting carried away. Don't tell him."

"Of course I won't tell him. Why would I tell him?"

"You swear you won't?" Cherry had a hold of Hope's arm now. It was surprising what a strong grip she had for such a petite person.

"I said I wouldn't." And then Hope shook her arm free and left.

She went back to her house and into her room where she closed the door and sat on the bed and attempted to process all she had just heard. Cherry wanted out of her marriage. She had wanted Nona's house and money as part of her escape plan. And then, after she'd had some "fun," she wanted to settle down into a respectable marriage with Lewis. But most of all, Cherry did not want Hope to tell Lewis.

She even tried to swear her sister to secrecy. And Hope had given her word.

Still, something about the whole thing was fishy. And Hope was pretty sure it was Cherry. Even so, Hope had no idea what to do about it. Or if she should do anything at all. And so she went into the kitchen, and after locating the celery-colored paint, she began to paint the wall above the lower cabinets. It might even be therapeutic.

"Hey, Hope," said Brian as he came into the house with a cardboard box. "How's it going?"

"Okay." She smiled. "Thought I'd get some painting done."

He looked surprised. "Don't you want to let Lewis finish that?"

"Huh?"

"The man does good work." He nodded toward the living room. "And I hear his rates can't be beat."

"What are you saying?"

Brian looked confused now. "You didn't know that Lewis did all this painting for you?"

"Not exactly." She set down her brush.

"Oh, man, I hope I didn't blow some surprise. I thought it was pretty nice of him." Brian cocked his head. "In fact, I thought maybe Lewis was putting the move on you. I mean some guys bring chocolates and flowers; I guess some come over and paint your house."

Hope didn't know what to say.

"And don't get me wrong," he said quickly. "I like you, too. But not enough to work for free. Lewis has been the one pushing me to get the place done while you were gone. And since he's the one cutting me my checks, I was motivated."

She looked at the clock on the stove. It was 10:27. "I heard there's a Habitat House dedication at ten thirty this morning. Do you know if that's open to the public?"

"Sure. Anyone can go. They even serve coffee and donuts. Not as good as yours, though."

She was putting the lid back on the paint can now. "Do you know where this particular house is located?"

Brian told her where it was then chuckled. "Let me guess, you're going over to tell Lewis thank you?"

"Something like that." She already had her car keys in hand. "See you later."

By the time she found the house, the dedication had already started, but she just parked her car then went over to stand behind the small crowd of spectators. Hope wasn't the least bit surprised to see Cherry up front. Dressed in baby blue Capri pants and a white sun-top that showed off her tan, she stood next to Lewis with a sweet smile on her shiny lips. Hope wondered if she still used Cheery Cherry lip gloss. Anyway, the girl was picture perfect. Fortunately, Cherry didn't seem to notice her sister. And Hope attempted to remain in the shadow of the large elderly man in front of her.

The mayor's speech finally ended, the ribbon was cut, and the family was presented with a key and several other things. Then Erica's friend Bobbie shot some photos for the newspaper. Hope wondered if Bobbie might try to cut Cherry out of the shot since she was at the end, almost as if she'd ducked in there at the last possible second simply to be close to Lewis.

People began milling about now, helping themselves to donuts and coffee and visiting. Some were taking tours of the house. As the crowd

of spectators loosened up, Hope went over to where Cherry and Lewis
were still standing together. Cherry's back was to Hope now, but she
was happily chattering at Lewis, telling him about how she'd made the
kitchen curtains at the last minute and how pleased the new owners
were and how she was going to give the teenage daughter sewing
lessons so she could sew her own curtains. But Lewis's eyes were on
Hope, and his expression was a mix of bewilderment and perhaps
even fear. Did he think Hope was here to knock off her baby sister? To
assure him she didn't have murder in her heart, Hope simply smiled.
He smiled back and Cherry turned to see who he was looking at.

"Hello, Cherry," Hope said casually. "Hey, Lewis."

"What're you doing here?" Cherry asked in an artificially sweet tone.

"I wanted to see the Habitat House." She turned her attention
to Lewis. "And I wanted to thank you. Brian just informed me that
you were the one who painted my house. I had no idea. That was
incredibly kind and generous." Now a part of her—a small and
childish part—was still a bit worried and slightly suspicious, because
there still remained the possibility that he had simply painted the
house to make it easier to sell. And yet Lewis was an intelligent man.
He could've easily hired someone else to do that. There had to be
another reason he had done it himself. And she was here to find out
why. "You do excellent work," she told him.

His eyes lit up. "Thank you."

"Lewis helped paint the Habitat House, too," Cherry said
importantly. "He likes helping out those in need."

"But you said you'd like to see the house." Lewis directed this to
Hope. "Would you like me to give you the grand tour?"

"I would love that."

And, just like that, he tipped his chin to Cherry then turned away, escorting Hope toward the front door.

"I want to apologize," she told him as they entered the house.

"So do I," he said quietly. Then, in a more formal voice, probably for the sake of the others touring the house, he told her about the volunteers and the construction. But as he spoke, he seemed to be directing her straight through the house then out the back door until they were standing by themselves on a small deck.

"And over there," he nodded toward town, which was just a block away, "is a place to get coffee. Would you like to see that as well?"

She giggled. "Yes, as a matter of fact, I would."

Chapter Twenty-five
....

"I really am sorry," Hope told Lewis once again. They were seated with coffee now, and though she felt nervous and there were butterflies in her stomach, she was finally ready to throw her cards on the table. "I can't believe I said all those horrible things to you, Lewis. My only excuse is...well, I was jealous."

His brows shot up. "*You* were jealous?"

"It's humbling to admit it, but *yes,* I was jealous." As embarrassing as this confession was, she was relieved to have it out there in the open now.

"Of who?"

"Cherry."

Lewis actually laughed.

"Why is that so funny?"

"Because it's so out there. Totally left field."

"Left field?" She considered this. "So are you saying that it's not even slightly possible that you might find Cherry to be attractive?"

"Oh, she's cute enough, in that bubbly cheerleader sort of way. But definitely not *my* type."

She could tell by his eyes he was being honest, and yet she still wondered. "So, tell me then, Counselor, why did you clandestinely meet my cute, bubbly, cheerleader-sort-of sister in a bar that day?"

His brow creased as if trying to recall this incident. "Oh, the lounge at the—hey, you mean you were there that day?"

"Never mind. I was there. I saw you two meet, embrace, then duck into the lounge. You were there at least thirty minutes or longer."

"You were timing us?" His dark eyes seemed to twinkle as if this was all terribly amusing.

"What were you doing there?"

He reached over and placed his hand on hers. "After your grandmother died, Cherry had called and left several urgent-sounding messages—both in my office and my home phone. I'd been pretty busy seeing to the details of the funeral service and all that, since it was my responsibility as trustee. Your grandmother didn't want to put that on any of her family, which I think was thoughtful on her part."

"Yes…?" Hope waited.

"So I finally called Cherry, and she said she needed legal counsel. When I told her to come on by my office, she said she couldn't."

"She *couldn't*?"

"She said that it was because of Josh Thompson. He's a surveyor who rents office space from me. She didn't want Josh to see her there and report back to Drew since those two are pretty good friends."

"So she didn't want Drew to know she was talking to you."

"No…" Now Lewis looked concerned—as if he'd said too much.

"And I don't expect you to tell me what she wanted to talk to you about." Hope nodded. "But I do appreciate hearing the circumstances surrounding it. And it makes sense."

"The reason I hugged her was because she was crying and your grandmother had just died, and it seemed like the normal thing to do. That's all."

"Thank you for explaining that. I do understand."

"Good." He shook his head and chuckled. "I still can't believe that you were jealous, too."

"Too?" She studied him.

"Wasn't it obvious?"

"What?"

"I figured I must've looked about as green as your guest room when I saw you catering to Brian with your little breakfast surprise yesterday. And then you seemed disappointed to see me and that stung a little."

"I was caught off guard. I fixed that for Brian because I'd promised him coffee a couple weeks ago. And I was so pleased with the work that had been done while I was gone. But now I realize that had more to do with you than with him." She gave him an apologetic smile. "And then I went and accused you of possibly selling my house out from under me. Will you forgive me?"

"Of course. The truth was, I had hoped that if your house was all put together and looking as nice as I suspect it will be in a couple of weeks…well, maybe that would've made you change your mind about living here. Well, that and something else…" He smiled mysteriously.

"And I had already changed my mind." She put her hand on his now. "I decided I was coming back no matter how bad things seemed. I was going to work through them because I was hoping there was a reward at the end. And I'm not talking about money."

"So…" He was beaming now. And she suspected she was, too. And whether or not they were being observed by onlookers, in a town so small that the news would spread like wildfire, she did not care.

"So…here we are." She felt slightly lightheaded.

"So, would you do me the honor of going out with me tonight?"

"On a real live date?" She feigned shyness.

LOVE FINDS YOU IN SISTERS, OREGON

"That's right. On a real live date."

"I would love to!"

His smile broadened. "And I would love to sit here and talk with you for hours on end, but I promised a client to meet him for lunch, and I'm already running late."

"As much as I hate to let you go, I will." She reluctantly moved her hands away from his and he stood. But then he leaned across the table, cupped her chin in his hand, and kissed her lightly on the lips. And she honestly thought she was going to faint. Or perhaps even swoon if women still did that sort of thing. Fortunately she was seated so there was no fear of falling too far. And she simply smiled and nodded as he told her he'd pick her up at six thirty then left.

She wasn't sure how long she sat there, just basking in the afterglow, but by the time she went back to the Habitat House to get her car, everyone was gone. And when she got home, she discovered that Monroe was up and had picked up painting where she'd left off. And he was doing a pretty good job of it, too.

"You look happy," he told her as she set her purse down to admire his work.

"I am happy," she told him. "I don't think I've ever been so happy."

"Cool." He dipped the brush into the can. "My mom called here."

"How did she sound?"

"Different."

"Different good? Or different bad?"

"Hard to say. She wanted you to call her. On her cell phone."

"Okay." Hope headed for the living room.

"And I think I should finish this up in a few hours. Then I'm going over to Alex's house, if that's okay."

"That's fine. But could you write down his number for me in case I need to reach you? And keep track of your painting time—remember you're getting paid."

Hope decided to call Faye in the privacy of her bedroom, just in case the conversation got sticky in regard to Monroe. But to her surprise, Faye sounded almost pleasant. "I heard you were back in town," she began. "Do you think we could meet for lunch?"

"Sure," Hope said eagerly. Perhaps if they were in a public place, Faye would be more likely to keep her emotions in check. "How about the deli?"

"I'm on my way. Want me to order for you?"

Hope told Faye what she wanted, and then finally took the time to clean up a little. She couldn't believe she'd just been sitting with Lewis, having that wonderful conversation, and she hadn't even brushed her hair today. Obviously he didn't mind.

Then Hope hurried on over to the deli. Faye was already seated at an outdoor table. As Hope got closer, she could see that her older sister looked much better than the last time she'd seen her. Faye was dressed somewhat stylishly, and her hair was different. "You look great," Hope told her as she sat down. "What did you do to your hair?"

"I put a rinse on to cover the gray. Then I went in for a trim."

"Very nice."

"So how are you? How is Monroe?"

"We're both doing well, thanks. Right now Monroe is painting my kitchen. And he's a good painter. I hope it's okay if I pay him."

"It's okay with me."

"And after he finishes, he's going to Alex's house."

Faye's brow creased. "Who's Alex?"

"A friend. He's into art and plays the guitar and wants to teach Monroe some chords. He told Monroe that Sisters has a great music and art program."

"That's what I've heard. So do you think Monroe really wants to stay here?"

"I think he's trying, Faye. But he's going to need some help from you, too."

"I went to see a counselor."

"Really?"

"She's pretty good. She gave me permission to be angry."

"You needed permission?" Hope tried not to remember the last time Faye had torn into her.

"Sort of. I mean, yes, I was blasting everyone around me. But then I'd feel guilty."

Hope just nodded.

"But Janna, that's my counselor, says that I have the right to be angry at Jeff and the way things have gone. But I don't have the right to hurt people with my anger. So I want you to know that I'm sorry. I'll try to control myself better."

Hope smiled. "She sounds like a good counselor."

"She really is. I'll meet with her weekly for a while, for an hour. Then pare it down later."

"Does she do marriage counseling?"

"Marriage counseling?" Faye looked confused.

"I mean for Cherry and Drew."

"Oh…I think so. Do they need help?"

"Don't say you heard it from me."

"I thought everything was peachy-keen with them. Cherry

always acts like they're the happy family—like her life's just a bowl of cherries." Faye chuckled at her pun.

"Cherry is a pretty good actress."

"Yeah, I remember her as a little girl, doing all sorts of things to get our attention, trying to act older, trying to keep up, whining when she couldn't. I still remember the time I caught her in my makeup. She'd made a huge mess, and I was so mad. That's when I got that lock put on my bedroom door."

"I remember that. And I have to admit I thought she was a totally spoiled brat. She was always conniving to get her way, manipulating people, trying to be the center of everything. But now, I wonder if all her antics weren't just a cry for help. Like she was slipping through the cracks."

"What do you mean, slipping through the cracks?"

"Well, you were all grown up and doing your own thing, locking her out of your room. I was always pushing her away, too. We might've been close in age, but we were so different. She wanted me to play Barbies, and I wanted to escape her. Plus, I had Nona. And Mom seemed like she was kind of tired of being a mom, you know, like she wanted to go climbing and hiking and have her own life. Sometimes I wonder if Cherry didn't feel kind of left out."

"Maybe so." Faye paused as the waitress set their lunches down. "And sometimes," she spoke quietly after the girl left, "I think if Mom hadn't been killed in that wreck…well, that our parents would've divorced on down the line anyway."

"Really?"

"Don't you remember how they fought at times?"

"I guess…but that's when I'd run over to Nona's. And I'd tell her about it, and she'd say that was just the Italian way. You fought and then you made up."

"Maybe so…but I don't know."

Hope took a bite of her chicken salad. "Life's funny, huh?"

Faye just shrugged as she picked up her burger.

"Things we thought were a certain way as kids start to look different as adults."

"You know what else Janna told me?" Faye said suddenly.

"What?"

"That I'm pessimistic."

Hope tried not to laugh.

"And that I always expect the worst thing to happen, and so I might even bring it on myself. Like I always thought Jeff would cheat on me. Oh, I never told anyone, but in my heart, I was afraid it would happen. And then it did."

"But you don't think you caused it to happen?"

"Not exactly. But my negative attitude could've had an impact. And then there's Monroe. You know how I'm always just sure he's going to ruin his life?"

Hope nodded as she chewed.

"Well, Janna says that I could be influencing him in that direction."

"Really?"

"So I'm trying not to be so pessimistic."

Then Hope told Faye about Monroe's observation—about how the three sisters named after the three mountains hadn't exactly been living up to their names.

"Monroe said that?"

"He did. And I had to admit that I haven't been very hopeful for most of my life. But that's changing now. I have more hope today than ever before."

"You do seem different."

Hope considered telling her about Lewis, but figured it could wait.

"And it's true that I tend to lack faith. That's something else Janna mentioned. That I don't have much faith in people, the human race, or life in general. She thinks it's associated with losing Mom like that."

"I think it took its toll on all of us." Hope suspected her cautious way of living the past twelve years had a lot to do with losing her mom.

"Isn't it weird how we all went our separate ways after she died? Some families are pulled together by a tragedy. Ours was blown apart."

"But maybe we're coming back together now."

"Maybe." Faye frowned. "So what about Cherry? Why are you suddenly so concerned about her? Did she tell you something?"

"Sort of. But I probably shouldn't say too much. Except that I think she needs a friend...and a sister. And I really don't think it can be me. At least not right now."

"So, it needs to be me?"

"If you have it in you, Faye. I'm worried about her."

"I know what I'll do." Faye set her soda down with a clunk. "I'll ask Cherry to help me decorate my condo. The sale closed Friday, and I already moved in, but all I have so far is a bed and a chair. I told Jeff to just keep the furniture and everything. I want a fresh start anyway. But Cherry's actually pretty good at decorating, and I want my condo to have that Sisters lodge kind of look."

"That's brilliant," Hope agreed.

"I wanted to get it all set up in time for Monroe's birthday." Faye looked uncertain now. "In case he decides to live with me."

"That's a great plan. And speaking of his birthday, do you think it would be okay if I got him a mountain bike?"

Faye looked disappointed. "It's okay...except that's just one more reason for him to like you better."

"I don't need to, if you'd like. I just thought he could use a way to get around. But I also have a feeling that he may want a guitar before long. He seems really interested in learning to play from Alex."

"A guitar." Faye's eyes lit up. "That might just work."

They talked some more, and the whole time Hope was tempted to spill the beans about Lewis and how excited she was...and yet she didn't think Faye was ready for too much good news about someone else's life. Not until she had a few more counseling sessions and moved further along in getting beyond her ruined marriage. It could wait.

Chapter Twenty-six

. . . .

"This all feels so right," Hope told Lewis as they were leaving Jen's Garden—a tiny but amazing restaurant where they'd had the best meal imaginable beneath the trees and the stars in a sweet little garden courtyard.

"Like it's meant to be," he added as he squeezed her hand.

"Exactly."

They walked through town, finally stopping at the Coffee Company where a bluegrass band was playing outside. They got coffees and sat and listened for a bit then continued walking until the mountains, where the sun was setting, came into sight.

"Summer solstice is only a few days away." Lewis put his arm around her, pulling her close to him.

"The longest day of the year...the best summer of my life." She smiled up at him. "Does it get any better than this?"

He shook his head then kissed her. Then kissed her again... and again. Finally they stopped, and she felt slightly breathless and lightheaded, but she didn't think she was going to swoon this time.

"If I weren't suddenly the parent of a teenage boy, not to mention the keeper of a certain little dog, I'd let you keep me out until the wee hours of the night," she told him. "But I should probably get home and check on Andy, and see if Monroe is back. He might need a ride."

"I have a feeling you'll make a great mom someday," Lewis said as they walked back through town.

"Do you want to have children someday?" she asked, knowing that this was quite a leap in a relationship where the word *marriage* had never even come up. And yet, hadn't they already made a big jump today? What was one more?

"I do want children," he told her. "But I'm not in any big hurry."

"I used to worry that I was going to wait too long," she confessed. "You know, you hear about women who get into their forties and find out it's not as easy as they thought. Now it doesn't concern me that much. Just having a dog and a nephew is a handful."

"But you do want children, don't you?" He turned and looked at her.

"Of course. Someday I plan on having a daughter that I will name after Nona." She laughed. "A little dark-haired Madolina. Can you imagine?"

"I can."

And although they hadn't said anything about this being their child together, Hope knew that it would be. Or at least she hoped.

Lewis took Hope and Monroe to church with him the next day. Hope had been surprised that Monroe had so readily agreed, but then she had sort of tempted him with an offer to go early-birthday shopping afterward. Lewis had told her he knew a thing or two about mountain bikes since he was on his third one now.

But what Hope hadn't considered, or remembered, was that Cherry and her family went to the same church as Lewis. And so when she, Lewis, and Monroe were seated in front of Cherry's family, it was a bit uncomfortable. Or perhaps as the pastor was saying, God was simply at work in ways that confused mere humans. Whatever the case, everyone was congenial when they stood around to visit afterward. And Drew even informed Hope that Avery was no longer grounded.

"Do you still need help at Nona's house?" Avery asked with big brown eyes.

"I sure do." Hope put an arm around Avery. "And I missed you."

"I missed you, too."

"I have things to unpack and put away, and there's still the garden to work on, and all sorts of things."

"Cool!"

Cherry didn't say much. But at least she tried to smile. Then, when she got her chance, she ducked away on the pretext of helping with the coffee table. "There goes our little Charity," Drew said with a sarcastic edge, "off to help anyone in need."

"We'll see you around," Hope told them.

"I'll come over tomorrow morning if it's okay," Avery said as they parted ways.

"That's perfect," Hope called back.

Then they went to look at mountain bikes. Lewis's friend owned the shop, and after Hope listened to him explaining what was good, better, and best in a bike, she decided that best made most sense. She also decided that her budget, which was already getting tight, could only afford one bike. And that would be for Monroe.

"What about you?" Monroe asked her. "I thought you were getting a bike, too, Aunt Hope."

"Not today." She pointed to the helmets. "You should also go pick out one of those. And if I ever hear of you not wearing it, I'll—"

"I know," he told her. "It's the law."

"I know Lewis has a bike rack," she told Monroe as she stuck the receipt in her purse, "but maybe you'd like to ride it home?"

His grin was her answer. "Thanks so much, Aunt Hope," he told her again. "And then, if it's okay, I'll change clothes and ride over to show Alex. Unless you want me to paint or some—"

"No," she told him. "I think we all need a day off." She also thought it would be nice to have some alone time with Lewis. Unless he had other plans.

But then he dropped them both off, told her he'd see her later, and then left. She couldn't help but feel a little let down. But instead of moping, she let Andy out and decided it was time to plant something in the window boxes as well as to get some mulch for the garden, and perhaps a new wheelbarrow. Surely her budget could manage that much.

She was just sitting in the backyard, making a list of things to get at the hardware store, when Cherry came through the back gate—and the way she was walking looked like she was on a mission, and not a good one, either. As Andy started to bark, an alarm went off in Hope's head, telling her to make a run for it. But it was too late.

"You told him, didn't you?"

"Told who?" As she scooped up Andy to stop his barking, Hope had no doubt about whom Cherry meant.

"Lewis, you told him everything. I could see it in his face. Yesterday, when you crashed the Habitat—"

"I was told that was open to the public."

"Whatever. Anyway, you told him then, didn't you? And then you probably acted all hurt and asked him to take you and Monroe to church…right?"

"Wrong."

"Oh, I know how you worked it. Don't think you can pull this over on me." Cherry's eyes narrowed. "But you won't get away with it."

"Get away with what?"

"Stealing him."

"Oh, Cherry…" Hope shook her head. She actually felt sorry for her baby sister. How could anyone be so delusional?

"Don't *oh, Cherry* me like you think I'm still a baby…like I'm too little, too dumb to understand. I *do* understand."

"Not really, Cherry. You don't."

"Well, then why don't you explain it to me, big sister?"

"It's impossible to steal something from someone who doesn't own that certain something."

"Of course I didn't own Lewis. No one owns a guy. But that doesn't mean you didn't steal him from me. Or at least you're trying to. Whether you succeed or not remains to be seen."

Hope didn't know how to respond. But instead of losing it, she closed her eyes and petted Andy. She was ready to silently count to ten if necessary.

"But you know how I feel about him," Cherry continued to loudly state her case. "I told you that I was leaving Drew—that I was willing to divorce him for Lewis—and then you went and told Lewis the whole thing. I know you did. And you probably made me sound like a wicked witch, scaring him off just so you could keep him for yourself."

"That's not true."

Hope felt Andy wriggling in her arms, and she opened her eyes to see Lewis walking toward them, wheeling with him the exact bike that she had wanted. But his expression was grim. "I'm sorry to have eavesdropped, but I heard voices back here…and then since you were talking about me, I listened."

"Oh, Lewis…" Cherry's hand flew to her mouth. "Those were just emotions doing the talking." She spoke quickly as if she thought she could sweep it all under the rug. And maybe she could, since Hope had no idea how much Lewis had heard. "I think I'm still getting over losing Nona. You know how broken up I was. And Hope's over here living in her house instead of Nona. And I suppose I'm just overreacting to everything—blowing it out of proportion. You know how sisters can be." She forced a smile. "We sometimes bring out the worst in each other."

He leaned the bike against a tree and walked over to stand by Hope, putting his arm around her in a protective way. "Well, what you said isn't true, Cherry. Hope never told me any of those things. And Hope certainly didn't steal me from anyone." He turned and smiled at Hope. "My heart was yours for the taking the moment we met—or re-met, since I've always had a fondness for you."

"Always?"

"*Good grief!*" Cherry turned away in disgust. But as she did, she let out a gasp, and both Hope and Lewis looked to see Drew by the fence. And judging by his face, he'd witnessed the whole ugly mess. "How long have you been standing there?" Cherry asked in a voice that was strangely void of emotion.

"Long enough." He just shook his head. "I'm glad the kids are inside, though."

Hope's heart went out to Cherry just then. Oh, she was thoroughly perturbed at her baby sister, not to mention hurt. But really, Cherry's life just seemed to get worse and worse. Unless Hope was mistaken, South Sister was getting ready to blow.

"Let's go inside," Hope said quietly to Lewis. He just nodded, and with Andy on their heels, they hurried into the house where Hope picked up the phone and called Faye. "I think Cherry could really use a friend today," she said quickly. "I can't give you the details, but trust me, the girl is in bad shape right now—and probably about to get worse. She desperately needs a sister, and I seriously doubt that it can be me." Faye promised to check on her, then Hope sat down and let out a loud sigh. "I'm sorry you had to see that," she told Lewis.

"Wow, I had no idea that was going on." He was sitting on the sofa with his arms dangling between his knees and a totally mystified expression on his face. "I mean Cherry's always been nice to me. Too nice, I'm thinking now. And she always seemed to be around, too. Whether it was a fund-raiser or Habitat or whatever—it seemed I was always running into that girl. And yet, she was pleasant, always saying sweet things. And sometimes we'd talk about your grandmother and how her health and spirits were doing. And it just seemed like she was being a good friend. Really, that's all I ever thought it was. Even yesterday when you told me you were jealous of her, I thought that was odd. But now I understand."

Hope wasn't sure if she was imagining it or not, but she thought she heard voices next door. She opened the door and listened. "Whoa," she said as she went outside. "That is not good. The kids shouldn't be hearing that." Lewis was behind her as she jogged next door, ringing the doorbell and knocking loudly. Avery answered, and her face was pale. "Go with Lewis," Hope told her. "I'll talk to your parents." Avery didn't even argue.

Hope could hear the voices coming from the den. Did they think their children couldn't hear them there? But before she confronted them, she ran to find Harrison. He seemed rather oblivious, plugged into his Gameboy. "Go on outside," she told him. "Lewis and I are going to take you kids for ice cream."

"Ice cream?" He nodded and, still playing his game, headed for the door. Once he was out, Hope braced herself as she knocked on the den door, barely cracking it open to call in. "Hey, you guys, I'm taking your kids for ice cream and to the park. I've got my cell phone if you need anything."

"That's right," Cherry yelled angrily. "Steal my kids, too."

"Shut up," Drew told her. "That's fine, Hope. Thanks."

And she had barely shut the door before they were yelling again. Hopefully they weren't given to violence. She had no reason to think Drew was that type, and Cherry was probably too small to do him much harm. And maybe Nona was right. Maybe Italians fought and then made up. She prayed that would happen, and that Faye would get here soon.

When she found Lewis and the kids, they had rounded up Avery and Harrison's bicycles and helmets and were wheeling them into her yard. "I thought we could all meet for ice cream since these dudes are under the impression we're doing that." He winked at Harrison. "That way your aunt can try out her new bike."

She had completely forgotten about the bike. "That's for me?"

"Of course. I would've gotten you a helmet, but I wasn't sure what kind."

"We have some extra helmets," Avery called out.

"Great," Lewis told her. "You guys get your helmets and I'll run home to get my bike. My guess is we'll meet up in about ten minutes or less."

"Less," shouted Harrison as he clicked the strap of his helmet in place.

And Harrison was right, because ten minutes later, they were sitting at a picnic table eating ice cream.

"Do you know why our mom is so mad at our dad?" Avery asked quietly.

"Not exactly," Hope told her. "But I do think they need to talk about it."

"They're not talking," Harrison declared, "they're yelling."

"Sometimes grown-ups act like children, don't they?" Lewis told them.

"And they get mad at us when we yell in the house." Harrison caught a drip before it fell from his cone.

"Aunt Faye is on her way over there now," Hope said. "Maybe she can help them to figure things out."

Before long, they were on their way to the park. It turned out that an outdoor market of crafts and things was in full swing, including music in the gazebo. Hope gave both kids five dollars and told them to meet them back by the gazebo after they found a treasure. "And stay together," she called as they left.

Then she and Lewis sat down in the grass amongst the bikes and helmets and just listened to the music.

"They're going to be okay," Lewis told her.

"Oh…" She nodded. "Do I look that worried?"

"A little."

She attempted a smile. "I was just thinking of the irony—the old maid aunt returns to Sisters and—"

"I wouldn't exactly describe you as an old maid." He pushed a strand of loose hair away from her forehead.

"You know what I mean. The unmarried and childless aunt returns and within a month's time she accumulates one orphan dog, her grandmother's house, one runaway teenager, two confused children—"

"And a partridge in a pear tree," Lewis finished for her.

Hope laughed. "But, seriously, is that weird or what?"

"I don't think you're going to get stuck raising your sisters' children."

"Not that I wouldn't take care of them…I mean if it were really necessary. Because I do love them."

"I know you do. They are all great kids."

"I'd just rather they had their own parents, but healthy, you know?"

He nodded. "I know. I also know that these kids need some relatives around for them. You know what they say about it taking a village to raise a child."

Hope looked around the colorful park where kids and dogs and grown-ups were enjoying the sunshine and music and crafts. "And this is one amazing little village for it, too." She reached for Lewis's hand. "You know, more than ever, I feel like I'm home."

"Me, too."

Chapter Twenty-seven
....

By Monroe's fifteenth birthday, Drew and Cherry had been to Faye's counselor Janna twice. Hope had no idea if it was going to save their marriage or not, especially since Drew had taken to staying at his folks' place—sometimes with the kids, sometimes not. But Hope felt encouraged that they were at least trying.

"No way," Monroe yelped when he saw his mom emerging from her room with a guitar case tied with a big red bow in her arms. "Last but not least," she told him. "Happy birthday."

With wide eyes, Monroe opened the case, removing a beautiful guitar, and immediately he began to play a chord, which didn't sound half bad. "I think it needs tuning," he told them.

"That's even nicer than mine," Alex said.

"We'll have to do some jamming."

"And I think I'll move in with my mom," Monroe told Alex. "Since her house is closer to you than Aunt Hope's." He glanced at Hope. "You don't mind, do you?"

Hope exchanged a look with Faye. "Not as long as you come by to visit."

"Of course."

Hope went over to where Cherry was standing in the kitchen, just looking out the window. They had barely begun to speak to each other and that was only a cautious "hello" from one yard to the other. But Hope thought it was time to push it a bit further. "You're really making Faye's house look great," she told her. "I can't believe how easily decorating comes to you. You're really a natural with color and texture and everything."

"Really? You think so?" Cherry seemed hungry for this recognition.

"I do. And when my furniture and things come from the city after the sale of my condo closes, I hope you'll come over and help me figure out how to arrange things. I'm worried my sofa might be too big and overwhelm that small living room."

"Sometimes a small room can handle one extra large piece of furniture," Cherry told her. "As long as it's placed right."

"Well, then maybe you can help me place it right."

"Sure."

"Are we still going to do some mountain climbing this summer, Aunt Hope?" asked Monroe. "Because Alex wants to come sometime, too, if it's okay."

"Absolutely," Hope told him. "I was thinking about attacking South Sister soon. It's a good warm-up climb since it's only a day trip. Maybe even by next weekend—anyone else want to come?"

"I'm in," Lewis told her.

"That's two." Hope held up two fingers.

"Don't forget me and Alex—that's four." Monroe glanced at his mom now. "How about you, Mom?"

"Oh, I don't think so. I'm not in very good shape."

"You've been walking a lot," Hope reminded her. "And you could go as far as you like up the mountain and then wait."

"Wait? By *myself*?" Faye cocked her head to one side with uncertainty.

"There are lots of climbers and hikers up there," Hope assured her. "Really, it's safe."

"I want to go, too," said Avery.

"Me, too," chimed Harrison.

Avery looked at her mom. "If that's okay."

"South Sister?" Cherry frowned. "Isn't that the one with volcanic activity? Sounds a little scary to me."

Now Faye laughed. "Don't worry, Cherry, I think South Sister already blew her top."

Cherry narrowed her eyes, and for a moment Hope thought she was going to blow again. But she simply smiled. "Right." She looked at Hope. "Fine then, if Avery and Harrison want to go, I better go, too."

"How about you, Dad?" Avery asked Drew hopefully. "Can you come, too?"

He shrugged.

"Come on, Dad," Harrison urged. "You're not afraid of South Sister, are you?"

Drew glanced at his wife then almost cracked a smile. "No, her blast is way worse than her bite."

"Great," Hope said, "and if the South Sister climb is a success, maybe some of us will want to tackle Middle Sister in August while the weather is still good."

The sale of Hope's condo unit closed the Friday before the South Sister climb. But in all honesty, Hope wasn't sure which was more thrilling, knowing she had made that final break from Portland or watching her family all climbing South Sister together. Sure, not all of them made it clear to the top—but still it was an amazing day. And nothing she would've predicted a month ago.

Faye begged out about two-thirds of the way up. "I gave it my best," she told Hope. And Hope agreed. Then Harrison, who looked a little wilted, offered to stay behind to "keep Aunt Faye company." And since they had a nice spot in the sun, and Hope was a little concerned that the thin air and cooler temps might not be the best for Andy, she asked them to doggy sit for her.

Avery was next to wear out. She was slowing down shortly before the summit, and Drew, who had been walking with her and holding up quite well, wanted to stay behind with his daughter. Then, to Hope's surprised delight, Cherry, unlike her last and only attempt to climb this or any mountain, decided to continue. Though she was obviously tired, she seemed determined to keep going. And in an attempt to give her baby sister the limelight she never seemed to get enough of, Hope asked Lewis to slow down so that Cherry could pass them and be the first in their climbing party to reach the top. And she did!

"South Sister finally conquers South Sister!" Cherry yelled loudly enough for God and the world to hear, as she struck the mountain-climber victory pose. A couple of startled hikers from California questioned her about her unusual statement, and when she explained her name and her sisters' names, the guys were so impressed that they took her photo and one of them promised to post it on his Facebook site.

Lewis and Hope waited again, allowing Monroe and Alex to be the next ones to the top. And, by their faces, it was plain to see that this was going to be an unforgettable moment, and they

posed so that Cherry could take their photo, too. And finally,
Hope and Lewis made their way to the peak, waiting for the
others to head down before they exchanged a kiss. Lewis had
promised to kiss her on all three mountaintops—maybe not all in
one summer, but in due time—and Hope planned to make him
keep his word.

All in all, it was a great day. An extremely great day. And at the
foot of the mountain, as the three tired but happy Bartolli sisters
locked arms and posed for a photo with the much larger Three
Sisters looming tall and majestic behind them, Hope wondered if
their mother—and perhaps Nona, too—might be smiling down on
them. And as they continued on to their cars, Hope remembered
how grief and guilt had been her constant companions when
returning to Sisters. But now they were replaced with joy and
peace…and wrapped in love. Truly amazing!

In the parking lot, they all went their separate ways. Faye took
the two unexplainably energetic teen boys, who were now begging
for pizza, with her. Without saying much to each other, as usual,
Drew and Cherry packed their own worn-out kids and gear into the
backseat. Hope was pretty sure those two wouldn't be complaining
about bedtime tonight.

Then Lewis and Hope, along with Andy, got into his SUV. But
instead of going straight home, Lewis went to a spot where they could
enjoy the last rays of sunlight.

"I hope you don't mind if we don't go straight home," he said as he
helped her out of the car. "But I packed us a little picnic dinner." Then
he produced a picnic basket and cooler and a nice thick quilt. Before
long, they were comfortably situated in front of what Hope felt was

the most beautiful scene on the planet. "You even thought to bring Andy's food," she commented as Andy slept peacefully in her lap. "You really think of everything, don't you?"

"I try." He grinned as he pulled out a bottle of sparkling cider, as well as two glasses, which he set on the cooler.

"Wow!" She was really impressed. "What are we celebrating?"

"Well, for one thing, a successful mountain climb." He was working on opening the cider.

"Yes. And kind of a family reunion as well."

He nodded. "And we can celebrate the closing of your condo in Portland." The cork popped out and went sailing.

"That's right. But how did you know that was going to happen today?"

"Just lucky, I guess." She studied his face as he took his time to fill the glasses. His expression seemed more serious than usual. But he smiled as he handed a sparkling glass to her.

"Thank you." She held it up as if to toast.

"But there is one more thing I would like to celebrate. Only I will need your permission."

"My permission?"

He nodded somberly. "I'm afraid I could be rushing things, but my only excuse is that I have absolutely no doubts."

"No doubts?" She felt her heart beating a little faster.

And then he took her glass back, set both glasses on the cooler, and proceeded to get down on one knee. "Hope Bartolli," he began, looking straight into her eyes, perhaps even into her soul, "I love you more than I ever thought possible. Will you do me the honor of marrying me?"

She sighed happily. "Yes, Lewis, I will."

Then he apologized for not having a ring yet. "But we can seal it with a kiss." So they kissed and a few minutes later he handed her back her glass, and they both made toasts to their future, which seemed brighter and better than Hope had ever hoped for. And they drank their cider and ate the delectable dinner that he'd had catered by someone who knew how to do that sort of thing. And finally, while there was still enough light to see, they piled everything back in the SUV and he began driving back toward town.

"So I guess we won't be able to get married until next June," Hope said a bit sadly.

"Next June?" He glanced at her. "Is that what you want?"

"Well, I wouldn't complain about a June wedding," she told him. "But for some reason I'd always dreamed of getting married in late September."

"Great, let's plan for a late September wedding," he said happily.

"But that's…let's see…" She did some quick mental math. "That's fifteen months away, Lewis."

"Oh, you mean September of *next* year."

"I know some people stay engaged for years," she said, "but I don't think I'm one of those."

"I'm with you there. So why wouldn't you want to get married this September?" he asked hopefully.

"I guess we could do that. But I figured I have to live in Nona's house for a full year, and it's a little bit small, but maybe it would be okay. Would you mind if—"

He laughed. "Oh, I almost forgot."

"Forgot?"

"Your grandmother had one more clause in her will, Hope."

"She did?"

"Yes. In the event that you should decide to marry—and I'll be honest with you, Hope, your grandmother had predicted this."

"This?" Hope stared at him in disbelief. "You mean you and me?"

He nodded and chuckled. "I thought she was nuts. But I tried to humor her. And she kept saying that we were perfect for each other."

"Nona was right."

"So she had this clause that if you should decide to marry before the year was up, and if I, as her trustee, deemed it a good and happy marriage, you would get her estate anyway. Because her whole purpose—the thing your grandmother wanted most—was to see you happy, Hope."

Hope threw back her head and laughed. "And somehow Nona knew…she knew that getting me to Sisters, connecting me with you…that somehow it would all make me happy."

"She was a wise woman."

"So, if the inheritance becomes mine when I get married, I'm free to do as I like with it, right?"

"Absolutely."

"So I can share it with my sisters or give it to the Humane Society or whatever."

He nodded. "Whatever makes you happy, Hope."

"Being with you makes me the happiest of all," she admitted as they were coming into town. "But being here in Sisters…being with my family…having a niece and two nephews…and having this funny little dog, too…well, Nona was right to bring me back to my roots." She reached for Lewis's hand. "Love found me in Sisters…and it's good to be home."

POST CARD
CARTE POSTALE

Love Finds You

Want a peek into local American life—past and present?
The *Love Finds You*™ series published by Summerside Press
features real towns and combines travel, romance,
and faith in one irresistible package!

The novels in the series—uniquely titled after American towns with unusual but intriguing names—inspire romance and fun. Each fictional story draws on the compelling history or the unique character of a real place. Stories center on romances kindled in small towns, old loves lost and found again on the high plains, and new loves discovered at exciting vacation getaways. Summerside Press plans to publish at least one novel set in each of the 50 states. Be sure to catch them all!

Now Available in Stores

Love Finds You in Miracle, Kentucky by Andrea Boeshaar
ISBN: 978-1-934770-37-5

Love Finds You in Snowball, Arkansas by Sandra D. Bricker
ISBN: 978-1-934770-45-0

Love Finds You in Romeo, Colorado by Gwen Ford Faulkenberry
ISBN: 978-1-934770-46-7

Love Finds You in Valentine, Nebraska by Irene Brand
ISBN: 978-1-934770-38-2

Love Finds You in Humble, Texas by Anita Higman
ISBN: 978-1-934770-61-0

Love Finds You in Last Chance, California by Miralee Ferrell
ISBN: 978-1-934770-39-9

Love Finds You in Maiden, North Carolina by Tamela Hancock Murray
ISBN: 978-1-934770-65-8

Love Finds You in Paradise, Pennsylvania by Loree Lough
ISBN: 978-1-934770-66-5

Love Finds You in Treasure Island, Florida by Debby Mayne
ISBN: 978-1-934770-80-1

Love Finds You in Liberty, Indiana, by Melanie Dobson
ISBN: 978-1-934770-74-0

Love Finds You in Revenge, Ohio by Lisa Harris
ISBN: 978-1-934770-81-8

Love Finds You in Poetry, Texas by Janice Hanna
ISBN: 978-1-935416-16-6

COMING SOON

Love Finds You in Charm, Ohio by Annalisa Daughety
ISBN: 978-1-935416-17-3

Love Finds You in Bethlehem, New Hampshire by Lauralee Bliss
ISBN: 978-1-935416-20-3

Love Finds You in North Pole, Alaska by Loree Lough
ISBN: 978-1-935416-19-7

summerside
PRESS